The Auction

By

Eve Vaughn

Dedication

To my mom who has always been my biggest cheerleader. Mom you gave me my passion for books and without you there'd be no Eve. Thank you.

The Playboy...

In a society where the divide between the haves and the have nots is distinctly drawn, Foster Graham enjoys the privileges of the ruling class to the fullest. With looks, wealth and a place in society that gives him access to anything he wants, the world is his playground. But behind his easy smile and suave demeanor lurks a demon he's managed to suppress. When a friend goes missing, he finds himself immersed in a world that forces him to unleash the darkness within.

The Captive...

Far removed from the glitzy lifestyle of the upper class, Tori Preston must fight daily for her survival. In order to support her family she is forced to participate in a barbaric ritual called The Run, for a second time. But she soon learns there are far worse things that could happen when she finds herself captured and sold off into a life of pure hell.

The Auction...

An underground organization formed by a group of depraved sadists once thought to be a ghost tale used to scare little children into behaving, no one believes in its actual existence. Tori, however, learns the hard way that this 'bogey man' is very much real.

Without hope, Tori fears she'll never see her loved ones again, until she comes face to face with the only man who ever managed to touch her heart. Seeing the woman who has haunted his dreams since their parting, Foster is determined to save Tori and never let her go again. But they just might find that someone has other plans for them.

Prologue

Tonight she would be punished.

Shrouded in total darkness, Tori was positioned into a kneel with her forehead pressed against the cold cement floor. The tightness of her back muscles indicated she had been like this for at least a couple of hours. Her knees ached, but she dared not move or else what *he* had in store for her would be much worse. Though there was no one else in the room, there were infrared cameras planted all around her. She also wore a collar that detected motion, picking up even the slightest twitch of a finger, so HE would know if she broke form.

Tori held her breath as the menacing sound of footsteps drew closer. Her brief act of defiance earlier would cost her dearly. At the time, it had been well worth it to release the frustration of her situation, but now she wasn't so sure. Her patron was an unbending beast with very little tolerance for disobedience. He was a sadist of the worst order, seeming to take pleasure in making her and the other girls under his patronage suffer.

Though she'd long since given up believing in any deity, she prayed that he would eventually grow bored and release her from this contract, freeing her to return home to her family. Tori promised herself if she gained her freedom, she'd collect her younger siblings and get out of this cursed city, and somehow make a way for them without falling victim to the sadistic enjoyment of people who had more money than compassion. Even though her middle sister was now of age to participate in illicit programs like The Run, Tori hoped it wasn't too late to save her.

Tori had survived The Run the first time in one piece, although she hadn't been completely unscathed. The scars she bore from that experience were all internal and in ways even more painful than the physical harm she endured now. The second time she found herself being hunted by a group of Elites as if she were an animal, led to an ordeal of brutality and mental anguish. Her new patron, who only allowed her to refer to him as Mr. X, made Tori wish she hadn't been born. She couldn't imagine either of her sweet sisters enduring the inhumanity of the horrible Run.

A shudder shook her shoulders as she imagined it. All her life she'd done her best to shield them from harm by working odd jobs, and sometimes doing things that made it difficult to look at herself in a mirror. She protected them from a lazy alcoholic father who was verbally abusive and expected to be taken care of. But now that she wasn't there, she could only hope that somehow they managed to pull through, despite the realist in her fearing the worst. She had to keep believing, however, that nothing bad had happened to them or else she'd lose hope and without that, she'd have no reason to go on. She wasn't positive how much time had passed since she'd been under the patronage of Mr. X, because she'd lost track months ago. But she figured it had to be at least a year. She muttered a silent prayer for the six people she cared about the most.

The clicking of booted heels clicked and clacked against the floor, making her stomach bubble as adrenaline pumped through her veins. Sweat beaded on her forehead and her breathing grew shallow. She could tell from the sound of his approach that he was wearing his steel-toes. The last time he'd worn them, she'd been treated for three broken ribs and a crushed hand. Tori still experienced pain whenever she balled that particular appendage into a fist. It wasn't that Mr. X couldn't afford the proper medical treatment to make sure every single nerve ending worked properly; it was just that he wanted the remaining pain to serve as a reminder to never step out of line again. Now that she had, she could only imagine that what was in store for her would be worse.

Much worse.

When the door creaked open and bright lights flooded the room, Tori nearly flinched from fright, but she barely managed to remain still. She bit the inside of her bottom lip to hold in a cry.

The footsteps stopped right by her head but she didn't dare look up.

"Pretty, pretty, kitty. You've done it this time." The sinister way in which he whispered his words sent chills down her spine.

Tori wanted to throw up the contents of her dinner at the name she'd been given. Her patron seemed to find it amusing to refer to all the woman in his 'harem' by animal names, completely robbing them of the humanity they deserved. When Tori had first arrived at his mansion of horrors, she'd dared to stand up to him. *So you have claws*, he'd said as he stroked her face, *just like a kitten. You'll be my pretty, pretty, kitty.* She hated the name just as much as she did the man who'd assigned it to her.

Mr. X stroked the back of Tori's hair. Her wild honey-brown curls hung around her face, masking the fear and contempt that must have shown on her face. "When I give you an order, I expect it to be obeyed. Do you understand, kitty?"

"Yes sir," she bit the words out.

A chuckle filled the room. "Still defiant until the end. That's why you've always been my favorite. The fight in you is what makes it so exciting." He ran an icy finger down her spine and Tori began to tremble. This was how it began. Mr. X liked to put his girls at ease with soothing words, making them think all was forgiven before he went in for the kill. Tori wasn't fooled for a second. The sweeter the words he spilled, the worse her punishment would be.

"You have pretty skin, a beautiful golden brown, not the artificial kind from the salon, but the genuine thing. I would so hate to mar it more than it already has been." He sounded as though he actually regretted putting her in this situation.

He was full of shit.

"Do you know why you're here, kitty?"

Tori tried to gulp before answering but she couldn't gather up enough saliva to wet her pipes. She was so thirsty, her throat felt raw. "Because—" She could barely get the word out.

"You may get into position two."

Pain seared through her body until she was in her new pose, resting upright on bended knees with her back straight and head forward. She kept her gaze focused on the spot in front of her, not daring to glance up to make eye contact.

Black gloved hands holding a bottle of water with a long straw sticking out of the top came into her line of vision. "Drink, kitty."

Without hesitation, Tori latched on to the straw and sipped as quickly as her parched mouth would allow. After a few life-giving gulps, Mr. X pulled the bottle away much to Tori's distress. "I require your answer now," he said calmly, as though he were a man who wasn't about to torture her within an inch of her life.

"I'm being punished because I defied you."

"And how did you defy me?"

She wanted to glare at him and scream, but thought better of it. "Because I didn't want to service your guest."

"And why was that?"

"Because he smelled horrible, like he hadn't washed in days. His scent was revolting." It wasn't a new occurrence for Mr. X to have guests over. Most of his friends were huge assholes like their host. When there was company, Mr. X expected his guests to be taken care of, which meant Tori and the rest of the girls giving them oral stimulation. There was no penetration because Mr. X declared that was reserved exclusively for him. But the guests were usually allowed to fondle the girls. The first time it had happened to her, Tori had smacked the guest in the face. She had been hung upside down and beaten with a whipping contraption that didn't leave permanent marks but she'd been sore for weeks. She'd learned her lesson after that. From then on whenever a guest touched her breasts or between her legs, she let her mind wander to another place. But tonight was just too much.

Earlier on, Tori and two other women in X's harem were summoned to entertain. Tori had caught the eye of one man who seemed no worse than any other of the men. He'd been non-descript and his appearance was inoffensive besides the small beady black eyes, almost like a rat. When she'd gotten closer and caught a whiff of an odor that threatened to knock Tori off her feet, she'd retreated. It was as if the man had taken a bath in shit. In that moment, Tori had chosen to take whatever punishment would be coming to her rather than put her mouth on something that smelled like raw sewage.

Mr. X actually chuckled, startling Tori enough to make her look up into malevolent eyes, the color of liquid sky. He stroked the spot on his face that he called his beauty mark although she saw it as a big hairy eyesore. Whenever he did that, Tori knew her punishment would be bad. Quickly, she righted her head before he could add another infraction against her. "You're right. My friend does have a unique odor to him." He laughed again, but just as quickly as it started it ended. "But he's a very important contact and for that violation you need to be disciplined. Unfortunately for me, as of tomorrow, you will no longer belong to me."

Before she could stop herself, a gasp escaped her lips. He was letting her go?

"But you're mine until the morning and you must pay for your little act of rebellion. I can't damage that pretty skin of yours; it's one of my favorite things about you, by the way. But I can do other things to make you rethink your actions, should you ever step out of line again. Because where you're going, you'll thank me for the instruction."

Tori didn't understand what he was talking about. If he was setting her free why did it sound like he actually wasn't?

Again Mr. X chuckled. "I see the confusion on that beautiful little face. So let me make this clear for you. Tomorrow begins your new life. As for your punishment tonight, the water I gave you was full of microbots, naked to the human eye. They'll eventually pass through you, but they'll expand and as they work their way out of your system, it will feel like being sliced by tiny razors. All internal. You'll cry, maybe even scream, but it will be over soon enough. The medics will monitor you throughout the night to insure you don't bleed internally. But look on the bright side," He stroked her cheek with the back of his hand. "At least your skin will remain untouched.

Mr. X backed away until he was out the door. Darkness once again shrouded her. Before she could make sense of what he'd told her, a pain so excruciating hit her, making it feel as if her insides had been set on fire. And just as Mr. X predicted, Tori began to scream, unable to stop.

Chapter One

"Give me one reason not to rip your fucking head off!" Foster tightened his grip around West's neck, daring the other man to even think about fighting back. He had enough of the guy's evasiveness and wanted, no needed answers. This was a matter of life and death.

West simpered like the piece of shit he was. "I swear I didn't have anything to do with her disappearance. I haven't seen her since you and O'Shaughnessy took her away from me. I didn't even complain when I wasn't compensated for her, even though I had every right to."

Foster applied more pressure, making the other man's eyes practically bulge out of his head, but much to his annoyance no information was forthcoming. He had been certain a spineless little weasel like West would have broken down by now. The fact that he wasn't talking could possibly mean that he really didn't know of Macy's whereabouts, even though Foster's sources had led him here.

Foster had tapped into connections that he long since believed he was done with and it angered him enough to take his frustrations out on his closest target. It wasn't as though Peter West didn't have this coming. The man was a slime ball, rumored to have killed his wife for access to her fortune. It was also whispered that he'd murdered several of the women he'd kept in his so-called harem, though no one could prove it.

The only thing that stopped Foster from actually killing this son of a bitch was that he wasn't interested in being involved in any investigation. West was still after all considered among the Elite in their community despite his sullied reputation. Attention from the law was the last thing Foster needed to deal with. He had the funds to grease the right palms and could afford a top-notch attorney, but it was a messy business he wanted no involvement in. Of course, there were ways to take care of this bastard and go undetected, but dead men couldn't talk and he needed some information.

"Then why do my sources tell me you know something?"

"I don't know who these so-called sources are." West gasped for breath as he spoke. "I swear on my dear deceased wife that I'm telling the truth. I don't mess with the traffickers anymore. You have to believe me. The last time I saw that girl was when she was taken out of here." Tears streamed down the bastard's face and suddenly a foul stench slammed into Foster, offending his nasal passages. He looked down to see his red-faced prey had shit his pants. Foster immediately released his hold, sending West crashing to the floor in a heap at his feet. He really was a disgusting piece of vermin. A slimy worm like him would have broken by now, so Foster could only assume he was either telling the truth, which put him firmly back at square one or that West was scared of who he was trying to protect. Foster suspected the latter.

Although West might not have anything to do with Macy's disappearance directly, Foster sensed he was hiding something. The longer his friend was missing, the less chance he had of finding her. She was no longer on the grid, which meant her vitals chip had been removed. Not only did the little implant read a person's health and could be used to spend and receive credits, it could also track a person almost anywhere in the world. It was one of the government's worst-kept secrets.

Though the citizens knew that their chips could lock on to their coordinates when necessary, most of them believed it was a matter of public safety or to track criminals. The tracking devices were extremely expensive, which was why not many people had access to them. But for the very rich, obtaining one of these machines wasn't very hard. His best friend had access to a couple of them which is how Foster had learned Macy couldn't be tracked. There was no telling where she was. For all he knew, she could be out of the country. And if that were the case, there weren't too many avenues he could pursue.

It was nearly a month since Macy had disappeared and the guilt was tearing him apart. He'd made a promise to protect her and he'd dropped the ball, all because he could no longer look her in the eye and be the man she believed him to be. What he saw in those big violet eyes was trust and adoration, two things he definitely didn't deserve. It had become evident to him that she had developed feelings for him and while he was flattered, they were emotions he was incapable of returning.

How he'd become her sort of protector had happened completely by accident. Macy had been a participant in a game called The Run, where women volunteered to be hunted by wealthy patrons. Though these women were handsomely compensated, most of them were basically at the mercy of their captors until they were formally released. As a patron who had participated in several runs, Foster saw it as a sport. Most of the women he let go. Some he kept for a few weeks to warm his bed, but they were never more than a pleasurable pastime for him, baring his one slip-up. He was, however, aware that there were several patrons who viewed The Run as a way to build their harems or to use these women as their personal toys.

It was rumored that many of these hunters never let the girls go, while it was also said that many of these volunteers died in custody of their patrons. There were laws against murder, but most of the patrons were so wealthy they could buy their way out of a messy situation by bribing the right authorities. West was one of them. He had been the center of much gossip regarding exactly this, which is why it was no surprise that Foster's sources had landed him on West's doorstep.

West had been Macy's patron and she probably would have died under his care had it not been for Aya, his best friend Dare's girlfriend, who had also been a participant. Apparently, the two women had bonded over the game and it was at Aya's insistence that Macy was tracked down. Going along with his friend as a favor, Foster was shocked to see the state the girl had been in. Covered in bruises and cuts, Macy had been missing a few fingers and several teeth. She had been so thin to the point of emaciation. Foster could tell that Macy had not been properly fed. Her face had been severely scarred. It was clear she'd been beaten to within an inch of her life and this asshole cowering at his feet was responsible.

Seeing the pathetic heap that Macy had been had brought out Foster's protective instincts, not to mention she reminded him of someone who still haunted every single one of his dreams. He couldn't quite put his finger on why. Both women had similar bone structure but where one was petite and pale, the other was tall and bronze, not to mention different ancestry. Yet every time he glanced into Macy's large violet gaze, he was reminded of a pair of hazel eyes that made him toss and turn at night.

Macy had clung to him because she viewed him as her rescuer so he'd taken her under his wing. He saw to it that Macy had gotten the proper medical care that she required by getting her teeth replaced, scars healed and fingers grown back. Within months, she looked nothing like the shell of a woman she had been. She started to smile more. The woman who had seemed afraid of her own shadow when they met had shed some of her timidity. But with her recovery, the resemblance between her and his ghost had become even stronger and he began to distance himself. He saw Macy's disappointment when he didn't come around as often or check in when he said he would.

And now because of his selfishness, she was gone. The last time she had been seen was leaving the bar she worked at, which happened to be owned by Aya's uncle. Apparently, no one knew where she was. It was as if she'd vanished into thin air. Foster was certain she wouldn't just run off, not when she had younger siblings to look after while her father drank himself into an early grave.

The only explanation was that she'd been taken but he had no idea by whom, at first. And then, he remembered. There was a legend about an organization that snatched women and children off the street in broad daylight, never to be seen again. Because it was so shrouded in secrecy, no one knew how to even become a part of the network unless they were already a member, and none of them were talking. This secret group was a tale people would use to tell their children in order to keep them on their best behavior. But since he'd begun his search he realized the stories might very well be real. He prayed Macy was not somehow entangled in that web because if she was, she might be lost to him forever.

"Please, I've told you all I know," West groaned from the floor.

Foster looked down at the piece of crap who also smelled like it. "If you're lying to me, I will be back and I will end you." He pulled his leg back and delivered a hard kick to West's ribs.

The cracking sound was followed by a loud scream, but Foster felt zero remorse as he thought of all the times this man had hurt Macy for his own sick enjoyment. When Foster was about to step over him and leave, he paused. Something that West had said suddenly registered. Foster hadn't brought it up, but now he finally understood why his sources believed that West knew something regarding Macy's disappearance.

Bending over he grabbed West by the collar, who was now clutching his side. "You mentioned traffickers. I didn't say anything about that. What do you know?"

"Please! I can't say anything or they'll kill me."

"If you don't tell me, I'll kill you. What do you know, you rat bastard? Start speaking before I break the rest of your ribs!"

West was bright red as he panted for breath. It was clear he was in a lot of pain, but Foster had no compassion where this man was concerned. "Most of my money is tied up in the business and this house. Sometimes, I need some credits to play around with."

Foster gritted his teeth. "Get to the point."

"Sometimes, I would sell the girls I got from The Run to them. They paid handsomely. But, I wasn't the only one. There were a few other patrons who fed them a steady supply of the women. They only wanted the cream of the crop. They didn't want attention drawn in their direction so this was the ideal way to get what they wanted. Now that The Run is shut down, they've been finding other means of getting the girls. I hear they're snatching them off the street, but from what I understand, they're only taking woman who won't be missed. Since you're looking for your friend, maybe it wasn't them. Just please….that's all I know."

"Who were the other suppliers who used the cover of The Run to sell women?"

"I… oh God, I need medical assistance,' he whined. By now, tears streamed down West's face.

"Did you give medical attention to all the women you hurt and tortured? Did you offer to get help for your wife before you killed her?"

West's eyes widened. "I loved Diane. I would never harm her. Those were just vicious rumors."

Foster delivered another blow to West's injured ribs, making the man howl in what sounded like pure agony. He wanted to do more than make the weasel scream. Foster wanted to rip his spine out. "You keep telling yourself that lie. Everyone knows you're a lying, murdering piece of shit. Now start naming names!"

"Please don't make me."

Foster rammed his fist into West's tender spot and then dropped him to the ground. He stood over the crying man once again ready to strike. "Talk."

"George Neville. Randolph Hutchins. Carline Davidson. That's all I know. Oh, God. I think I'm going to die if I don't get to a medic soon." And without warning, West stopped moving.

Foster leaned over and checked the man's pulse. It was still beating and strong. He probably just passed out from the pain. Pussy. He probably dealt out much worse to the women who were once under his care, but now that he was on the receiving end, he couldn't take it. Scumbag.

At least now, Foster had more leads which he intended to follow up on. His friend's life depended on it.

Chapter Two

As consciousness slowly seeped in, Tori opened her eyes and immediately closed them against the bright light of the stark white room. She squeezed her lids shut before gradually opening them again, giving herself a chance to adjust to the brightness. As she took in her surroundings she saw that she was in a part of the mansion she'd never been in before. Normally, she was kept in the basement for 'instruction' and only brought up to the main room for entertainment. Sometimes she was taken to Mr. X's bedroom but she'd never stayed there for more than a couple hours at a time. It was strange that he'd decided to change up the routine after all this time.

Every muscle in her body ached as Tori forced herself to move. The last thing she clearly remembered was experiencing the most excruciating pain in her life. She'd been beaten, whipped, choked, kicked and even stomped, but she would have taken any of those punishments over that last punishment she'd endured. Knowing there was torture far worse than anything she'd gone through before scared the shit out of her. At least with the other things, she could somehow transcend to another plane and push through the agony. With that she couldn't. Mr. X had spiked her water with things he called microbots which meant that any food or beverage served to her would need to be eyed with caution. Being scared of food was another level of psychological warfare.

Tori recalled screaming until her throat burned. Even now it felt dry and scratchy, and her skin felt as if she'd been scorched, but at least most of the ache had subsided. Forcing herself into a sitting position, Tori realized she was on a bed. She hadn't had the luxury of a real bed for longer than she could actually recollect. It was nice and soft and the temptation to roll around on the fluffy comforter was strong, but she didn't dare. This could be some trap set up by Mr. X.

She studied the room and wasn't exactly sure what to make of it. Besides the bed, the room was sparse. There were no windows, and everything was coated with the brilliant artificial lights hanging from the ceiling. There was a table by the bed, white like the sheets, blankets and walls. Everything was so sterile. No door seemed to be present. It was as if she was inside a big box, like some kind of sophisticated prison.

Swinging her legs over the edge of the bed, she touched her bare feet to the chilly surface of the uncarpeted floor. A burst of cold air shot through the room, possibly from some central cooling system, making Tori aware of her nudity. That didn't bother her much considering she'd spent the majority of her time in Mr. X's care in the buff. He preferred to have his woman ready to "serve his needs" as he'd put it.

Grabbing the top cover from the bed, she wrapped it around her body to stave off the chill that seemed to have seeped into her bones. Was this a new form of torture she wondered? Not knowing what to expect was part of the cruelty of the punishment.

As different scenarios ran through her mind, she heard the whoosh of an opening panel. Startled, Tori turned around to see that a portion of the wall had opened up to reveal a hidden door. A rail thin woman, dressed in black from head to toe with cat-eye glasses walked in. Her iron gray hair was pulled back into a tight bun, highlighting the sharp angles of her face. The red lipstick that decorated her thin, pinched lips looked like an angry wound. Tori could tell she was a tall woman, but she wore what appeared to be six inch stilettos that made her seem larger than life.

Tori took a step back as the woman walked further into the room. It was then she noticed the newcomer was not alone. She was flanked by two men also encased in all black, with sunglasses that made their expression unreadable. They didn't appear overly large or intimidating size-wise, but Tori sensed the danger in each man. She was sure they were hired with good reason.

Tori returned her attention to the woman who now eyed her dispassionately. Her dark eyes looked like mean little raisins behind those glasses. It was rare to see someone who was clearly privileged sporting any kind of visual aid. Laser eye surgery was so common among the people who could afford it hardly anyone wore glasses except for fashion reasons. This woman didn't strike Tori as the type to make such frivolous choices.

"It's a good thing you were awake. You've been out for quite some time." The woman's voice didn't quite match her appearance. In fact it sounded masculine. The voice wasn't the scratchy tone of one who partook in too much tobacco, but a natural deep timbre.

Tori looked the woman up and down and noticed her figure was more square than gently curved, and she sported a codpiece over her tight leather pants. Perhaps she was born as a man and now identified as a woman, or it was quite possible she was into gender experimentation. For a while, it was a trend among some of the edgier Elite to go through gender body modification. Men would sport breasts, women would have a penis added, and men a vagina. Some people would have both organs. Though she wasn't sure if the person standing in front of her had any enhancements, it did appear that she was sporting a little something extra.

"Are you finished staring?" The woman inquired.

Tori blinked and nodded, not sure whether the question required a verbal response. Flashbacks of all the times she'd been smacked for speaking out of turn entered her head.

"Good. I'm Zee. I will guide you through the next several days you're here until it is your time to go up on the block. You will be given a thorough medical examination where any physical ailments you may have will be taken care of. Afterwards, you'll be groomed and then briefed on how you will conduct yourself. Failure to comply with any part of this process will result in punishment that may or may not include death. I would so hate for that to be you because I think you will bring us a lot of money."

Tori wrinkled her forehead in confusion. The block. Bringing in money? Where was Mr. X? Curiosity getting the better of her, she couldn't stop herself from asking her questions out loud. "I don't understand. Are you trying to tell me I'm being sold? What about my patron? Once he releases me, I should be free to go."

The two men each took a step forward but Zee held up her hand to halt them. "You don't know the rules yet so I'll allow you this one faux pas. You will not speak unless an answer is required of you and I will tell you when that is. If you speak out of turn again, I will have your tongue removed. I'd rather not do that because it would depreciate your value. Our research shows buyers prefer their women with tongues. It's better for oral pleasure. Even still, we'd make a nice profit from you. Exotics always go for a little extra, since they've become so rare in the last few decades. People always pay more for things out of the ordinary."

Tori flinched at that word. She hated being referred to as an exotic like she wasn't a human being. Sure she had more melanin in her skin than most but she was still a person.

Zee stepped forward and ran a sharp nail-tipped finger down the side of Tori's arm. Tori braced herself not to flinch away in case it earned her some kind of demerit.

Zee gripped Tori's face in her hands and gave her an examination. "Yes, you'll do quite well. Your eyes really pop out against all the pretty brown skin. Hmm, you'll last a long time with your buyer because of it. And should your owner ever get tired of you, he could always sell you to the harvesters. Your natural melanin is a valuable commodity, what with this blazing sun of ours. People burn so easily around here. You look to be of mixed breeding, though. Shame. You'd go for more if you were full-blooded." It was almost as if Zee was talking to herself instead of to Tori. She could have been talking to an inanimate object.

"Drop the blanket," Zee requested gently, although there was no doubt in Tori's mind that the other woman could turn ugly if her order wasn't immediately obeyed.

Tori let the comforter fall in a pool at her feet and kept her arms rigid by her side.

Zee palmed Tori's breasts and squeezed her nipple until she gasped. "Hmm." Making a twirling motion with her finger, she directed Tori to turn around. "Nice backside. Breasts are a little on the small side, but this rear more than makes up for it. Good curve in the back. These whip marks we can heal along with the other cuts on your body. Seems your previous owner liked a bit of rough play. Perhaps your next one will be a bit gentler but there's no telling. Yes, you'll fetch top money. What do you think boys? We could probably get a half a mil for this one depending on how we can market her."

"Yes, she'll do well on the block." One of the men who had been silent responded.

"I think so too." Zee seemed quite pleased with herself. "I'll leave you now. Someone will be in here shortly to groom you and then you'll be served a meal."

Without another word, Zee turned on her spiked heels and strode out of the room with her lackeys following close behind. The door closed, leaving Tori standing alone and wondering what the fuck had just happened.

Foster stepped into the bar called *Arthur's* reluctantly. He could have contacted his friend by holophone but felt she deserved to hear his news face to face. Sighing heavily, he glanced around him. The bar, which had been fixed up in the last few months was still not a place most people in his circles would step foot in, but he liked the welcoming atmosphere where hardworking patrons came for a drink to take their minds off of the everyday grind of life. He was sure some of his so called friends would refer to these people as Dregs. To his shame, not very long ago, he would have done the same.

He spotted Aya laughing with one of the customers. When she raised her head, their eyes locked. She smiled before walking over to him. "Hey, I haven't heard from you in a couple days. I was beginning to wonder when you'd check in. Why don't you grab a seat and I'll get you a drink. Whiskey on the rocks, right?"

"Actually, I don't want to drink right now. But we need to talk."

The smile that Aya had sported only a few seconds ago fell. "You sound serious."

"This is serious."

"Okay. Give me a second. We're training another girl while Macy...well you know, until her return. She's getting the hang of things but I've never left her on her own before. I just have to tell Uncle Arthur to keep an eye on her."

Foster nodded. "Sure. Take your time."

He watched as Aya disappeared into the kitchen behind the swinging wooden doors. Foster wished he had come with good news but it was better than keeping Aya in the dark.

When Aya returned, she gestured for him to follow her. Aya lead him through a door at the side of the bar which led to a flight of stairs. He'd never been in this section of the building before and he was almost certain his friend Dare wouldn't approve of him being in his girlfriend's home. Aya placed her thumbprint on the identification pad until the indicator turned green. It then triggered the door to open.

Aya's apartment was small, but neat.

"Please have a seat."

"What do you think Dare would say when he finds out I've been in your place?"

Aya waved her hand dismissively. "I don't know, but he has to realize that the two of us would never do anything to betray his trust. So even if he doesn't like my entertaining you in my home, he'll get over it."

"Or he'll punch my heart out."

She threw her head back and gave a boisterous laugh. "Don't tell me you're frightened of Dare. You two are best friends."

"That doesn't mean a thing when it comes to you. Dare can be quite possessive."

"True, but I very much doubt you have cause for concern. Besides, behind that playboy persona of yours, something tells me that you'll be able to hold your own. Anyway, Dare's bark is far worse than his bite."

Foster raised a brow. "I wouldn't let him hear you say that. He might take that as a challenge."

"Well, we just won't tell him then, will we?" She winked. "So tell me what it is that put that ferocious frown on your face. It's about Macy, isn't it?"

"Yeah. Uh, I did some asking around and it looks like there has been heavy trafficking activity around here lately. What I learned was that some of the patrons who participated in The Run were capturing girls to sell them off to groups, which places them on something called a market, which is basically a code word for an illegal auction."

Aya shook her head. "No. Not Macy. How can you be certain that she's involved in this? Did you visit that Peter West character? Maybe he's upset because he had to release her. He could have kidnapped her and has Macy hidden away somewhere." She scooted closer and gripped his arm as she stared at him pleadingly. "We both know that he's no good and probably has something to do with her disappearance. Can't you make him talk?"

If Foster told Aya exactly what he did to get West to talk she'd probably get away from him as quickly as she could. Instead he tried to choose his words with as much finesse as possible. "I did follow up with him, actually, and she was nowhere to be found."

"But I'm sure he has secret rooms in his house. Servants that might be bribed."

"I thought about that. There were still a few women he had under his care who I questioned. They said that Macy hadn't returned since she left that house. I convinced West to set them free so they had no incentive to lie. As for West, he was able to give me some helpful information. I got the name of the other patrons who served as go-betweens for the market. One of them was very forthcoming."

Foster left out the part where he had broken the guy's arm to get the info he wanted. Hutchins had squealed like a wild animal. "He told me that they were being paid handsomely to get these women because going through that route wouldn't raise suspicion. Now that Dare has shut down the Run, their supply has been cut off. It's forced them to scout disenfranchised neighborhoods like this. It's likely that Macy was taken by one of their operatives and without her chip, there's no telling where she is now."

"Oh no. What about her siblings? They've been worried sick about her. I know you have taken the responsibility of supporting them financially while she's gone but they would rather have her than the money. After what she went through with that rat-faced bastard, I don't know if Macy can survive another ordeal like that. She's my friend and I feel that there's something I can do for her rather than sit here and wait."

"There's nothing you can do, and if I got you involved in this, Dare would have my head"

"I am my own woman and he can't order me around. Please tell me what I can do."

Foster shook his head. "There's really nothing you can do without putting yourself in the line of danger. You have to realize that the people involved in this are not only wealthy, but their heavily connected and extremely dangerous."

"I don't care. My friend is out there and if we don't find her, maybe she won't survive. Macy helped me during The Run, and she has become very dear to me. It'll weigh on my conscience if I sit back and do nothing."

"Aya, now isn't the time to be stubborn. I know you want to get involved but I don't want you to go missing as well. I couldn't live with myself if something were to happen to you too."

Aya looked as if she wanted to argue the point but Foster held his hand up to stop whatever it was she was about to say. "No Aya. It's for the best. If you want to help, just be here to support her when we do find her. Keep your ears open in case you hear something."

Her dark eyes gleamed with newfound hope. "So you're saying there is a way to get her back?"

Foster sighed. "Yes, there may be a way to track her down. I'm not giving up on her yet."

"How? What's your plan?"

"I'm going on the inside."

Chapter Three

Tori paced around her room waiting for something to happen. She was going crazy in here without any stimulation. It felt like hours since Zee had left, leaving her to wonder what the hell had happened. Suddenly she halted. Something Mr. X had said came reeling back to her. He'd mentioned it being her last night with him. Had she been sold? This wasn't supposed to happen. Per her contract from The Run, he was to release her on her own recognizance. She'd silently wished to be rid of him since they day he'd tagged her but now she found herself in a situation that could turn out to be infinitely worse.

She sank to the floor, feeling defeated by the unknown. Tori wasn't sure how long she lay there but she was pulled out of her temporary misery when the sound of the door opening indicated she was no longer alone. She looked up to see a young girl wearing a green sarong, with song black hair. The girl, who didn't look a day over sixteen, definitely wasn't as intimidating as Zee.

"Rose, I'm Shia. I'll be assisting in your grooming."

"My name is Tori."

Shia raised her a dark brow. "Perhaps that was your name before you came here, but now you are Rose. Perhaps it slipped Zee's mind to inform you of this."

"My name is Tori," she said more firmly than before. They'd taken everything from her, she wouldn't allow them to take her name as well.

Shia shrugged before walking to the far corner of the room. "Well, you can be Tori all you want, but don't let anyone else hear you say that. Until you're sold and renamed you're Rose. All the girls are given code names while they're here to maintain anonymity." Shia placed her palm against the wall and a panel appeared revealing several buttons which she proceeded to push. "Step back, please."

Tori moved in time to see the opposite wall open up and the bed recede behind it. Then, where the bed had been, the floor opened up and a large square tub appear. Water began to spill from filters on either side of it while a stream of soap poured out from a slot in the corner of it.

"You don't have to hold that blanket so tightly against your body, you know. There's nothing I haven't seen already." Shia gave her a polite smile.

Tori licked her parched lips. Her throat ached slightly, possibly from screaming so much. "This bath is for me?"

"Yes, you must be thoroughly cleaned and groomed before I take you to the medic to have your scars healed. The buyers won't settle for anything less than perfection."

Tori had no clue what was going on and she wasn't sure how much she was allowed to ask. After hesitating for a moment she figured she'd suffered a lot already, if they tortured her some more then at least she'd know what she was up against. "I don't understand what's going on here. What is this place? Where am I?"

Shia gave her a funny look. "Don't you know?"

"If I did I wouldn't be asking."

"In ten days you're going to go on the block. You'll be auctioned off and from there, I guess it will be up to your new master."

"Auctioned off? Yesterday I was under the patronage of a man who only referred to himself as X."

"Well, I guess he sold you and now you're here. Look, I can imagine this is all confusing for you, but there's really no point in getting yourself worked up over this. The only escape from this place is death. Zee would never let you go because there's a lot of money to be made with you." Shia sat on the side of the tub and dipped her hand into the soapy water as if to test it. "Come on, get in."

When Tori remained frozen to the spot, Shia sighed. "Please don't make this harder on the both of us. My instructions are to give you a bath. If I'm not done by a certain time, the guards come in and take matters into their own hands and I'm sure you wouldn't like that. And personally, I don't want to be punished because you don't want to comply."

It was on the tip of Tori's tongue to tell the girl to fuck off but she thought better of it. Even if the girl was a little pushy, Tori didn't want to be responsible for getting someone else in trouble. With a sigh she dropped her blanket and stepped into the steaming hot water. Gingerly she sat down in the tub, flinching a bit as her body adjusted to the heat. She hadn't had a proper bath since she was under the care of her first patron. Growing up in a poverty-stricken neighborhood, they didn't have the luxury of baths, instead they washed in ancient shower stalls that were made in the twenty-first century. Sometimes they didn't work properly because of the plumbing issues.

"How's the water?"

"Nice."

"Good. I'll give you a minute to soak and relax before I get your back. I have a variety of scented soaps. Would you prefer something flowery or citrusy?"

"You choose. I don't care."

"Okay."

Silence fell between them as Tori tried to wrap her head around everything happening to her. When she was a child, her father used to tell her and her younger brother and sisters stories about the child snatchers. They would come around and take bad children away. Those stories used to terrify her, but as Tori grew older she realized they were simply tall tales from a drunken man meant to keep them afraid. She didn't think she would find herself embroiled in something even worse The Run. At least with The Run, there was a possibility of freedom; with this she wasn't so sure.

"You're different from the other girls who've been through here," Shia spoke, breaking into Tori's thoughts.

"How so?"

"Most of them cry the entire time. But not you. You seem, I don't know, almost angry about this."

"Of course I'm angry. Who wouldn't be? I signed up for a game because I had no other means of supporting my family without completely losing every bit of self-respect I had. And now to find out that I'm going to be sold off to the highest bidder is just fucked up."

"Maybe it won't be so bad. You might get a master who treats you well. It's not unheard of."

"Or I may not. Tell me, how are you involved in all this?"

The girl frowned. "I'm not sure I understand your question."

"You seemed very young to be involved in something so sinister."

"I wouldn't use so strong a word. I was born into it. My mother was pregnant with me before she was put on the block. Unless a buyer is specifically looking for a woman with child, the auctioneers prefer to abort the child depending on how far along the woman is. My mother was near the end of her final trimester when they took me from her womb. I've been raised to serve ever since."

"So you're basically a slave?" Tori was horrified at how calculated everything was. But what bothered her most was Shia's easy acceptance of it.

Shia shrugged. "What you see as slavery, I see as the only life I've known. I'm not sure what I would do in the outside world. Besides, I'm not treated unfairly. If I get my work done, I get rewarded with treats. We even get to watch shows on holovision in the privacy of our quarters. Besides, it's better than the alternative."

"The alternative?"

"I could have been born a boy. They don't have it as easy as the girls."

"How so?"

Shia glanced at a point above their heads. "I...I really shouldn't say."

"Are we being filmed?"

"Yes, but there's no audio. It's just maybe the less you knew the better, for your own piece of mind."

"But you brought it up. Tell me what happens to the boys?"

"Well..."

Tori was a bit uneasy now. What could the girl possibly be holding back?

"Well, when they turn eight, they're sold off. You see, since men outnumber women by such a large percentage, the bidders are only interested in the young boys."

Tori wanted to vomit as she imagined what these bidders would want with small children. She'd seen a lot of sick things in her life, had even experienced some of it herself but knowing these people had no problem selling children made her stomach turn.

"And the girls are never sold?"

"Sometimes. Every now and then one of the buyers may request a certain type and if one of us fits the bill then we're put on the block."

"Aren't you worried that one day you'll be sold?"

"No. If that's what my masters have planned for me than so be it. My entire life has been designed to serve others. I see no difference from one master or another."

Tori strongly disagreed with that statement, however she saw no point in arguing with the girl. It was clear Shia was so ingrained in this culture there was little chance of changing her mind.

Shia produced a sponge and gently pushed Tori forward before running it up and down her back. "I know you're probably worried about what will happen but if you're good to your buyer, perhaps they'll be good to you. You might even get an owner who takes very good care of you."

Tori froze. She'd heard that line before. Her father had basically uttered something similar to her just before she sighed up for The Run, the first time.

"I don't see what the difference is between you signing up for The Run and turning tricks to earn money," Carl Morton slurred his words, drunk from the bottle of whiskey he'd consumed. "The way I see it, you'll earn a lot more for less work. Ten thousand credits is nothing to sneeze at. That will take care of this family for a while."

It was like a slap in the face to be reminded of the one time she'd resorted to giving a handjob to one of her father's drinking buddies for the few credits it took to buy her little brother some much needed medication. "I do not turn tricks *as you so delicately put it. I did what I had to do because you don't want to work."*

"You know I have a disability," he whined.

"Called alcoholism. Look, you may have the rest of my brothers and sisters fooled with this sick act of yours but I can see right through you. You're a lazy, good-for-nothing bum. Mom worked herself to death while you sat back and let her instead of taking care of your family."

"You watch your mouth, you little bitch. You've forgotten that you're only in this house because of my generosity. After your mother died, I could have kicked your ass out on the street. It's not like I can afford another mouth to feed."

The Auction

Tori had hardened her heart against Carl's insults. He let her know in many ways, blatant and subtle, that she wasn't his biological daughter. If it weren't for her siblings, she would have left a long time ago. She narrowed her eyes and poked her finger onto the drunk's chest. "No you watch it. You won't kick me out because I'm the only one bringing in enough money to keep us from starving. I bust my ass from sunrise to sunset working any kind of odd job I can get because you want to play the victim. The only disability you have is in your head, so go ahead and just try to put me out."

Carl opened his mouth as if to argue the point with her but then thought better of it. "Well if you care about your brothers and sisters like you claim, I see no reason why you can't enter The Run. I hear most of those girls are with their patrons for a few weeks, a month tops, but in return you get all those credits. The way I see it, if you don't do it, you're being selfish. Besides, it may not be so bad. You might even get a patron who will take really good care of you and treat you well. Imagine that, living it up in the lap of luxury and you get all that money to boot."

Tori had wanted to punch him square in the nose, but when it was all said and done, she had no valid argument to counter his reasoning. The restaurant she had waited tables at had shut down due to lack of business and the factory where she worked part time had laid off hundreds of employees including herself. She had been an errand girl in the shopping district for a while, but she didn't earn enough money doing just that to keep food in everyone's belly. With no work prospects in sight her only option was to work in a brothel, which meant she'd have to move and live in one of those houses and she wanted to keep an eye on siblings. It was a daily struggle to keep her brothers from getting involved in illegal activity which was a powerful lure for kids in her neighborhood. As much as she hated to admit it, The Run was probably her best option. She only hoped she'd get a patron who would lose interest in her quickly, just like Carl said.

Tori however, truly learned the meaning of being careful for what she wished for, because not only did she get it, her heart was shattered in the process.

Chapter Four

"Foster, are you sure you want to do this?" Dare's holographic image paced from side to side.

"Can you think of a better way? Just being wealthy isn't sufficient to get into an organization like this. You need connections and references."

"Yes, but you swore off that life. There has to be another way. If we put our heads together we can come up with something."

"Don't you think I've run different scenarios in my head? There's no other way. I know these types of people."

"What's your plan when you learn who she's been sold to? I seriously doubt her buyer will willingly hand her over."

"I'll figure it out when I see her. Look, I appreciate your offer of help but I need to do this alone so as not to draw suspicion my way. If any of the proprietors get wind of me being on a rescue mission, bad things can happen. These are dangerous people and no amount of wealth and influence can save me."

"And that's exactly why you need some backup."

"Dare, this isn't your battle. Let me handle it. I know what I'm doing."

"This is my business. Granted, I'm not invested in whether this girl is found or not, but my woman is. And if she's unhappy, so am I. So for her, I'm offering you any kind of assistance I'm able to give."

"I appreciate it, but the best thing you can do for me if to keep an ear out for anything you hear on the outside. You have plenty of contacts, powerful ones with lots of secrets. It wouldn't surprise me if some of our public officials are involved. It would explain why this organization has been able to cover their tracks so well. Dare, these are the types of people you don't want to be involved with."

"But you're willing to."

"I made a promise and I intend to keep it"

His friend sighed heavily, expression stern. "Just watch out for yourself."

Foster grinned. "Careful, O'Shaughnessy, you're going to actually make me think you care."

Dare glared. "Fuck you."

Foster chuckled. "That's the Dare I know. I have to sign off now, my two o'clock will be here shortly."

Dare raised a surprised brow. "I'm surprised you're actually in your office today. You're going to end up ruining your playboy reputation."

Foster took his friend's good-natured ribbing in stride. "Never that. I'll check in with you later."

"Sounds good."

Foster pressed the side button on his holowatch, making his friend's image disappear. Dare was the only friend who knew a little about his past, but not much, just that Foster used to be involved in illegal activities. And then there were those who were fully aware of what Foster had once been involved in but were too scared to speak of it because of fear from retaliation or for incriminating themselves. Foster had never fully opened up to Dare about his past because there were some things better left unsaid.

Over the past several years, Foster had done his best to cultivate an image that most people found pleasant. He said the right things, attended the right parties, rubbed elbows with the right people. His one vice was the women which most people expected of a good looking man of wealth. Many thought of him a playboy who coasted through like without a care in the world never lifting a finger to maintain the corporation built by his grandfather.

Foster didn't have to work another day of his life if he didn't want to, but he chose to handle all business matters behind the scenes. Foster believed this was for the best. He figured if people saw him as someone content to spend his money without taking anything seriously, they could view him as non-threatening. The alternative was not a path he'd intended to go down again. Until now.

The thought of immersing himself in a world he'd left behind made him shake. Several questions ran through his mind. Would he run into old contacts? Would he have to do things he swore off? But most of all, would he like it? Foster pressed a button beneath his desk, making the drink panel appear. A tumbler full of bourbon, an ice bucket and an empty glass popped up. With unsteady hands, he fixed himself a drink before downing it in one gulp, hoping it would steady his nerves. When he was younger, it was a given that he'd eventually take over the family business, although it never occurred to him exactly what it all entailed. He'd never forget when he found out.

"Foster, you're thirteen years old today. That's practically a man. And as a man, you're entitled to know the truth. Your father may want to coddle you for the rest of your life, but if you want to survive in this world, you're going to have to grow a pair." Andrew Graham stared at his grandson with steely blue eyes that seemed cold and calculating.

Though Foster adored his grandfather, who was always generous with his gifts and made allowances for him that his parents wouldn't, he was also a bit frightened of him as well. His larger than life grandfather, with a brash manner that demanded respect, often said whatever was on his mind regardless of whether the other person would like it or not. A self-made man who had clawed his way from poverty to become one of the wealthiest men in the city, he didn't play along with society's rules, refusing to participate in any of its niceties. He would sooner blow cigar smoke in a person's face than shake his hand if he didn't like him. Foster always admired that about his grandfather and wanted to be more like him. He could never understand why his father didn't seem thrilled about the prospect of him bonding with his grandfather, though Foster could never remember a time when the two adult men in his life got along. It almost seemed like they simply tolerated one another.

Even though it was apparent his father didn't approve of Foster's relationship with his grandfather, he never interfered in their relationship. While he was in awe of his grandfather, Foster still had a decent relationship with his father, who tried to instill in him the importance of putting his best foot forward and being responsible.

Once they were in his grandfather's chauffeur-driven car, Foster could barely contain his excitement. It was a rare treat to spend this time with him. "Where are we going, Granddad?"

"Like I said, I'm going to show you our business."

"But Dad has taken me to the bank before. It was kind of boring." The Grahams owned banks all along the coast, which was no small feat considering they weren't as old as many of the chains that had a history which dated back to the twentieth century.

"Of course it was because your father would rather keep you in the dark than to tell you about your heritage. I blame myself for why your father is so soft. I wanted to give him the things I didn't grow up with. I indulged him, so he took this life he was born in for granted and doesn't like to get his hands dirty. Apparently he wants to do the same to you but I see too much of myself in you. You're not like your father. I know you're strong enough to handle what I plan on showing you."

Foster hoped he could live up to his grandfather's expectations. So when the car stopped in front of one the main branches of Graham's Bank, he couldn't hide his disappointment. His grandfather must have noticed because he chuckled. Andrew patted Foster on the knee. "The first rule of business is to never take anything at face value. Sometimes there's more than meets the eye." Foster sulked all the way inside the building. Once the employees noticed them, they sat up at attention and pasted smiles on their faces.

"Good afternoon, Mr. Graham," echoed throughout the halls as they greeted the man who could end their means of making a living and send them to the slums if he so chose. For his part Andrew, walked with his head held high, accepting the effusive acknowledgments as his due. Seeing how respected and revered his grandfather was made Foster puff his chest out a bit. Sure, his father was treated respectfully whenever he made an appearance at the bank, but not quite on a level of this magnitude.

The security guards who shadowed them backed away at Andrew's signal once they made it to the elevators. Foster thought they'd go to the top floor where all executive offices were housed, but his grandfather punched in a series of numbers on the keypad which took them to the thirteenth floor. That number hadn't been on the panel.

Foster frowned and it was on the tip of his tongue to ask his grandfather the meaning, but the older man held up his hand, silencing him. He walked silently, following the older man down a long dark corridor until they reached another elevator. This time, they went down. Once there his grandfather took them to a large room, sparse of furniture. Two large men in all black with shoulders so broad they seemed to go from wall to wall stood by the door.

"Is he here?" Andrew asked one of the men as he shrugged out of his suit jacket. He handed it over to the closest one to him.

"Yes and he's all ready for interrogation."

"Good. Come on, Foster. Time to see what you're made of."

As they walked further into the room, Foster noticed several hooks hanging from the ceiling and a number of knives on the wall, all different shapes and sizes. There were also whips and chains and what looked to be weapons used by enforcers.

Foster couldn't wrap his head around why these items would be in a bank or what purpose this secret room served. What he saw next made his heart beat faster. There was a man tied to a chair in the corner of the room. A large wound was on the side of his head that dripped with blood. One of his eyes was swollen shut and his lip was busted. If it weren't for the man's gasps for air, Foster would have been certain that he was dead. Foster bit his tongue hard to hold back a gasp.

"Addison, the brass knuckles please." Andrew rolled up his sleeves and loosened his tie.

The tallest of the two men in black grabbed the requested item off the wall and handed it to his boss.

Foster watched in horror and amazement as his grandfather slipped the instrument over his fingers and flexed as he stalked over to the injured man. "You see Foster, the bank is diverse in its activities. We don't only loan, invest and transfer credits. We're also heavily into collections. You're about to witness firsthand the collection portion of our business." He smirked down at the unresponsive man. "Phillips, wake the fuck up. I know you're just pretending."

The broken man raised his head. A tear ran down his cheek from his good eye. "Please, Mr. Graham, I'll pay you back, every single credit. I just need a little more time."

"What kind of fool do you take me for? I've been more than generous already. I gave you an extra week and you played me for an idiot. You tried to skip out of town, didn't you? We both know I'll never see that money again because you blew it gambling. Seeing how I won't be recouping my money, you'll have to pay me another way."

"Please, I have a family to feed. I'll do anything!" The man pleaded.

"Were you thinking about your family when you were spending credits on back alley dice games and cheap women in brothels? And before you deny it, I have eyes everywhere and *even if I didn't I know your type. You see, I grew up with people like you, always making excuses instead of making things happen for themselves."*

"Then why did you lend me the money?" The man glared at Andrew through his one good eye in an act of defiance.

Without missing a beat, Andrew slammed his fist into the victim's jaw. Foster winced when he heard a loud crack. That had to have broken his face. The man let out a pathetic whimper because he probably wasn't able to release a proper scream.

"Looks like I'm going to have to see if his organs are salvageable. I could probably get a return on what I let this punk borrow and make a little profit. Give me the scanner." He held out his hand waiting for one of his men to comply.

This time Foster couldn't hold back his gasp. Kill him? If someone would have told him he was about to witness a murder, committed by his grandfather no less, he would have called them a liar. He'd never seen a dead person before besides watching shows on holovision or looking at pictures during his history lessons. His hands began to shake and he wanted to run away but his legs wouldn't cooperate. He pinched himself to see if he'd awake from this nightmare before him. Foster had heard whispers about an underworld within their community, crime syndicates run by people who presented a respectable front. Hidden behind their perfect masks was something no one talked about in polite company.

With scanner in hand, his grandfather moved the infrared light over the man's body. It beeped several times before Andrew seemed satisfied with the results. With a grim expression, he read the results on the device's monitor. "Hmm, the liver is no damn good, neither are the kidneys but I can still salvage the heart and lungs." He clicked the scanner off and handed it to one of his men before turning to Foster."

"Now it's time to see what you're made of." Andrew walked toward his grandson.

Foster didn't know where the knife that was now in his grandfather's hand had come from.

"Slit his throat from left to right and make the cut deep. This can be done slow or quick. The more quickly you do it, the more humane, however this piece of shit doesn't deserve mercy. Go as slow as you can." He placed the knife in Foster's hand.

What happened next changed his life forever.

"Mr. Graham, your two o'clock is waiting. What should I tell him?" His executive assistant's image waited patiently for his response.

"Go ahead and send him in, Serena."

"Yes, Sir."

Foster braced himself as he waited for his visitor to enter. The last time he'd seen this man, he thought it would be their final encounter and now he was the one in need of a favor.

"Well, well, well. If it isn't the golden boy? How's life on the other side of the fence?" Marcus Freeman strode into the office like he owned it. Without waiting for any indication to sit down, he took the seat opposite Foster's desk.

"I appreciate you coming to see me on such short notice." Foster tried to be as polite as possible but he was having difficulty doing it when this man was little better than the traffickers Fosters wanted to infiltrate. Their last face to face had not been on good terms.

Marcus smirked. "What are friends for?"

"Cut the bullshit. You and I both know we're not friends. We're not even business associates and if this was five years ago, things would be very different between us."

Marcus raised a brow seemed surprised by Foster's candor. "Pretty hostile words from someone who's looking for a favor."

"A favor you owe me."

"You can't prove I did it, you know," he responded cryptically.

"Oh, but you know I can or you wouldn't have come. Do you have the invitation?"

Marcus dropped his cocky demeanor for a moment. "Are you sure you want to do this? These people don't fuck around."

"I'm sure."

"Okay. It's your funeral, bro." Marcus reached into his jacket pocket and produced a gold-gilded card. "These weren't so easy to come by. I trust this makes us even?"

"What do you think?"

"I think if I could, I'd gladly switch places with you. You're actually one hundred percent legit and you're willing to fuck it up over a whim. I don't get you, Graham."

Foster shrugged. "No one is stopping you from turning things around."

Marcus rolled his eyes. "Yeah, right. I don't have the fancy contacts and powerful friends you do. That makes all the difference in the world and you know it. So, are we done?"

"Yeah. We're done."

Marcus stood up and just as quickly as he'd entered the office, he walked out, leaving Foster holding the gold card.

The card read: *The Auction begins at midnight. Contact number below to learn the coordinates for the secret location.* The date read a week from today. Now that he was completely committed to his plan. There was no going back.

Chapter Five

Tori felt as if she'd been scrubbed and groomed to within an inch of her life. Since she'd been here in this facility she'd been bathed, waxed, buffed and brushed. Her teeth were whitened; every single strand of body hair had been removed. She'd been poked, prodded and examined all under the watchful eye of the intimidating Zee who demanded that every single one of her commands be obeyed.

She was even given a full body scan to ensure that there were no major medical issues. The only upside to that was having the nerve damage in her hand repaired. The residual pain she had experienced on and off from Mr. X's cruelty was gone, leaving only mental images of his torture as a reminder of her time with him. She should have at least been grateful for the medical care but she couldn't help thinking that her new owner wouldn't undo it all through cruelty and abuse.

Tonight was the night.

Zee had informed her that the buyers would be in residence and she would have to be prepared. Shia had spent the better part of the day getting her ready.

"I don't understand why they would go to so much trouble if I'm just going to be sold off," Tori said with a frustrated huff.

Shia stared at her thoughtfully. "These bidders will be paying top dollar. They expect a certain aesthetic from their girls. I wouldn't be surprised if you are the top moneymaker tonight."

"What does it matter to me what I'll bring in? It's not like I'll ever see any of it." Tori couldn't help but feel bitter as she thought of all the credits that would be spent on women who would be treated as property and would have no say in their futures. She had a deep-rooted disgust for the Elite class, who treated people from a lower economic background like her as if they were objects, things to amuse themselves with. They came up with games that preyed on poor people like The Run.

It was the government that started the hunt not long after the female population dipped dramatically because of an unregulated vaccination for breast cancer that was introduced to the market. It knocked out over fifty percent of the women in the country. Other parts of the world had been hit even harder. In Tori's mind, it would have made more sense if women were cherished and revered. Instead, they had become a commodity for wealthy men to play with. It was a dangerous world for a woman, where they were fewer in numbers with most of their basic human rights stripped away.

Women who managed to find jobs made only a fraction of that of men. There were certain jobs they weren't allowed to have. They couldn't hold public office, and most women born in squalor had few options to earn a decent living, which was why many of them turned to earning money on their backs by either working at brothels or finding rich patrons. And then there were more sinister options like The Run where volunteers earned ten thousand credits, which in most cases was more than they could possibly earn in weeks. The downside, however, was that the women had to trade in their self-respect and strip naked and run away from "hunters" who pursued them in the name of gamesmanship. Once these so-called hunters, also known as patrons, caught the woman, they could do whatever they wanted to their prey. In a lot of cases, these patrons ended up keeping the woman they caught.

In Tori's case, both her patrons had left her shattered. Mr. X had broken her body, while the first patron, Foster Graham, had broken her heart.

Tori wasn't sure how long she'd been running but her legs were tight and ached from excursion. Her lungs were on fire and sweat dripped down her body like rain. As much as it hurt to keep going, she couldn't stop. She figured if she got a safe enough distance away from the starting point no one would find her.

Perhaps if she could locate a suitable hiding space she'd be able to rest for a bit and continue on later. She didn't want to get caught. She had to get back to her siblings and take care of them. She'd already authorized for the credits she'd earn for participating today to be transferred to her father since he was technically the legal guardian of her brothers and sisters. But she couldn't trust that he'd use that money to take care of them properly. He'd probably spend it all on alcohol, drugs, or gambling, or maybe even all three.

With her mind momentarily occupied, Tori lost focus on her task causing her to stumble over a large rock. "Ah!" she cried out as she landed on the ground, face first onto the moss-covered forest floor. Rolling over, she reached for her ankle which now throbbed in pain. She touched it as gently as she could but winced when her hand made contact with the sore spot. She hoped it wasn't broken, because even if it was, she had to somehow keep going or be caught. Tori gave herself a moment to recover, hoping the ache would subside a bit. When it didn't, she realized she had no choice but to keep going.

Tori attempted to stand, but the minimal amount of weight she attempted to put on her injured foot sent her crashing back to the ground. She bit her lip to stop herself from crying out. The last thing she needed was to draw attention to herself in case someone was headed in her direction. She looked around, hoping to find some kind of hiding spot where she could rest and look through her supplies to see if there was something to wrap her ankle with. After taking a brief survey of her surroundings, she spotted a large bush with an opening just big enough for her to crawl through. She figured she could keep herself cloaked by covering the opening with branches and leaves once she was inside.

She crawled to her sanctuary, and cursed under her breath as she squeezed through the tiny space, getting scrapped by the sharp edges of exposed twigs. It was the hazard of playing this stupid game. She wasn't allowed a stitch of clothing besides running shoes. She cursed the sick bastard who originally thought of this idea. There was no space to move and if she did, Tori feared she'd make too much noise, so she kept very still and quiet, ignoring the pain in her ankle.

After what seemed like several minutes, she realized her injury wouldn't get any better even with her being off of it. She had no choice but to keep moving, but as she was about to leave her hiding place, the sound of leaves crunching beneath booted feet caught her attention. Someone was near. She and the rest of the women had been given an hour head start, so she must have been in this spot longer than she thought.

Gazing through the leaves, she wasn't sure whether to be frightened or relieved, because the person who came into her view was none other than the one patron in this horrible game that didn't make her skin crawl. It relieved her because he hadn't pawed her like she was a piece of meat as the others had done. But it scared the hell out of Tori that she actually thought it wouldn't be so bad being caught by him.

Earlier, before the games had started, the patrons were allowed to check out the volunteers. As each of those Elite bastards degraded the women like insignificant little nothings, some going as far as to touch their genitals, Tori had wanted to punch, and lash out but knew those actions could cost her. But finally a tall blond man stood before her. She literally gasped when she saw him. When he'd introduced himself as Foster, it didn't quite register because she couldn't tear her eyes away from him even if she wanted to.

His crisp blue eyes a shade so vibrant, they held her mesmerized. He had a face that seemed to be chiseled from granite, all perfect angles and planes. Dirty blond hair that hung past his ears seemed elegantly tussled in effortless waves. Tall, and broad-shouldered, he was surprisingly well built for a man who probably didn't know what the meaning of hard labor *was. He certainly looked as if he took good care of himself. Tori could think of no other word to describe this man other than beautiful. Despite the easy smile tilting his lips, there was a hardness about him that lay just below the surface. Behind that sapphire gaze, were secrets. It frightened her a bit, because she knew better than most that looks could be deceiving.*

She tried to huddle as inconspicuously as she could inside the bush, so as not to draw attention to herself. It didn't matter how attractive she found this man, he was a danger to her as long as he threatened her freedom. He casually strode in her direction, seeming to be in no hurry. As he got closer, she heard a beeping noise. Tori bit the inside of her lip to hold back a gasp so she wouldn't give herself away. She focused on his polished black boots which seemed to be the kind worn by the military, but fancier.

He took a few paces away from the bush only to return. "I can wait this out as long as you can, although I can't imagine that it's very comfortable in that bush." He spoke with such confidence, if Tori didn't know better she would have thought he'd actually seen her enter her hiding spot. But that wasn't possible because she'd crawled inside before he'd come into sight.

She remained very still, not daring to move. There was no way she would surrender so easily. She thought of trying to make a run for it but realized it wouldn't do her much good on her bad ankle.

Foster chuckled. The sound was tinged with just the right amount of sinister intent that sent chills down Tori's spine. He could have reached inside the bush at any second but it felt like he was toying with her somehow. "It's only going to end one of two ways, you can either come out on your own volition, or I come get you, and I've been told that I can be...rough. Come out and play."

Tears stung her eyes. This wasn't how she envisioned the game to go. She was so certain she could somehow find a way to dodge all the patrons but she was wrong. Suddenly realization hit her. That beeping sound. He'd been using a tracking device. How else would he know exactly where she was hiding? The fucking game was rigged! Tori's fear quickly transformed to anger. There was no way any of the volunteers were meant to get out of here without being hunted down and captured.

"Bastard!"

His response was to once again chuckle. "I assure you, sweetheart, that my parents were very much married when I was born. Come on out."

"What do you think people would say when they learn this game is fixed?"

"Fixed? In what way."

"Clearly you have a tracker."

"Your point?"

It was disheartening that he didn't seem the least bit concerned about her accusation. The fact that he didn't bother to deny it seemed to support the fact that even if she became a whistleblower, no one would care, at least no one who had the power to do anything about it. "Why me? You could have tracked any of the other women."

"If I wanted another woman, I'd be with her right now, wouldn't I? Look, it'll be dark soon, come out."

"Fuck off. Do you honestly think I'll come to you willingly?"

"Have it your way."

Before she could reply he reached inside the bush. He yanked her by the forearm with enough force to send her colliding against his chest. In the process, however, her injury was aggravated. She let out a howl. "Oww, you asshole!" she screamed in pain.

Foster held her away from him, staring down at her through now narrowed eyes. He must have discerned that she was in agony, before he sighed and lifted her in his arms. "Where do you hurt?"

Surprised that he bothered to show concern, Tori answered honestly. "My ankle."

"Well, we have about a six mile hike back to the main house where someone can give you treatment. In the meantime, I guess that I'll have to carry you, not that I mind." That easy smile of his returned.

Tori wasn't sure what to make of him. One second he was the cheerful charmer, and the next, he was the dark menace. And both sides of him scared the hell out of her.

"I think you're all ready." Shia glanced at her, seeming satisfied with her handiwork.

Tori hadn't been paying attention as Shia had dressed her in a sheer black dress that clung to her body like a second skin. Though she was given a tiny metallic G-string, Tori wasn't offered any other undergarments. She felt just as nude now as she had when she'd participated in The Run.

Shia pressed a button on the room's control panel and a full length mirror rose from a slot that opened on the floor. Tori stared at the image looking back at her. She barely recognized herself. Her face was caked with artfully applied makeup, and her normally riotous curls had been straightened and now hung to the center of her back. Her bronze skin seemed to shimmer beneath the lights which made the green in her hazel eyes really pop. She looked like one of the workers in the fancier brothels.

When Tori used to hold a job in the shopping district as an errand girl, many of the high class prostitutes would stroll down the street clothed in the latest fashions, carrying an armful of bags. They held the title of courtesan because of the price they could demand for their services and were held to some degree of esteem in their twisted society. But while they may have walked around with their noses in the air, looking down on the workers in the seedier bordellos, they still made their livings on their backs. Tori never wanted that for herself, but now she was in a situation far worse. At least the sex workers chose their profession despite the circumstances which lead them there.

Tori was so deep in thought, she didn't hear the door to her room open.

"Is Rose ready?" Zee's no-nonsense voice brought Tori out of her musings.

Zee stepped inside, flanked by her bodyguard. Her small dark gaze roamed over Tori, inspecting her, not seeming to miss a single detail. "You were a bit heavy-handed with the makeup, Shia. You've aged her. Do it over."

"Yes, Zee." Shia guided Tori to the chair where she'd made up Tori.

Tori tried not to fidget as the girl cleaned her face and proceeded to reapply the makeup under Zee's watchful eyes.

"You should be honored, Rose, we're having some very important visitors tonight. That means we'll probably get more for you than I anticipated. The foreign ones almost always seem to prefer the exotics, and you're one of two we have going on the block tonight, although I think you're the more attractive of the pair."

If that was meant as a compliment, Tori didn't appreciate it. How could this bitch so casually discuss selling her off as if she were nothing more than a piece of furniture? "Fuck you," she muttered, fed up with this woman, and this place.

Zee raised a brow before stalking across the room to where Tori sat. She pushed Shia out of the way and raised her hand. Tori felt the sting of Zee's backhand before tumbling off her chair. She fell into a heap on the floor. Not giving herself time to absorb what had just occurred, Tori leapt to her feet. Rage boiled over from the depth of her being. She was tired of being used, tired of others deciding her fate for her. Tori charged at Zee and managed to wrap her finger around the woman's throat.

Squeezing with her all her might, she was determined not to let go until this bitch was dead.

So focused on her task, Tori didn't realize one of Zee's goons approaching. A sharp searing pain shot through her as she dropped to her knees. When she looked up to see what had happened, a large meaty fist flew in her direction only to be caught by Zee. "Enough, Xander. No bruises. We want to make sure she's in the best condition possible when she goes on the block. Grab her arm. Bronte, you get the other."

The two guards grabbed Tori by either arm and held her up as she struggled. Zee stood directly in front of her and stroked the dark marks that began to form on her pale, slender neck. "You're quite fortunate that tonight is exchange night or else things would go quite differently."

Tori glared at Zee. This was the bitch who'd tormented her for the past several days with her constant demands and psychological torment. She spit in Zee's face.

She was answered with another backhand. Zee then wiped off the spittle dripping off her cheek. "Listen you little cunt. Exchange night or not, you keep it up and I will make sure you experience the worst pain you've ever been in. Don't fuck with me." Zee turned her beady gaze toward Shia's direction. "Get me the neutralizing serum."

Shia nodded before scurrying out the room.

Zee returned her attention to Tori and grasped her by the chin. "You will not ruin this night for us, because if you do, you will live to regret it for the rest of your life. And no, that doesn't mean we'll kill you. We'll make you suffer and I'll see to it personally. Do you know what we'll do to you?" Zee smirked and continued without waiting for Tori's reply. "First I'll cut your tongue out with no anesthesia. I'll make sure it's slow and you feel every agonizing second of it. Then I'll puncture your ear drums, so the only thing you hear for the rest of your life is ringing. It'll make you want to scream but you won't be able to because you'll have no tongue. Then I'll pluck one of your eyeballs out and make you watch me stomp it beneath my heel. Afterwards, I'll take the remaining one and feed it to the dogs. Finally, I'll chop off your hands leaving you with no way to communicate. Your world will be completely dark and soundless but we'll keep you alive so you can live in your own isolated hell until you draw your last breath and trust me, my dear, I'll personally make sure that will be for a very long time."

Tori shivered because she believed this twisted bitch would actually do it.

Shia returned holding a large syringe.

Zee took it from the girl and promptly jabbed the needle into Tori's chest.

Tori tried to pull away, but as the liquid that had been injected into her, spread through her body, she felt as if she had been turned to stone. Her tongue felt heavy and she could no longer move her lips or any other part of her body. She couldn't even blink.

Zee attempted a smile, revealing large teeth that had been sharpened to fine points. "The serum should immobilize you temporarily, but as your muscles relax, so will your mind. You can't escape because you won't want to." She ran her knuckles over the curve of Tori's breast, grazing her nipple. Tori couldn't fight off the horrid woman's touch if she wanted to.

"Shia, see that she's ready within the hour." Zee backed away and gave Tori another long inspection before spinning around and leaving the room, her guards close behind.

Shia practically dragged Tori's stiff body in front of the mirror and proceeded to repair her makeup. "You shouldn't have done that, Rose. It's not good to make Zee angry. I've seen her do things far worse than what she threatened to do to you."

Tori could only stare at herself in the mirror. The stranger who started back at her looked like a frozen doll, with a tear sliding down her face.

Chapter Six

Foster took a deep breath as he stood outside the building he'd been given the address to. On the outside it looked like an old abandoned structure that had seen its glory days many years ago. To the untrained eye it probably should have been condemned, but he knew more than most that looks could be deceiving. It was now or never. If there was any chance of getting Macy back, this was it.

Just as the instructions had said, he found a metallic door at the side of the building, with a small black star painted in the center. The decoration was so small, it could have been a smudge, but it was obvious if one was actually looking for it. Foster knocked three times, then paused. He knocked two more times and stopped again. He rapped on the door four more times in rapid strikes. After a few moments the door slid open, and he barely managed not to let out a sigh of relief that he'd gotten the secret knock correct. He was sure he had been monitored from the second his driver dropped him off, so he couldn't appear as anything other than confident. He needed to look as if he belonged.

The last thing he wanted to do was raise suspicion. He'd heard about these people and what they could do to infiltrators. His contacts were useless now that he was on the inside. Almost as soon as the door shut behind him, Foster was approached by two large men in black suits. It was rare for Foster to feel small in any situation, being a few inches over six feet, but these behemoths were close to seven feet and wide to boot.

"Thumb." The closest doorman requested as he held up a handheld identifier.

Foster pressed the pad of his thumb against the device's green screen. A line moved across it to capture his identity.

"Foster William Graham. CEO and President of Graham Banks. Cleared." the identifier read back.

Seeming satisfied with this information, the guard nodded. "This way Mr. Graham. I'm Dino. I'll personally escort you to your box."

Foster noticed this guard's face had several deep scars over his cheeks and forehead as if those marks had been carved into his skin as some form of initiation. Foster knew a little something about scarification as it was once a tool he'd used himself to get something he wanted out of an uncooperative target. He wondered who might have done this to a man who was the size of an oak tree, or even had the power to do so.

He followed his guide down a narrow hallway. Foster wasn't given much time to take in his surroundings but what he did see was mostly shrouded in dim light. The large floor was completely barren. The scarred guard halted in front of an elevator. Foster stiffed. It was like déjà vu of that fateful elevator ride he'd taken with his grandfather. He braced himself when the doors opened and he stepped inside. Just as he suspected, they went down. There were no numbers that indicated just how deep their descent was but it felt like a big one.

Once the elevator came to a halt Foster flinched as he was hit with a bright light when the doors opened. He stepped off the elevator and found himself surrounded by gold-gilded walls. One of the largest chandeliers he'd ever seen hung from the center of the ceiling. It most certainly seemed to be made of the rarest gems, in nearly every color on the spectrum, dusting the room in a rainbow of light.

Everything about this room screamed luxury, from the marbled floors to the precious works of arts decorating the walls. Whoever the actual owner of this organization was, they'd certainly spared no expense. A handful of people he assumed were guests littered the room, casually chatting with one another, drinking various glasses of alcoholic beverages.

A young girl dressed all in black appeared by his side. Her hair was pulled back in a severe ponytail and her skin was impossibly pale as if she hadn't seen the sun in years. She had to be in her early teens. "I'm Remi. May I get you some refreshments before you're taken to your box?"

Foster needed a clear head to get through the night but he noticed the rest of the people in the room held drinks. He had to fit in. "Yes, I'll have a bourbon, no ice."

"Will that be all, sir?"

"Yes, please." She raised a brow, almost seeming surprised by his response and he wasn't exactly sure why. But she said nothing before hurrying away to fulfill his request. Foster now wondered what it was he'd done to throw the girl off. He noticed that even Dino eyed him curiously. Foster glanced toward the other guests. Many of them seemed to be from foreign countries judging from the different languages spoken around him. Some chatted with each other while other stood off by themselves. No one had handheld devices or watches which were forbidden on the premises.

As he glanced around him, he discovered a familiar face, one he hadn't seen in years. As if they had a mind of their own, his legs propelled him to the person leaning causally against the wall, not really looking in anyone's particular direction. He straightened up as Foster drew near.

The only sign of recognition from the older man was the light twist in his lips; otherwise, they could have been strangers. "Winthrop," Foster greeted when he halted in front of him.

"Fancy seeing you here. One would think a Graham wouldn't compromise their dignity by being in a place like this. But of course, your family isn't quite as dignified as you'd like to present yourselves to be. You do all your dirty work behind closed doors, don't you?"

Foster glared at the man who was the son of his grandfather's former business partner. Foster was well aware of the fact that when Graham Bank was originally started, his grandfather had had a silent partner, which had been Eli Winthrop, father of Eli the second standing before him. When he was a child, Foster used to be quite friendly with Eli III until his childhood friend had gone missing. Not long afterwards, Foster had learned the partnership between Graham and Winthrop had dissolved over some business disagreements and Foster's grandfather had bought Winthrop out, gaining the controlling shares to take the company in the direction he wanted.

Before the falling out, the Winthrops and Grahams had mingled frequently at social events and informal family dinners. Foster remembered his childhood friend fondly, but there was always something about Eli II that made him a little uneasy and he could never figure out what it was. Seeing the man now, older and slightly grayer, he felt a similar dislike that he had as a child.

When Foster had learned the other side of his grandfather's business, Andrew had assured him that the Winthrops had nothing to do with it. Judging from the bitterness in Eli II's voice, Foster wondered if the falling out had something to do with them finding out the truth about his grandfather. The Winthrops had at one point been one of the wealthiest and most respectable families in their circle. Shortly after the business partnership had dissolved, however, it was like all the Winthrops had fallen off the face of the Earth. Some speculated that they'd moved overseas and were living quite comfortably off of what they'd made after selling out.

"You seem to know a lot about my family considering we've had no contact for years. Besides, you should be careful about spreading rumors. They have a way of coming back to bite you in the ass."

The other man snorted. "I see you're no different than that brute of a grandfather of yours. Weren't you involved in his dirty little side business?" If looks could kill, the one of pure hatred Winthrop shot his way would have killed Foster on the spot.

He didn't get a chance to immediately reply because Remi had once again appeared by his side. "Your drink, sir. Is there anything else I can get for you?"

Foster plastered a smile on his face as he took the drink from the girl. He gave Remi a wink. "Nothing right now, darling."

A deep red blush creeped up Remi's cheeks and she gave him a shy grin. "If you need anything else, just snap your finger and I will be at your service." She then looked to Winthrop. "Mr. Winthrop, can I refresh your drink?" she asked with noticeably less enthusiasm, although she maintained her polite demeanor.

Winthrop leered at the girl. "You know I'm interested in more than just a drink, but if a drink is all you're offering, get me some scotch, and be quick about it."

Remi nodded.

As Remi turned to do the older man's bidding, Winthrop reached out and pinched the girl's bottom. To her credit, Remi took it in stride before walking away.

Foster had participated in The Run several times, hunting naked women for his amusements, but even he drew the line at children. As much as he wanted to give this asshole a body blow, he couldn't draw attention to himself. But at least he understood why Remi had looked at him so surprisingly earlier. If Winthrop was any indication, none of the other guests were polite in their requests either. It made sense that a place like this would attract assholes no matter how fancy they were dressed up. It was probably part of the appeal of the organization. One could be as rude as they wanted to be without having to worry about the rules of polite society.

Once Remi was out of earshot. Foster returned his attention to Winthrop. He learned closer, making sure the other man would be the only one to hear what he had to say next. "You don't know shit about my family and I suggest you keep your opinions about them to yourself."

"Or what? You'll make me disappear like my son?"

Foster reeled back at that accusation. "What the fuck are you implying?"

"I'm not implying a thing, but I would like to offer a word of warning. You're a newbie here. This is my territory and you'd better not cross me. The Grahams have no power here."

Foster clenched his fists at his sides to keep himself from beating the hell out of this piece of shit. Whatever bad blood there had been between his grandfather and Eli the First, he couldn't let it affect him now. It didn't matter if Winthrop knew of his past because he would have a hard time proving it. If he had any hopes of getting Macy back he had to play it cool. He smirked, masking his murderous thoughts. "Of course we don't. We're just humble bankers."

The other man flared his nostrils and looked as if he wanted to hit Foster, but remained where he stood. "Keep it up, Graham. You won't be grinning for long."

"It was nice catching up with you, Winthrop."

Foster turned away from the other man, not bothering to wait for a response. Dino came into his line of vision. "Sir, the bidding should be starting soon, and I'd like to show you to your box."

"Will you be individually escorting the rest of the guests to their spots as well?"

"No sir. The others have already been shown to their boxes. Since you got here later than everyone else you missed some of the activities. We had a dinner laid out for the invitees, but I could send one of the girls to your box to bring you a meal so you can eat in private as some of the other guests prefer. You should still have time to go through our catalogue to see what offerings we have going up on the block tonight."

Foster nodded in response. This outfit seemed well run. He followed Dino out of the luxurious room and down a long corridor. When they reached the end, Dino pressed a button on the wall which opened a small door. Foster had to duck in order to go through. The box as it had been described was stark white, from the thick white carpet to the plush chair and desk sitting in the middle of the room. The furniture took up most of the space, making it cozy.

"The organizers believe the fewer distractions the better. This way the buyers can fully concentrate on the merchandise. On the desk you'll find a control panel that will generate the holoscreen. The other buttons control volume. This red button means that you want to place a bid and the light beside it will turn on when you've been outbid at which time, you can press the red button again. If your bid is successful, the light turns green. All transactions will be squared with Zee at the end of the auction. You won't be able to leave until all the bids are final. In the meantime, you bring the holoscreen to peruse through our catalogue of who will go on the block tonight. Some of our guests prefer being surprised. Do you have any questions, sir?"

Foster shook his head. "I think I can figure it out. But I was wondering, do you ever see the girls? The offers I mean? Are they housed in this building?"

Dino shifted from side to side, his eyes darting back and forth. "I'm not sure what you're asking, sir."

Foster had already known that the auction only took place once a month. Macy disappeared close to two months ago, so she most likely would have been sold off in the last auction if she were sold. "I think my question was pretty straightforward but here's another question for you. What happens if the person on the block gets no bids?"

"That's never happened to my knowledge, sir. As for your other question, I'm not at liberty to answer that question. If there's something here not to your liking, I can certainly relay that information to Zee."

"Is he the one in charge?"

"*She* runs things around her. Perhaps I should bring your questions to her attention so that you can have your questions answered to your satisfaction."

Foster smiled. "That won't be necessary. It's my first time, so naturally, I'm curious."

Dino nodded. "Naturally. The bidding will start in less than twenty minutes but someone will check on you about that meal."

Once Dino left the room, Foster cursed under his breath. He'd come on way too strong. He was almost certain the guard would tell his boss about the questions he'd asked. At this very moment they could be watching him. "Fuck."

Remi entered the room next. "Mr. Graham, is there anything I can get for you? Another drink? Maybe something to eat. Our chef can whip up anything you require."

"No, sweetheart. I'm fine."

She blushed. "If you need me, press the blue button on your panel."

"I'll keep that in mind."

"Well, if that will be all, I'll check on the other guests." She smiled, backing away slowly, in no particular hurry to leave.

He winked again and she nearly stumbled over her feet.

She stopped at the door. "You know, Mr. Graham, anything you require of me, I'll be happy to do. I mean, if you have any special needs, I'll take care of those as well." The bright red blush coloring her cheeks made it very clear what she was offering. He doubted this was something new for her and he was quite sure others had taken her up on her proposal. Some probably demanded it.

"I just might take you up on that, but later. I have a little business to conduct first, darling."

She giggled before leaving him alone.

He wouldn't take her up on her offer of course, but he did himself no favors to make his disgust known that this place was using children to entertain guests. Foster didn't consider himself a prude, but he preferred his partners to be of age and fully developed. In his former life, if he knew someone was a pedophile, he took extra care to make them suffer.

His thoughts drifted to his brief conversation with Dino. If what the scarred man had said was true then there was no way Macy was here now. She'd be long gone. But he could probably find out who bought her if he asked the right person. Winthrop might have the answers since it was apparent this wasn't his first time here. Maybe he was one of the guests when Macy went up for sale.

Foster was deep in thought when a bell sounded. The holoscreen appeared and a holographic image of a woman dressed all in black, a codpiece and spiked boots, appeared before him. "Welcome to tonight's events. I am Zee for our first time guests. We have a large assortment of offerings tonight. Bidding will start at one hundred-fifty thousand credits." Then Zee's image disappeared to be replaced by a petite woman in a see through dress. Long red hair cascaded around her shoulders, and she was heavily made up. She was quite attractive. The woman seemed slightly dazed which meant she was possibly drugged. Foster wouldn't purchase any of these women but he had to put in a few token bids.

By the fourth woman, he was bored out of his mind, not really focusing on the women, but trying to figure out his next move. He barely paid attention when number five was called, but he happened to glance at the woman's holographic image before him and froze. It couldn't be. He reached out but his hand went through the hologram. She was fixed up, but he would recognize that body anywhere, after all he'd spent many hours tasting every inch of it. He remembered the nights when he held her in his arms and how he'd fucked things up in the end out of some misguided sense of nobility. But here she was at the mercy of anyone with enough credits to have her. Judging from the glazed look in her hazel eyes, she wasn't completely there. Drugs. Despite the superficial changes, she was just as beautiful as he remembered. "Victoria."

Chapter Seven

Some of the drug Zee had administered had worn off but Tori's muscles refused to obey her command. She'd been led to a pedestal that rotated slowly enough not to give her vertigo. Shia had explained to her, once Tori was put on the block, that she wouldn't be able to see who actually placed bids on her. This was something Tori was grateful for because this entire process was sickening. She wasn't sure how long she remained in the spot she'd been planted but it seemed like an eternity.

Finally, one of the guards stepped forward and lifted her off the stand. He led her toward Zee who for the first time since Tori had met her was actually smiling, or at least her version of a smile. Zee's face was so stiff, probably from injections, that Tori was surprised the woman could actually form any kind of facial expression. "You've set a record for us tonight, Rose. Ten million credits. You make me think we should be exclusively selling exotics. Your kind always goes for top dollar. Like I've already said, these buyers always pay top dollar for things out of the ordinary." It seemed Zee's musing was more for herself than for Tori's benefit.

"Bronte, you can take her out with the other girls in the waiting area until everyone has gone on the block," Zee instructed.

Bronte practically dragged Tori's uncooperative body to another room where she saw a group of women sitting around. Some looked frightened while others seemed unaffected. The guard placed her against the wall before leaving.

One small woman, who looked to be mixed like Tori but was of Asian descent approached. "How much did you go for?"

Was this woman kidding? They'd just been auctioned off like slaves and the price for which she was sold was a point of interest? Tori opened her mouth to tell her exactly that but the drugs made it difficult for her mouth to move.

"I see that they must have given you the neutralizing serum. They gave some to Pansy over there." She jerked her thumb in the direction of a redhead who looked slightly dazed. "But from the looks of it, you got a larger dose. You must have really pissed Zee off."

"Why…does…it m-matter?" Tori was finally able to get out.

"Why does what matter?"

"How much? It d-doesn't matter because…we're being…sold…like…animals."

The other woman shrugged. "It's not like our lives were going so great before we ended up here. I worked a dead-end job to help my family and I've got nothing to show for it. The way I see it, anyone willing to pay top dollar for us must live in some big fancy mansion. I'm ready to be pampered for a change. Oh, I'm Lily, by the way."

Was this real life? Even though Tori couldn't speak without great effort at the moment, her mind was just fine. It was clear to her Lily didn't understand the gravity of the situation. Tori had been in mansions before, and she would have traded her old life for what she'd found behind their closed doors. She wasn't sure what Lily's life was like before this but she couldn't have suffered through what Tori had if she still had an idealistic view of the Elite. Tori then realized Lily wasn't quite a woman. She might have been developed like one, but upon closer inspection, she couldn't be that old.

"Lily, how…old a-a-are you?"

"I'll be fourteen next month."

This poor child had no idea what was in store for her and Tori didn't want to be the one to disabuse the girl of her fantasies. For all Tori knew, Lily might very well go to someone who would treat her fairly. But deep down, Tori didn't think that was likely. She'd suffered through way too much to believe otherwise. Anyone who would participate in an event that involved snatching women and children off the streets against their will couldn't be good people.

"Good...luck, Lily." Tori sincerely wished this girl the best.

The door opened and Zee called out a girl's name. "Violet, it's time for you to meet your buyer."

A tall blonde who had been huddled against the wall walked toward Zee. It almost seemed as if she was heading toward her execution. The blonde burst into tears causing Zee to glare as they led her off. One by one the girls were taken, leaving Tori in the room by herself. She wondered why they'd saved her for last. She hadn't been the last one to go on the block.

With anxiety brewing in the pit of her stomach, it was tough for Tori to remain calm as she contemplated her fate. Just when she thought she couldn't take the waiting another second, Zee returned. "We had a to take care of a few minor details before handing you over to your owner but everything has been resolved to our satisfaction. I'll take you to him now." Bronte and Xander each took one of her arms and guided her to her fate.

She was taken down a long hall and then on to an elevator. They entered a large empty room. Standing by the entrance on the other side, was a tall blond man. She couldn't quite make out his features, but as she got closer, her brain screamed his name. It couldn't be. But how?

Overwhelmed by everything that had happened, she felt dizzy, and suddenly, everything went black.

Foster had been worried when the transaction took longer than he believed it should have. Once the credits had been transferred, Zee seemed very interested to know how he had heard of their organization and who had recommended him. He'd practiced his story several times before he arrived so he wouldn't raise suspicion. Zee had left twice to discuss a matter of business with someone. When she returned, he noticed her murmur something in an earpiece.

Just as Foster had suspected, Zee might have run the operation side of things, but there was no way she was the head of this criminal organization. There was someone else behind it and he had to know who. Foster realized they were probably suspicious of him because of the questions he'd asked earlier, but fortunately he seemed to check out. That didn't mean he wouldn't be looking over his shoulder for the next few weeks. He planned on being cautious, especially now, when he had someone special to protect.

He looked down at the woman whose head rested in his lap. This definitely wasn't part of the plan, but when he saw her on the block there was no way he would allow anyone else to have her. He'd made the mistake of letting her go once, but this time it was for keeps.

Foster didn't know whether the emotion he felt toward her was love but he knew that he'd been miserable without her. Sure he had put on a smile for the world to see but when she left, she'd taken a part of him with her and it was his own fault.

It had been a long night. He let out a sigh of relief when he pulled his vehicle into his multi-car garage. Many of his peers used drivers to navigate the busy streets. He had one as well but most times, he preferred to drive himself. It relaxed him and gave him a chance to think and there was definitely a lot on his mind tonight. The fire in one of his downtown banks was fortunately contained, but it was no accident. Tracking down the responsible party was what had taken up the majority of his day. And meting out the perpetrator's punishment had been draining.

His past had come back to haunt him in his business life. How much longer would it take before it caught up with his personal one? There was only one thing he could do.

The moment he stepped inside his house, she was there waiting for him, without a stitch of clothing, just how he liked her. His Victoria. *Foster was aware that she preferred to be called Tori, but Victoria was much more worthy for his queen. She was so beautiful she took his breath away.*

As she stood in her glory, he admired every single curve and dimple on her body. Her breasts were a nice handful, capped with nipples as dark as juicy blackberries. He could spend hours sucking on them. A light dusting of hair rested over her pussy, giving the hint of mystery that drove him insane with lust. He loved the way her honey brown curls rested on her shoulders, framing her pretty face.

His cock was rock hard and despite knowing this night would not end well, he had to have her. With a growl, Foster advanced, yanking Victoria into his arms. He covered her mouth, devouring her. Her plump lips were soft and pliant beneath his. He loved the way she tasted of cherries and chocolate. He pressed his tongue against the seam of her lips, demanding entrance to the sweet recesses of her mouth.

He cupped her round ass, molding her body against his hardness. Victoria returned his kiss with enthusiasm, giving him as good as she got. Foster had lost track of all the times he'd sampled her mouth, but he never grew tired of it. Digging his finger in her thick curls, he yanked her head back, making her gasp. He stared down into her lovely face, taking in every single one of her features before once again covering her mouth with his.

He took complete charge thrusting his tongue forward, demanding total dominance. Victoria twisted her head away and gasped for breath. "Slow down."

"No." Foster captured her bottom lip between his teeth and gave it a sharp nip. He trailed hungry kisses all over her face and along her neck.

Victoria moaned his name. "Foster."

The soft caress of her breath against his ear was enough to drive him beyond reason. Foster wrapped his arms around her waist and lifted Victoria off her feet. He didn't have the patience to carry her all the way to the bedroom, so he took her to the first room they came to, the kitchen. The need to reunite his tongue with her clit was overwhelming. He plopped her on the edge of the island and pushed her knees apart before kneeling directly in front of her cunt.

Her scent was intoxicating. Her dark folds were puffy and glistened with her juices. He looked up at her with a raised brow. "Have you been playing with my pussy while I've been gone?"

Victoria bit her bottom lip. She didn't have to say a word because her face said it all. Her eyes darted away from his and her guilt was apparent.

"What did I tell you about playing with my pussy when I'm not here? This belongs to me. It's mine and you didn't have my permission to touch it."

"I was so horny. I was waiting for you to get home."

Without warning, he smacked her pussy.

Victoria cried out.

"Say you're sorry."

A string of her liquid slid down her inner thigh and she began to wiggle. "I couldn't help myself. I got so hot thinking about you."

Smack!

"Ahh!" she groaned.

"You're not the least bit sorry are you? Because you're a dirty little slut who can't get enough, can you?" Smack!

"Oh, shit, Foster. I'm going to come!"

"You'd better not."

"Please. Let me come."

"Tell me how badly you need it."

"I need it bad."

Smack!

"Please! This is torture!"

Foster smirked, loving how responsive she was to his touch and how turned on she got whenever he talked dirty to her. "Ask me nicely."

"Please. May I come?"

"After I've had a taste." He parted her warm brown slit to expose the pink treasure inside. Foster buried his face in her cunt and slid his tongue inside her moist channel. Her juices coated his tongue and it was pure heaven.

Victoria dug her fingers in his hair as she grinded herself against his face. "Yes. Just like that."

As he fucked her with his tongue, he pinched her clit between his thumb and forefinger. He rolled it and applied enough pressure to make her cry out. He fed off the sound of her screams. Her honey dribbled down his chin and he could tell she was on the verge of release. He licked and laved her pussy with long broad strokes. Foster spread her cheeks apart and circled the tight ring of her anus with his tongue. He left not part of her unexplored.

"Foster, please! I can't hold back any longer."

Victoria began to wiggle and convulse, signaling her climax. Foster gladly lapped her cream, not wanting to spill a single drop. She was his addiction he couldn't get enough of and he was far from finished with her.

Without giving her a chance to recover, he yanked Victoria off the counter, set her on her feet, and positioned her body so that her back was flush with his chest. "Place your hands on the counter and spread your legs."

Victoria's breathing was ragged and she trembled as if she was still coming down from her high, but she obeyed him nonetheless. Foster quickly unbuckled his belt and undid his pants to free his cock. His need for her was too urgent to admire the beautiful curve of her ass. He slid inside her with ease. Her pussy encased his cock like a warm embrace. It felt like home, because there was nowhere he would rather be in this moment than with her.

"So fucking tight," he groaned, before pulling out enough so that only the tip remained. Foster then slammed into her, going deeper still.

"Yes!" she cried out. "So good."

"Damn right it is." He took a fistful of her hair to use as leverage before pounding into her over and over again. Something came over him in that moment, a demon of some sort that made him plow into her harder and faster with each stroke.

Victoria however didn't seem to mind, in fact, with each thrust, she threw her hips back to meet his cock, thrust for thrust. He pushed away all the troubles he'd dealt with earlier and focused completely on her, this beauty, because nothing else mattered right now besides being here with her like this. If he could, he'd fuck her forever. Foster held on for as long as he could but when Victoria clenched her muscles around his dick, he exploded inside of her.

He gripped her hair even tighter and let out a roar of satisfaction. Once he'd spilled every drop of his seed, he relaxed his grip and eased out of her.

"Oh, my stars," she panted. "That…was intense. It may take me a while to recover from that."

"You make it sound like I'm finished." Foster adjusted his pants before scooping her up in his arms. "I'm not finished with you yet. We have all night."

After that session in the kitchen, he'd carried her up to the bedroom and made love to her in various positions. At times they'd both drift off but he'd wake shortly after, eager for another round with her.

The Auction

And in the morning, he kicked her out of his house.

Chapter Eight

Tori stretched her arms over her head and let out a loud yawn. She couldn't remember the last time she'd slept so well. The warmth of the thick down comforter tempted her to sleep a little longer, and then she remembered the events from the night before. She opened her eyes and sprang into a sitting position. She looked around her and recognized the bedroom immediately. How could she forget this place when it was where she'd experienced her greatest joy and even greater pain?

Foster had bought her but she didn't understand why; in fact when he'd gotten rid of her she thought for sure that she'd never see him again. He was just like any other member of the Elite who took pleasure in using people until they grew bored. He made her believe that he actually cared and then stomped on her heart when she expressed her feelings for him.

One thing was certain, she had no plans of sticking around just to be toyed with by him again. Besides, she had to get back to her family. She'd been away from them for too long. At least she was in a familiar place. She just had to figure out a way to get out without being noticed. She was sure this mansion had top notch security. There was no telling what kind of system Foster had put in place to keep her prisoner.

Sliding out of bed, she realized she was stark naked. Had Foster undressed her? Heat flooded her cheeks and a warmth spread within her core. "Shit." Why did her traitorous body still react to even at the mere thought of his touch? It frustrated her because she believed she'd made herself numb to him. But even seeing Foster last night after all this time sent her into a dead faint. He hadn't changed much since they'd parted ways. His hair was slightly longer and he still had that devil-may-care grin.

No matter what, she couldn't afford to let her guard down with him again, because once he was done with her this time she wasn't sure she'd recover. She quickly pushed all thoughts of him from her mind. She'd have to plot her next move with the end result being a successful escape.

Tori looked around for something to wear and remembered the closet full of clothes Foster had bought for her when she was last here. She walked over to the control panel and pressed the button to open the wardrobe door. A gasp escaped her lips. The inside was exactly like she left it. The beautiful peach blouse she loved so much was laid over the cushioned chair in the center of the closet. She didn't hang it up so she'd have easy access to it. The dresses and shoes were arranged in the same order which meant no one had gone through this stuff, not even to tidy up the mess she'd made when she was last in here. Tori was well aware of how meticulous Foster's housekeeper was about keeping the mansion clean. She couldn't imagine why she'd left this untouched.

She grabbed a terrycloth robe off the hook to cover herself.

"Ms. Preston, I've been alerted that you're awake. Should I have some breakfast prepared for you?" Mrs. Gordon's voice came through the intercom.

The housekeeper spoke as if Tori had never left instead of being absent for the last couple years.

"No thank you. Uh…Do you know where Fos—Mr. Graham is?"

"He left earlier this morning but he said he shouldn't be long."

"Okay. Thank you."

"Will that be all?"

"Can I ask you as question?"

"Certainly. That's what I'm here for."

"The items in the closet don't seem as if they've been touched."

"They haven't, Ms. Preston."

"I don't understand why. I mean you do such a thorough job of taking care of this house."

"Thank you, ma'am. But it was Mr. Graham's wish that your room not be touched."

This surprised Tori. Why wouldn't Foster want anyone to touch this room? It couldn't be because he actually missed her. She wasn't fooled by the idea that he brought no other women to his house. He'd been a regular participant in The Run. Surely, there were several women after her. Whatever his reasons, it probably wasn't due to sentimentality.

Bastard.

Just thinking about his callous treatment made her want to leave as soon as possible. "Um, Mrs. Gordon, do you think I'll be able to leave the mansion for a walk in town?" When she'd been here before, Foster had allowed her walks in the neighborhood as long as his security detail was in tow. She figured if she could get outside, she could somehow lose them and make her escape. She simply wasn't interested in facing Foster again.

"I'm sorry, Ms. Preston, but under no circumstances are you allowed to leave the grounds. There are guards monitoring every sector of the premises and should you attempt to exit, you will be bought back."

"Do you understand I'm being held here unwillingly?"

"I'm sorry, but you'll have to take your concerns up with Mr. Graham. I wish I could be more helpful to you, but like I said it shouldn't be long before he returns."

That's what she was scared of.

"It's okay. I know it's not your fault."

"Well, please don't hesitate to call on me if you need anything."

"Thank you, Mrs. Gordon."

"You're welcome."

Tori dropped to her knees. She didn't know what Foster's reasons were for bringing her back. But this time around she refused to fall for his bullshit.

"Are you certain he's the one?" Foster stared at the images on the holoscreen of an unassuming looking man who didn't seem like he was involved in one of the largest trafficking organizations in the world.

"Yes, this man is the sole owner of the account your money went to. It took me several hours to track it because once you made your initial transfer, the money bounced to over a thousand accounts. It finally landed in one that belonged to this man. Now, I can't be certain that he won't end up transferring the funds elsewhere, but I'm sure he'll know some of the big players in this game."

"Thank you, Gareth. I'll handle things from here. Your payment has been sent."

"If you need anything else, you know how to reach me. I hope you're careful though. As I was scrolling through some of those names this guy is associated with I got a little worried. These are the types of people who could wipe you out. It doesn't matter how much money you have."

It was a sentiment that Foster had already heard. "I understand, which is why I'm not going to further involve you in this. Now I have a starting point at least. Thank you."

"You're welcome. As always, it's nice doing business with you." Gareth nodded in Foster's direction before sliding out of the booth.

Foster took a sip of his coffee and winced. It was too bitter for his taste. He'd only ordered it so as not to draw suspicion to himself. This wasn't his part of town but there was no telling who was watching, especially when dealing with people who didn't want their secrets exposed.

Finding Macy would be like tracking a needle in a haystack. One of the reasons he'd gone to the actual auction was to determine the flow of the operation. It hadn't been his intention to purchase any of the women on the block, but when he'd seen Victoria, there was no way he'd allow her to go to anyone else. When he'd paid his credits for the transaction, an idea struck him.

One thing Foster understood more than most was money and how the intricate system of transfers worked particularly on the black market. It occurred to him that the account his money was going to had to be a dummy. It wouldn't be smart business for them to have an easily traceable account. Even with the lax rules from the government regarding bank accounts, underground business still was at the mercy of the whims of any official who wanted to cause trouble. Though it wasn't typical since most politicians were mouthpieces for the highest bidder, it wasn't something unheard of. In his former life, Foster had worked with hackers to get information needed that wasn't readily available. One of the best he'd ever done business with was Gareth.

The guy knew his way around a computer and could get into any system in the world. As soon as Foster had seen that Victoria was safe and sound in his house, he'd made a call. He wanted the funds he'd spent at the auction to be traced. Since everything was computerized through the VC implanted in their bodies, Gareth would be able to use a tracker to find the money trail.

Foster had wanted to be home when Victoria awoke so he could talk to her, but he'd received a message from Gareth stating he'd found what he was looking for, hence the meeting on the outskirts of town.

Foster had recognized the man in the scans that Gareth had shown him. He was a former senator who had given up his government position to go into the private sector. No one knew for sure what he did exactly to maintain the lavish lifestyle he led, but most assumed he'd made most of his money through the government. Foster knew that couldn't be the case. He was aware of what the salaries for many politicians were, because they had accounts with his bank. Most could live quite comfortably off a government income, especially with the bribes they received from special interest groups. None of them, however, made enough to sustain this man's lifestyle. Learning that he was in the trafficking business made sense.

Ruben Myers.

The former politician now had a target on his back that he didn't realize. To find out what this man knew, Foster would have to do something he swore he never would again. He'd have to tap into the savage side of him. It was the part of him that made him less than human, the side that threatened to destroy his soul. And if he got out of this ordeal alive, he wasn't sure if he'd ever be the same again.

Chapter Nine

Tori was on edge as she paced back and forth in her room. After showering, dressing and eating she was bored out of her mind, despite being offered a number of items to keep her entertained by Mrs. Gordon. Foster had yet to return and she wasn't sure what would happen when he did. The only thing she could think about was how she'd felt the day he'd told her in no uncertain terms that he no longer wanted her.

The first thing Tori noticed when she woke the morning after a marathon sex session with Foster was that he wasn't in bed with her. She'd grown accustomed to waking up in his arms, or being roused with his head between her legs or him sucking her breasts. The only reminder she had from the night before was the delicious ache between her thighs. Her muscles were slightly stiff as well. Foster had a habit of being rough, not that she minded because he always made her crave for more. Last night was different, however. He seemed more ferocious, needier, as if he couldn't get enough of her, not that she was complaining. She loved every single minute of it.

There were also those moments of tenderness. He'd caressed her body and took her so gently Tori cried tears of happiness. She wasn't sure how it had happened, but she'd fallen for Foster Graham. Hard. From the moment he'd captured her on The Run, she'd been defiant, unwilling to bend an inch to his will, but Foster wasn't what she'd expected. He actually seemed to care about her feelings and took the time to find out about who she was as a person. And then there was the sex. He'd given Tori her first orgasm. It took a while to reconcile how she could respond to him so willingly when he technically owned her per the contract she'd signed.

Foster didn't act that way toward her, however. He showered her with presents and treated her as a valued guest. The only time he was aggressive with Tori was in the bedroom or wherever it was his fancy to take her. He was a kinky son of a bitch who constantly pushed her boundaries over and over again until there were none. He dominated her, making Tori bend to his every command, and she'd become his willing slave. Outside of the bedroom, he was charming, sweet and considerate.

She was almost certain he returned her feelings because of the little things, like the stolen kisses, or the way he'd look at her when he didn't think she was paying attention. Foster would find excuses to touch her and then there were those moments when he just held her. Tori lived for those moments.

She decided right then that she'd tell him how she felt. Tori wanted him to set her free so that they could be together for real and not because they were brought together in fucked up circumstances. She'd also be free to see her family. It didn't hurt that she'd be in a better position to help her siblings.

With her resolve firmed, she slid out of bed. As she headed for the bathroom to shower, Foster walked into the room. Tori didn't bother to cover herself. She saw no point in playing coy around him. They'd met when she was stark naked and he'd made no secret of the fact that he preferred her that way. Foster, however, was fully dressed and the expression on his face was grim.

She sauntered over to him with a huge smile on her face. "Good morning." When she attempted to put her arms around him, he backed away. "What's the matter?"

"Not now, Tori. Why don't you get dressed so we can have a little chat? I'll be waiting for you downstairs in my office. Take a shower while you're at it. There's an odor lingering on you." Foster didn't wait for her to reply before he walked out of the room, leaving Tori with her mouth hanging open.

What the hell was that about? Foster had never been so cold toward her, or even rude. Something had to be wrong. He'd called her Tori. He never did that. She went through the motions of taking care of her hygiene and getting dressed. By the time she made it to the designated meeting place, her stomach was all in knots. She couldn't figure out what had happened between this morning, when they'd fallen asleep exhausted from sexual exertion, until now. Maybe there was some kind of personal emergency. Several scenarios ran through her mind and none of them were good.

She knocked on his office door and waited for a response. The door slid open and Foster beckoned her inside. "Come in and have a seat, Tori."

She cautiously did as he bade, sitting on the edge of her chair. Tori laughed nervously. "What's going on, Foster? You never call me Tori."

He raised a dark blond brow. "Isn't that your preference?" His tone was so icy, he could have been talking to a stranger off the street.

"Well, yes, everyone calls me that but not you. I've just gotten used to you calling me Victoria."

"I didn't call you down here to discuss your name. I just wanted you to know, that'll I'll be sending you an additional ten thousand credits. It should show up on your chip by the time you leave. You can also take everything you were gifted during your stay here which included the jewelry and clothing. Mrs. Gordon will be on hand to help you pack. I think that takes care of everything. You may leave now." He then turned his attention to a holoscreen that appeared to contain documents of some sort. He'd dismissed her as if they didn't spend hours making love the night before, like he'd never called her beautiful before. Like she didn't matter.

"Leave? What are you talking about, Foster? Why do you want me to leave?"

"Tori, please don't make this more difficult than it has to be. I think my offer is pretty generous considering I don't owe you a thing. You were already paid by The Run organizers. Maybe you can make extra credits by selling off the jewelry."

"I don't care about the jewelry. I want to know why you're doing this." Tears stung the backs of her eyes.

Foster let out an exaggerated sigh. "Must you be so tedious about this? You had to know this arrangement we had would come to an end. Don't take it personal my dear, I prefer *variety so it was eventually bound to happen that I'd grow bored with you. You should actually be proud of yourself. You've managed to keep me interested longer than the others. Give yourself a pat on the back."*

That was it? She'd been ready to pour her heart out to him and he could just callously treat her as if she wasn't worth a damn? "No. There's something you're not telling me. Why are you really acting this way?" The tears that she'd felt only seconds ago ran freely down her cheeks.

Foster slammed his palm on his desk. "Tori, stop it! I've participated in several runs before you and I'll be in many more after you. It's a sport to me. The fact that I get to fuck my catch is an added bonus. You couldn't have possibly thought that this was permanent. You're a Dreg, and you belong in the slums with the rest of your kind. Tori, you were just a convenient fuck and now I'm tired of you. Frankly, I've grown bored with this conversation. There. Have I made it clear enough for you?"

The disbelief she felt was replaced by anger. Tori sprang to her feet. "So this is the real Foster?" She walked around his desk and smashed her hand across his face so hard, his head turned. Tori raised her hand to do it again, but Foster caught it.

"You only get one. Do it again, and I'll hit back even harder." He tossed her hand away. "Now get the fuck out of my office. You have an hour to get your shit together and get out of my house as well."

"Fuck you, Foster Graham, and fuck your money! I don't want a single credit from you! Yes, I thought I cared for you but I had to be mistaken because you're an unfeeling piece of shit!"

Foster rolled his eyes. "If you're finished being dramatic, leave."

Tori realized there was nothing she could say or do. The Foster she thought she knew didn't exist. All her life she'd been shit on by the Elites. They'd taken her mother away from her, they made it impossible for her to earn a decent living to *support her family. They destroyed her neighborhood to make more space for themselves forcing her family to live in a run down shack. But none of them had ever hurt her quite the way Foster had. And she'd never forget it for as long as she lived.*

"Ms. Preston?" Mrs. Gordon's voice on the intercom broke Tori out of her painful memories.

"Yes? Mrs. Gordon?"

"Mr. Graham is home and he'd like for you to come downstairs and join him in his sitting room."

Tori flared her nostrils. Did he think he could snap his fingers and she'd come running just like that? She wouldn't make it easy for him this time around. She'd be damned if he made a fool of her again. "Mrs. Gordon, could you kindly tell Mr. Graham to go fuck himself?"

There was a pause on the other end of the intercom before the housekeeper responded. "Are you sure that's the exact message you'd like for me to relay?"

"Word for word."

"Very well, Ms. Preston."

There was no response after that. In fact nothing happened right away, so she shouldn't have been surprised when the door to her room opened and Foster walked in. The shock of seeing him so suddenly made her take a step back. Regaining her bearings, she squared her shoulders, preparing herself for this showdown.

Foster wasn't surprised when Victoria rejected his invitation to meet him in his office. It wasn't as if they'd parted on good terms and that was the way he intended it to be. He'd hurt her and as a result hurt himself, but at the time it couldn't be avoided. He had to do what he felt was necessary to keep her safe. And now he had to do it all over again. If she still hated him, then so be it. He wasn't letting her go, not until everything happening was resolved.

She looked so beautiful. He appreciated that her face had been scrubbed of the heavy makeup she'd worn the night before. She was a natural beauty who needed no enhancement. It took everything within him not to pull her into his arms and fuck her senseless, but he managed to remain where he stood.

"Victoria, you're lovelier than ever. Time has been good to you."

She narrowed her eyes, giving him a death stare. "It's Victoria now? Call me Tori. Only my mother is allowed to call me that and she's dead."

"I used to call you Victoria as well."

"And you lost the right to. So why am I here?"

He expected her to be angry with him, but her hostility still hurt. "Because I bought you which means you belong to me."

"Right. Until you get tired of me being just a convenient fuck. What's the matter? Now that the Run has been disbanded you've resorted to flat out buying your women? How pathetic are you? Can't you get women on your own? You sick bastard."

Foster realized her words came from a place of hurt but hearing her lash out at him pissed him off. He was under a tremendous amount of stress with figuring out what happened to Macy and who had her. He'd involved himself with people that made him look over his shoulders again. What was worst, after his meeting with Gareth, he'd received a mysterious call on his holophone, no image had been available, but an unrecognizable scratchy voice had sent him a warning. *"You're sticking your nose into business that you shouldn't be. Be careful, Graham, or else you'll lose everything you care about."*

There were very few people who had his personal access number but he knew there were always ways to obtain things if one wanted it badly enough. This had happened to him one other time and that had led to him letting Victoria go. Having her rage to him, no matter how much he deserved, it was the proverbial last straw.

"Regardless of the reason why you're here, this is where you'll stay until I say so. You have free run of the house but you will not be able to leave."

Victoria folded her arms across her chest and pursed her lips. "It seems like I have no choice in the matter of my comings and goings, but I'm damned sure not going to make it easy for you. Don't even think about touching me."

"Do you honestly think that if I wanted you, there's anything you could do to stop me? You've forgotten, *Victoria* that I've heard this line from you before. You pretend that you don't like my touch, but in the end, I'll have you begging for it."

"If you touch me, I'll scream."

Foster chuckled with amusement. One thing he'd always admired about Victoria was her spark. Despite all she'd been through, no one had managed to break her spirit. Seeing the fire in her eyes turned him on and he wanted her more than any woman he'd ever had. He'd never stopped wanting her. "Oh? What do you think is going to happen when you scream? Who's going to come running to your rescue? Do you believe someone in my employee will call the enforcers on me? And what do you suppose will happen if they did? Do you honestly think I'd be arrested? Tell me, Victoria."

She backed away from him. "Touch me and find out."

Curiosity got the better of him, making Foster advance toward her. When he was only a few feet away from him, he noticed Victoria bringing her knee up. He barely missed getting kneed in the balls, but she did catch him on the thigh. "Shit. Don't ever do that again!"

She pushed him away from her. Then she got closer and pushed him again. Victoria balled her fists and began to pound against his chest. Foster allowed her the first few blows. After what he'd done to her, she deserved some kind of retribution, but when she smacked him across the face, he'd had enough.

Foster caught her by the wrists and dragged her toward the bed. She attempted to pull herself out of his grip but to no avail. He tossed her on the bed and fell on top of her.

The brief second he loosened his grip Victoria began to lash out again. "Let me go!" she screamed

"Never." Foster captured her hands and held them above her head as he pressed his weight into her. She squirmed and wiggled beneath him.

"The only thing you're accomplishing at the moment is making my dick hard." His erection rested hot and heavy against the junction between her thighs.

As if realizing this, she stilled. Victoria shook her head back and forth. "Don't," she whispered.

He looked down into her large eyes that now glistened with the suspicious sheen of tears. He really should have gotten off of her, but he couldn't move. The feel of her beneath him was too much of a temptation for him to resist. Since their first arrangement had ended he'd lived with the regret of it every single day. Each night his dreams were filled with images of her. He'd never forgotten the taste of her lips, or the way her eyes lit with wonder whenever he stroked her the way she liked.

"I can't help it." He then lowered his mouth to hers.

Chapter Ten

The slow descent of Foster's head gave Tori enough time to turn away. His lips grazed her cheek. She didn't want to be affected by him but the feel of his body, his scent, and just the lust in his eyes, reminded her of how good things had once been between them.

He nuzzled her neck and began to suck the skin just above her shoulder.

He remembered.

That was the spot that made her knees weak. Tori squeezed her eyes shut, trying not to give in to the masterful caress of his lips. She tried to focus on how much she hated him, on how much he'd hurt her, but it was all to no avail. The heat within her core was too hot to ignore. Her breasts felt heavy and her nipples tightened.

Foster transferred both of her wrists to one hand, but she still couldn't break his hold. "Why are you doing this to me?" He was too strong for her to overpower. Tori also doubted she could appeal to his sense of decency because he didn't have any. The best she could hope for to distract him enough to loosen his hold. Then she could get away and find some kind of weapon to use against him.

He raised his head. Foster's bright blue eyes had darkened to near black. "Because I want this, and you want me, too."

"If you're so certain that I do, then why don't you release my hands?"

He chuckled. "Because I'm not an idiot. The second I let go, you'll either attack me or try to push me off. You'll put on a nice show of resistance because you feel you have to in order to justify the inevitable."

Her breath hitched in her throat. "And what's that?"

"Me claiming every inch of this delectable body and you loving every second of it. I promise you this, sweetheart, by the time I'm finished with you, you'll be screaming my name until your throat hurts."

His arrogance was even greater than she remembered. "Don't count on it."

"How about we put it to the test?"

"If you try to kiss me, I'll bite you."

"Promise?" He pressed his lips against her neck, again finding that spot that drove her wild. Foster sucked and nibbled on her skin, applying just enough pressure to make her squirm.

Tori steeled herself to remain motionless, but that delicious ache she'd fought so hard to ignore would not be denied.

He moved his hand between their bodies and slid it beneath her blouse, not stopping until he held her breast in his palm. Giving it a squeeze, he kept his eyes trained on her face. Tori closed her eyes tight so that she couldn't see the smug smirk she was all too familiar with.

"Open your eyes, Victoria," he softly commanded.

"No."

"Why not? Because you don't want to watch when I do this?" Foster removed his hand from under her shirt only to rip it down the center, exposing her to his hungry gaze.

She squeezed her lids even tighter. Tori couldn't bear witnessing his moment of triumph.

"How about this, Victoria?"

Foster pushed her bra up, freeing her breasts. He then circled one nipple with his the tip of his of his finger. The already taut tip, puckered until it was completely stiff. She willed herself to resist but a sigh escaped her lips.

"You like that, don't you, sweetheart?" Foster paused as if he expected a reply. She refused to give him that satisfaction.

"I missed this so much, touching you and feeling your soft skin. And I especially loved doing this."

Tori felt the warmth of Foster's breath on her nipple before it was surrounded by the wet heat of his mouth. She tilted her hips in an attempt to buck him off but he would not be moved. Instead, he bit her tender flesh hard enough to make her cry out. This time she did open her eyes. Seeing that blond head sucking so forcefully on her breast sent a wave of heat shooting to her core. She couldn't keep still even if she wanted to.

Tori was unable to stop the moans that came tumbling from her lips as he licked, sucked and nibbled the tight bud until she was delirious with pleasure. He transferred his attention to the other breast and she thought she'd combust from bliss.

Without warning Foster released her wrists as he made a decent down her body, dropping kisses on her skin as he went. He laved her belly button and caressed her abdomen. He'd always been so thorough, and it was apparent nothing had changed in that department.

Now that her hands were free, she could finally push him away but it seemed as if they had a mind of their own. She found herself digging her fingers through his wavy blond locks, actually giving him a slight push in the direction where she wanted his mouth the most. Her pussy.

Foster eased her pants down her hips, taking his time to give every bit of exposed skin with a kiss. She whimpered with delight. Every single place he touched turned into an erogenous zone. The man seemed to have some kind of sexual hold over her that she didn't have the power to fight. Though he'd taken off her pants with artful precision, Foster tore her panties off without a care.

"You know I don't like it when you wear these. A pussy this pretty should never be covered," Foster said as he parted her thighs. He bumped his nose against her clit and inhaled. "I missed this so much." He captured the nubbin between his lips and sucked gently at first but with each passing second, he became more aggressive in his attack.

Tori yanked at his hair and grinded her hips against his face. She was so hot she could barely think straight. All she could focus on in that moment was having Foster ease the ache within her that he'd created.

"Oh, yes," she groaned.

Foster slipped his finger inside of her as he clamped on to her clit again. Pulling his finger in and out of her, he managed to hit the right spot with enough friction to drive her near the point of completion. He added another finger, stretching her channel and giving Tori the maximum amount of enjoyment.

When he added yet another digit she couldn't hold back any longer. A bolt of electricity raced through her body sending Tori to a quick and explosive orgasm. It had been so long since she'd experienced anything so intense.

Foster, however, continued to assault her pussy with his fingers and mouth, not giving her a chance to recover. He feasted on her like a man starving and pushed her to yet another powerful climax before pulling away.

Foster flipped Tori onto her stomach without warning. "On your hands and knees."

Tori was too turned on not to obey. She eagerly complied with his command.

"Stay just like that." He slid off the bed and quickly undressed before positioning himself behind her.

Tori looked over her shoulders to see him lick his fingers before placing his cock against her already throbbing pussy. It was still as thick as she remembered.

"You're so wet and hot for me aren't you, sweetheart? You need this, don't you?" "Mmm," she moaned in response.

"Tell me you want it."

"I-I want it."

"Ask for it nicely."

Her juices dripped down her thighs. Despite already experiencing two orgasms, Tori still felt the need to be filled with his hard cock. "Please," she whimpered.

"Tell me how much you want it."

"I want it. Please stop teasing me. I need it! I want it! Are you satisfied?"

"Not quite but I'm getting there." The smugness in his voice had returned, but she didn't have a chance to dwell on it because he slammed into her with enough power to rob her of all her immediate thoughts save being so thoroughly taken by him.

Foster grabbed her by the shoulders and began to plow into her hard and fast. There were no gentle strokes, no soft caresses, just hard core fucking. This wasn't sex, it was complete and absolute domination and he was her master. And to Tori's secret shame, she loved every second of it.

He went so deep inside of her, she could feel him in every single spot in her body. Foster gripped her hair as he sped up. "You are mine, Victoria. You will not deny me again because you belong to me."

He slammed into her over and over. Even when she came yet again, he continued. Finally, just at the point when Tori thought she'd pass out from sensory overload, he yelled out her name. "Victoria!" He shot his seed deep into her core before collapsing to his side, panting for breath.

Foster didn't stay put for long. Instead, he rolled off the bed and got dressed quickly. He stared down at her. She was exhausted, barely able to lift her head, and he'd recovered like it was nothing. He smiled at her before leaning over, moving a stray curl away from her forehead. "I told you I could make you beg for it. Keep that in mind the next time you think to deny me again." Without another word, he turned and left the room.

His words had the same effect of a bucket of water thrown directly in her face. He'd hurt her before and apparently, it looked as if he wanted to continue doing it. This was the real Foster, a sadistic bastard who enjoyed playing games. Mr. X had tortured her in ways that had made her wish she were dead, but he didn't come close to hurting her as badly as Foster did. What scared Tori the most was the knowledge that when Foster touched her again, there wouldn't be anything she could do about it.

<><><><><>

Foster wasn't sure what had come over him but the need to dominate had taken over. It was a part of him that he thought he'd had a handle on. The look in her beautiful eyes nearly crushed him. What he really wanted to do was go back to Victoria's room and pull her in his arms. Foster wanted to tell her how much he missed her and that he thought of her every single night since they'd parted. He wished he could let her know that no other woman could compare to her, and that no matter what, he would always take care of her. Instead, he'd hurt her again.

"Fuck!" he cursed under his breath and slammed his fist into his palm. Something about delving into the crime underworld had brought out a side of him that reveled in other people's pain. It was the demon within that craved destruction and chaos.

One thing was certain; he had to find Macy before he completely lost all of his humanity. In the meantime, he knew of one way to get the process going.

He made his way into his office and pulled up his contact list before taking out a handheld cellular phone. The archaic device was rarely used anymore except in museums and exhibitions that demonstrated old technology, but they were still useful in the underworld. In his old life, these devices were frequently used because they were untraceable on the grid. But a very cleaver hacker had figured out a way to rig them to tap into the towers that gave holo devices their signals.

Personally, Foster hated using them because they were only voice capable. He liked to see who he was talking to. The other downside, was when the cellular phones were used just once, they had to be destroyed because though they couldn't be traced on the grid, if the authorities got a hold of it, they could be hooked up to computers that were able to determine all outgoing and incoming calls.

Foster still had a few he'd never gotten rid of just in case an emergency. He'd debated on keeping them, wanting to destroy all traces of the life he'd once lived, but now he was thankful for his foresight.

He pressed the button on the phone but nothing happened. He then remembered it required an adapter in order to charge it up instead of the graphite batteries that were used as the main power source of small devices. Foster dug through his desk until he found a charger and plugged it in. He waited a few minutes before the screen lit up and a red light shaped like a battery came on the screen. He punched in a number on the keypad that he hadn't utilized in years.

He didn't expect anyone to answer right away, so Foster was unprepared when a voice spoke on the other end.

"Name."

"FG. 09823469797."

"Will call back in ten minutes upon verification."

Ten minutes later, the cell phone vibrated. "FG, here."

"0589525698." A click followed.

Even though it had been a while since he'd contacted anyone like this, the process had come to him so naturally, as if he hadn't been away for several years. To get to certain people, he had to call a dummy number and leave his name and the number he could be reached on. The caller on the other end would verify the number to make sure it wasn't on the grid and then the name of the person calling. If the verification went through, the person who he wanted to contact would either return his call or the go-between would give a time when that person would call back. Sometimes the person one needed to reach didn't want to call back, which meant they weren't willing to do business with you. So when ten minutes passed without a callback, Foster started to worry. Maybe no one wanted to work with him because he'd distanced himself from that life. The possibility was there.

After twenty minutes he had all but given up getting a call back. Someone would have contacted him by now. With a heavy sigh he began to put the cellular phone away but then it vibrated.

"Yes?"

"Thought you were done. Turned your nose up and decided you were too good to associate with the likes of us."

Foster pinched the bridge of his nose, feeling a stress headache coming on. "Did you only call back to gloat?"

"Not at all. I just wanted to know what could possibly be the cause of you contacting someone like me. Tired of rubbing elbows with all your fancy friends?"

Lars Anderson was what some called a finder. He could locate anyone at any time and he'd retrieve them. Foster had worked with him several times before. The other man, however, always seemed to resent the fact that Foster was born into wealth and did little to hide his disdain, although he never flat out said anything until now. Since Foster had gone completely legit, the other man probably felt comfortable enough to say the thing he probably always wanted to.

If Foster wasn't in desperate need of his services, he'd just say fuck it and hang up, but a job like this required the best and Lars was the best. "Are you finished?"

"Not by a long shot, but I'd be interested in knowing why you've contacted me. I almost didn't call you back. But my curiosity got the better of me."

"Of course it did. Or perhaps you couldn't pass on the hefty fee I'm willing to pay for your services. We both know I'd never contact you any other way."

A chuckle greeted him on the other end of the line. "Of course. There's the arrogant rich boy I remember. So what do you want?"

"What I want is for you to do what you do best."

"I'm listening."

"I need you to locate a certain gentleman. This one might be a little tricky because he has some high-powered connections."

Lars chuckled. "Connections never bothered you before."

"I've never dealt with a situation like this before."

"Who do you need me to find?"

"Name's Rueben Myers."

There was a pause on the other end.

This was exactly why Foster hated these phones. He couldn't tell why Lars had suddenly gone quiet and he couldn't read the other guy's expression. Finally, Lars whistled. "You're serious?"

"I've never been more serious in my life."

"Wow. For someone who hasn't been in the game for a while, you're sure asking for trouble. Look, Graham, I'll be the first to admit that you're not my favorite person. But if you go after this man I can almost guarantee there will be some retaliation."

"I'm prepared to take that chance."

"Okay, but for getting me involved in this bullshit, I'm going to have to double my fee."

"Of course." Foster expected this based on Lars's reaction.

"So do you want the usual?"

"Just find him and bring him to the old location. I'll handle the rest."

"Shit. What did this guy do to you?"

"Let's just say he stands in the way of me getting something I want."

"Okay. Give me twenty-four hours. These things take a bit of time. I want half of my fee upfront and the rest when the job is done."

"Deal. Just send me the account you need me to transfer the credits to."

"You can count on it." Foster clicked the off button before tossing the phone in the pile of items to be incinerated.

Foster leaned back in his chair, contemplating his next move. Part of him wanted to check in on Victoria but she needed her space. He vowed when this was all over, he'd make it up to her, that was if he made it out of this ordeal alive.

Chapter Eleven

His toolkit was right where he'd left it, another reminder of his old life. The more he thought about it, the more Foster realized that he hadn't gotten rid of many of the old toys associated with his past. Did he keep them because subconsciously he knew he'd fall back into an underworld that none of his current associates knew about? His best friend Dare knew some of it, but what would the other man say if he knew the entire story? Dare didn't exactly have clean hands himself, but Foster was certain Dare had never done the things Foster had, or was about to do this very night.

When he'd gotten the call from Lars, stating that Myers had been found and secured, Foster had battled with himself internally. Did he really want to take this step, and immerse himself so deeply into the mind of the madman he'd once been? Then he remembered that sweet girl he'd made a promise to. He'd done a lot of shitty things in his life. Finding Macy seemed like a step toward real redemption. But he couldn't help but wonder if it was worth the cost.

With his toolkit in hand, he got into one of his of his older vehicles, one no one would recognize him in. On his drive to the designated location he purposely kept his mind blank and concentrated on the road. The more that he thought about the task at hand the more anxiety it caused, and he needed a completely clear head.

Foster parked his vehicle down the street from the spot he needed to go and walked the rest of the way. It had been a while since he'd been in this part of town, full of abandoned buildings and old businesses barely managing to hang on. The streets were mainly empty because there were very few residents in this section. It was one part of town where a lot of the underworld players conducted their illegal activities.

He quickly made it to the designated building and headed to the side entrance. Foster gave the door a special knock and it slid open. He walked inside to see one of Lars' men gesturing for him to follow.

He was taken upstairs and down a hall that led to a metal door. Foster's guide placed his hand against the hand sensor to get inside. Lars was waiting for him.

Foster squinted from the brightness of the light. The room was covered from wall to floor in plastic. In the center, was a man in a metal chair with a ball gag in his mouth. His hands were tied behind his back, his feet were tethered to the chair with thick ropes and he was blindfolded. It was pretty safe to assume that he wasn't going anywhere.

Lars nodded in his direction before heading out the door, his man following behind. Foster acknowledged him with a nod of his own. Finally he was allowed in the room with his prey.

His heart started beating and his pulse raced. Sweat beaded his forehead and the adrenaline began to flow in his veins. It was the old rush, back in full force. He took a deep breath to calm himself. He had to have a steady hand for what he needed to do.

Foster placed his toolkit on the table next to the bound man.

His victim grunted through his ball gag as drool ran down his chin. He struggled against his restraints. He seemed desperate in his movements and Foster couldn't exactly blame him.

In most cases Foster left the blindfold on while he did his work, but not to keep his identity hidden. In fact, he preferred his victims to know it was him. No one who'd had a session with him told tales because they were either too scared, in hiding or dead. The dead ones weren't killed by him. A dead man couldn't remember the lesson. Usually those people had other enemies who caught up with them. Foster kept the blindfold on because it enhanced the torture. When the person couldn't see what was coming, the mind could sometimes be a man's worst enemy.

With Myers, Foster didn't fool himself into thinking this wouldn't be traced back to him. His identity in the underworld was a well-known secret despite him being away from it for so long, and his handiwork was very distinct. Someone had already tapped into his line. It was clear he was already being watched. That was fine because now they knew that he couldn't easily be fucked with.

Slowly, he rolled up his sleeves. He then reached into his bag and placed each of the instruments inside his kit on the table lining them up by size from biggest to smallest. He then pulled out a pair of black rubber gloves that covered him from fingertip to elbow. Finally he donned a pair of clear goggles, and tied a surgical mask around his neck to fend off any blood splatter.

Foster moved behind the still squirming Meyers and unlatched the man's ball gag.

Myers screamed! "Who's there?"

Foster walked around the chair so that he was facing his captive. Part of him wanted to walk away and never look back, but he'd already set off on this course and he intended to see this to completion. Besides, the other part of him was secretly thrilled, the side of him that got a rush from hearing someone's scream when he applied just the right amount of pain. Most of his victims were scumbags, people who deserved every bit of torture they got, while others were those who had crossed him in some way. Myers had never done anything to him personally but he definitely fit into the scumbag category.

Foster had taken the liberty of collecting information he could dig up on this guy in the past couple of days. He'd been a low-ranking government official who was controlled by a handful of corporations to do their bidding. There wasn't anything unusual about that but what was interesting was one of those companies had funded his legal defense when children of a prominent family went missing. They were able to make those charges disappear and payouts were made to the family. There was another incident involving a young boy, no older than ten, who was found brutally beaten, raped and unresponsive in his home. Again, it had been a child of a family with means. In this case, the family wasn't willing to go quietly. There were a couple of articles regarding the incident, but just as quickly as the scandal had broken out, it went away when the family, the boy included, mysteriously disappeared.

Shortly after that, Meyers retired from his government job and began working as a consultant for this company. Based on this information, Foster came to the only logical conclusion: the business was a somehow involved in the trafficking. Foster was determined to get to the truth, and figured when he was through with Myers he'd hopefully have the answers he needed. One other decision Foster had come to was that Myers was a disgusting pedophile. Any remorse that Foster might have felt for what he planned on doing quickly disappeared.

"Who's there? I want answers dammit."

Foster chuckled. "You're not exactly in a position to demand anything. But I'll answer your question. I'm someone who is in need of information and you're going to give it to me."

"Fuck you! I'm not giving you a damn thing. You had someone take me from my home. Don't you know who the fuck I am? I can destroy you. And don't think for a second just because I'm blindfolded it doesn't mean I won't figure out who you are."

Foster leaned forward, and yanked down Myer's blindfold. "There. Now you don't have to guess."

The older man's eyes widened. "I recognize you. You're...you're that banker! Why do you have me here?"

Foster walked over to his table of tools and picked up a scalpel. "I've already answered that question for you. I'm in need of answers." He held the instrument up to make sure it was sharp enough since he hadn't used it in a while. It was perfect.

"W-what are you going to do with that?"

"Hurt you."

As Foster walked over to his prey, Myers began fighting against his restraints in earnest. Foster sliced the sleeves of Myers' shirt to expose his skin. He then popped each of the other man's buttons, slowly just to fuck with the other man's mind. Once that task was complete, Foster ran the scalpel down the front of Myers' undershirt, making sure that the tip nick the skin from chest to bellybutton.

"Ow! That fucking hurt. Wait a minute. If you let me go now I promise there won't be any consequences. We'll pretend like this never happened."

Foster's only reply was a smirk. He walked back to the table and picked up a vial and syringe. Sticking the needle into the clear liquid, he drew out precisely, 10 cc's. He plucked the syringe to get rid of the excess medicine before placing it back on the table.

"What the hell is that?"

"Adrenaline. I'll administer it to you in case your heart stops."

"Let me go, you fucker! What kind of sick bastard are you? If you're going to kill me, you might as well just do it now because if I get out of this alive, you're going to regret that you messed with me. I have very powerful friends. They'll retaliate. They'll destroy everything you care about."

"Interesting. Who might these friends be?" Foster asked without turning around. He faced his tools, deciding which one he'd use first, and then his gaze landed on a small velvet pouch.

He approached Myers. "How much I hurt you will depend on you. If you tell me the truth I'll show some mercy. If you lie to me or fail to answer my questions in a timely manner, you'll pay the price. First question: what is your involvement with the auction?"

The man's eyes widened before he shook his head. "Auction? I don't know what you're talking about."

Foster sighed. "And here I was hoping you wouldn't be so tedious." He then pulled out a small steel pin. Moving behind the chair, Foster knelt and lifted one of Myers' forefingers. He shoved the pin beneath the man's fingernail and pushed until the pin was completely embedded.

Myers howled in agony. "Nooooo! Please don't do this. I'll pay you whatever you want. Just let me go."

Foster took out another pin and forced it under Myers' thumbnail.

"Oh, God! Please no!"

"Lie to me again, and I'll jam them beneath the rest of your nails. Now tell me why money from the auction is being transferred to your account."

"I'm just a middle man. I swear I have nothing to do with that money. I mean, I get a small fee for being an intermediary but that's it."

Just as he promised, Foster proceeded to shove a pin beneath each of Myers' fingernails.

The other man howled in pain. Tears streamed down his ruddy face.

"If you're only the middle man as you claim, where are you transferring the money to?"

"Another dummy account. I don't know where it goes from there."

Foster sighed. "I see you're going to be difficult about this. "I'll tell you what. How about we just cut to the chase? I had planned on using every single one of those tools on you, but tonight I have something even better in mind." Foster stood up and walked to the table. He picked up the scalpel and a small black plastic disc about an inch in diameter.

"Wait, wait. I'll tell you what you want to know!" Myers screamed.

Foster ignored his pleas. He'd done this enough time to realize what Myers would tell him: just enough, while still withholding the most vital information. He sliced Myers' forearm open, careful to avoid any vital veins and arteries.

"Oh Christ! What do you want from me? I fucking told you I'd tell you. Please just stop! I swear I'll tell you!"

Foster slashed another line across the cut he'd already made, tearing into muscle tissue, before shoving the disk into the wound. He pressed it deep to assure it would do what it was meant to.

His prey cried, sniveled and screamed, alternating between begging for mercy and cursing everything about him. Foster returned to the table and picked up a tiny remote. "I just implanted a muscle stimulator in your arm. These little babies were originally invented to ease back and muscle ache for people who suffer from chronic pain. A doctor implants it and when the patient is hurting, all they have to do is press a button and this tiny disc sends soothing waves throughout the body. Funny thing about that is the device wasn't properly tested before it went out on the market because the company who manufactured it wanted to save money, so they didn't run the proper tests. Anyway, when these things were used on real people, instead of the disks causing relief, it had the opposite effect. It caused severe pain. In the older patients, it even caused death. I heard it once described as razors moving beneath your skin. I've always found this thing to be the most effective when I need to make people talk. Although I usually save it for last, I'll make an exception for you. Now here's what's going to happen, I'll ask you a question and you're going to answer. If I don't like your answer, I'm going to press this button which sets it off. And if your heart stops, I'm going to stab this needle into your chest to bring you back."

Myers eyes were as wide as saucers. "You crazy bastard!"

"Wrong answer." Foster pressed the button and watched him let out a blood-curdling, high-pitched scream. The sound of the man's pain made Foster's heart race. He actually took pleasure in watching Myers fall apart. Foster bet this guy didn't show the children that he raped, beat and trafficked, any mercy.

When Myers stopped convulsing Foster stood in front of him. "You don't get to talk unless I ask you a question. Do you understand?"

The other man didn't respond so Foster pressed the button again.

"Yesssssss!" his victim screamed.

Foster waited for the shaking to stop and asked again. "Just so we're clear, do you understand?"

"Yes…I understand," Myers slurred his words.

"Good. Now tell me where you sent the money?"

"After I take my cut, I…I transfer it to an account outside of the country. As far as I know, it bounces around a few more dummy accounts before going to an account registered to Hemmel Corporation."

That was the company who had funded several of this man's campaigns, and also to his legal defense in the cases of those missing children. From what Foster had gathered in his research, Hemmel Corporation was a supplier of energy and other power sources. The problem he'd come across was in searching for the records of this company was that Foster couldn't find out much about them besides the fact that they donated heavily to politicians. There were no records of who they did business with. Even the CEO listed in their bio was someone Foster had never heard of. Being in a prominent position himself, there weren't many who were in or above his income bracket he didn't know, or at least was aware of.

"Who is Edison Wallace?"

"I told you all I know. Please let me go!" Mucus ran freely from Myers' nostrils as a he cried. Foster wondered if the children Myers hurt cried and begged for mercy. He was certain this motherfucker didn't give a damn. It made it easy for him to decide what he'd do next.

He pressed the button and counted down from twenty to zero. Myers began to jerk and shake as he screamed. The snot that flowed from his nose was now bright red, indicating some internal bleeding.

When Foster took his thumb off the button, he noticed a foul stench in the air. It was a familiar odor that wasn't uncommon during one of his torture sessions. Myers had shit his pants.

"Just…please…just kill me," Myers begged.

"I'm actually insulted that you think I'm a murderer. And here I thought we were getting along so well." Foster picked up his scalpel again and this time sliced into Myers' other arm. "You see, I was going to hold back on you, but you've hurt my feelings." He produced another muscle stimulator and like the first one, he pushed it inside of Myers' flesh, making sure to go slow and to cause the most discomfort.

"I swear I don't know who Edison Wallace is. I've never met him. No one has! I assumed he was a made-up person used as a cover for the business."

"And exactly why would said company need a cover?"

"I….like I said before, I just get the money."

Foster sighed. "It strange you would say that when you're listed as one of their consultants. You obviously think I'm fucking around with you because you're not telling me what I want to hear." He pressed the button. Myers screamed louder than ever from the intensity of two disks implanted inside of him. Drool, blood and tears streamed down his face." And then he stopped moving.

Foster put the button down and checked Myers' pulse. There was none. He retrieved the needle and jammed it into the man's chest right over the heart. When he injected the medicine Myers gasped as he raised his head in surprise.

"Welcome back," Foster taunted.

"Please, you have no idea who you're dealing with. These people have a lot of money and are very powerful. They have a lot of people under their thumb."

Foster walked to the table and picked up a jagged-edged knife. "That's nice. Here's what's going to happen now. I'm going to start cutting off pieces of you."

"No! I, they'll kill me."

"That's hardly my problem." Foster pressed the tip of his knife against Myers' chest and inserted it just enough to penetrate several layers of skin. He then dragged it down and drew a square in Myer's chest, all while ignoring the man's cries of pain. He managed to gouge out a chuck of flesh about two inches wide. "The next piece will be on your dick."

"Okay, but....please don't hurt me anymore."

"I won't make any promises but start talking."

"When I was running for the seat in the local senate's office, I was losing badly because my competitor was outspending me. But he'd made some pretty powerful enemies. I started getting donations from an anonymous source. They said they could help me win if I did this thing for them. I never knew with whom I was speaking and when they called there was never an image on the holophone. I couldn't even tell if the voice belonged to a man or a woman because it was disguised. I started getting money in my private account and all I had to do was make some transfers. I got elected and they got what they wanted. I fought for the bills they wanted passed. It was as simple as that. But...they were watching. They found out about my taste in companionship."

"That you like children?" Foster wanted to spit on this toad.

"They were compensated! These Dreg children would never have seen the kind of credits I offered them. It was a mutual exchange. I got something, and they got something in return."

"Go on," Foster prompted.

"My contact said they needed me to collect some children for them. They didn't say why. I just needed me to bring them to a certain location and they would take care of the rest. I did it because of the extra credits I received. I don't know what happened to them afterwards, but I didn't think it was a big deal. They were just Dregs, no one would miss them."

"Except maybe their families."

Myers snorted. "How do you think I got access to these street rats? Their own families sold them off to me. These filthy people demand rights but then they act like animals. They can't even take care of their own children but they keep popping them out. At least I compensated them."

Foster balled his fists at his sides. He was aware of how most people in his circle viewed the lower class; he'd witnessed it first hand, he'd even said something similar. That was until he actually got to know some of them. People like Victoria, Macy and Aya helped him to see how sheltered he'd been most of his life.

Hearing Myers discuss these people as if they were nothing when he was the one exploiting them pissed Foster off. He took the knife and gouged out another piece of the man's flesh, creating a larger hole in his chest.

"Oww! I answered your questions. Why did you do that?"

"I'm not interested in the extra commentary. So get back to your role in this mess. How many children did you provide these people and how often did you do it?"

"About two or three. But I only did it a handful of times. They stopped asking me when people got suspicious of me. Some visiting dignitaries came to my house. They had their children with them. I had a few children in a room that I'd marked as off limits. They went exploring in the house and discovered the room. I had no choice but to get rid of them too. These families made a fuss and they had to be paid off to make the allegations go away."

"And that boy you beat?"

"I didn't know who he was. I swear. He was just some kid off the street. I didn't know his family had some pull in the city."

"And that makes it right?"

Myers lowered his head.

"So then what?"

"They told me no more children. At that point I just did the money portion. I made the monthly transfer when credits ended up in my account."

"When was the last transfer?"

"A few days ago."

That was just after the last auction.

"Did you also take women?"

"No. They didn't ask for women but...there was someone who collected the children whenever I would drop them off. I once saw another man with a couple of women."

"Where is this location?"

"It's about an hour outside of the city." He rattled off an address. "It's in front of a big blue building, you can't miss it."

"Who was this other man?"

"I don't know. He had a medium build. Light brown hair. Thin mustache. A weasely looking guy."

"West," Foster muttered. The bastard had withheld information and had probably lied to his face.

He had something in store for that guy when he caught up with him. He glanced at his tools. By the time he was done with Peter West, the other man would be begging for Foster to kill him. In the meantime, he owed Myers a lot more pain.

Chapter Twelve

Tori was determined to remain strong and resist Foster at all costs. After that incident where he proved to be an even bigger bastard than she remembered, she stayed in her room, not bothering to come out except to eat her meals. For the most part she'd managed to avoid him. But by the third day it occurred to her that he hadn't bothered to seek her out. There were no invitations to join him for meals and he didn't barge into her room.

It almost seemed like he'd forgotten she was in residence. There were a few times she'd actually run into him but he never gave her anything more than a polite hello. She didn't understand what game he was playing, and why he'd made her believe he'd come to her room for nightly visits. But that wasn't the case.

It shouldn't have bothered her but it did. Tori curled up in her chair, trying to keep herself occupied with a book on the holopad Mrs. Gordon had given her. All the words seemed to blur together and she could barely concentrate. She wondered if this was Foster's way of getting her to drop her guard around him. She'd fallen for it once before. She couldn't afford to do it again.

Tori ran her hands over the expensive knick knacks that decorated the living room. She'd spent most of her morning exploring the house. It was hard to reconcile that only a few days ago, she had shared a run-down, two bedroom house with six other people. The roof leaked, the walls were cracked and the carpets were dirty and stained. There was a faint scent of smoke that permeated the entire house. Victoria had tried her best to keep her house as tidy as possible, but it was difficult when there was another adult in residence who refused to pick up after himself. The kids often had accidents and broke things and they weren't always the neatest.

And now here she was in a house so large, it could have fit several families very comfortably. It was the kind of opulence she'd only heard about. Tori felt guilty being here when her siblings were still where she'd left them.

"Do you like to read?"

Tori nearly jumped out of her skin when a voice cut into her thoughts. She turned around to see Foster watching her. She gulped, taking a step away from him. She'd forgotten how handsome he was. His looks were almost surreal. She could almost forget that he wasn't the jerk who'd hunted her down and was virtually holding her prisoner until he said she could leave.

"Why do you want to know?"

He smiled revealing even white teeth. Tori shivered as she remembered those perfect teeth nibbling on her neck the night before. She shoved her carnal thoughts away and told herself that it was just her body that responded to him. None of that mattered. Sooner or later, he'd get tired of her and she could go back to her old life.

"Relax. It's just a question. Do you?"

"Do you mean for fun?"

"Of course for fun. I noticed that watching programs on the holovision doesn't seem to interest you. I figured you may like to read."

"And how would you know what I've been up to? I barely see you around except...at night."

He smirked. "Missed me?"

"Don't flatter yourself. I'm only here because of that stupid game."

"Oh? Was it that stupid game that had you moaning for more last night?"

She turned her back to him. Tori refused to think about how she'd acted. It had been her intention to resist him but after a while, she'd melted. He wasn't the first person she'd even had sex with but he made her experience things she hadn't before.

He chuckled. *"You don't have to respond. We both already know the answer to that."*

Tori didn't dare acknowledge that statement. *"So, how do you know what I've been up to?"*

"There are cameras all over the house. I can look in any room any time I want with a click of a button." Tori turned around to see Foster He hold up his wrist. He pushed the button on his watch and a hologram popped up with a picture of the living room. She could see the two of them.

She frowned. *"Have you been watching me?"*

"Just to check in on you. Don't worry. I haven't been spying." Foster pressed the side of his watch again and the image disappeared. *"So you never answered my question. Do you enjoy reading?"*

"I don't know. I mean, I haven't read for pleasure since I was little. My mother used to read to me on an old electronic reader. It was so ancient that when it finally broke, there wasn't anyone in town with the capability to fix it and we couldn't afford a holopad."

"I'm sorry to hear about your mother."

"You say that as if you mean it."

"Why wouldn't I?"

"Because someone like you is only kind if they want something."

"Someone like me? Interesting." Foster's expression had gone blank and Tori couldn't tell if she'd offended him.

"It's just, these aren't the best circumstances. Even you have to admit I have no reason to trust you."

Foster nodded. *"I get it. But how about we make the most of it while you're here?"* He waved her forward. *"Come with me. I have something to show you."*

"Where are we going?"

"If I told you, it wouldn't be a surprise."

She followed him to the East wing of his house to a room she'd already been inside of. *"This is the library."* He hit the control panel and the wall in front of her opened. He touched a large black box with a keypad on top "This computer is an electronic library. It can pull up any book ever published."

"Wow. I thought only the record halls had equipment like this. Do you read a lot?"

"I used to when I was younger, but when I finished all of my schooling, I didn't have the time. My holo devices are synced to this computer so I can read any book I want at any given time. But this isn't want I wanted to show you."

"What?"

"Second panel."

Another portion of the wall split open to reveal shelves of books.

Tori gasped in awe. "These are real?"

"Of course."

Tori was amazed. Paper books hadn't been made in at least fifty years. People kept them as collector's items and they were valuable, the hardback covers being the most expensive. "They must be very old."

"They are. Some of them are hundreds of years old."

The cynic in her reared its head. "I suppose you have them to show off. I can only imagine how many credits this is all worth."

"No. Actually I don't. I've only ever shown my friend Dare who also has his own impressive collection. These used to belong to my father." There was a sadness in his tone at the mention of his father.

"Is he...?"

"Dead? Yes."

A twinge of guilt tweaked her heart at the casual way she'd dismissed something that seemed to have a lot of meaning to him. "Sorry."

"There's no need to apologize. It wasn't your fault."

"Were you close?"

"Yes and no. We were closer when I was a child but we often butted heads because we didn't always see eye to eye. When I look back on some of the advice he'd given me, I wish I would have taken it." He ran his hand over the books. "I *sometimes come in here and think and I wonder what he'd do. Being close to something that he once enjoyed makes me feel a little closer to him."*

Though it had only been a few days since she'd been brought here, Tori couldn't quite figure Foster out. At night he was the aggressor, bending her to his will, making her ashamed of how much she liked the things he did to her. And then there was this. It warped her perception of Elites. This man actually had feelings and he wasn't the one-dimensional villain she'd conjured up in her mind.

"Why?" she wanted to know.

"Why what?"

"Why are you showing this to me? This room obviously means a lot to you."

"Because despite what you think of me, I don't want your stay here to be unpleasant. I know you're not here by choice, but I think the two of us can get along quite nicely. How about we call a truce?" He held out his hand to her. Foster seemed so sincere.

Then, Tori placed her hand in his.

That had turned out to be the biggest mistake of her life. It was the moment when she'd started to fall for him. He made her believe in something that wasn't real.

She was so deep in thought it startled her to hear Mrs. Gordon's voice. Tori looked up to see the housekeeper leading a woman into the living room. "You can wait in here, Ms. Smith. Mr. Graham has been informed of your arrival and he said he'll be home within five minutes. May I offer you something to drink or eat?"

"Nothing for me. Thank you, Mrs. Gordon."

Once Mrs. Gordon left the room, the woman turned focused on Tori. "Hi. I didn't know Foster had company. Sorry to interrupt."

Tori stared at the other woman, wondering who she was. She was small in stature and dressed in a pair of jeans and t-shirt. But even so casually dressed, she was one of the most stunning women Tori had ever seen, with her large brown eyes in a heart-shaped face. Short fluffy curls crowned her head and she had flawless skin, even darker than Tori's. Her beauty was almost unreal.

Tori couldn't help but wonder what this woman was to Foster. She felt a sudden dislike toward her and Tori couldn't figure out why.

"You're not interrupting me. I was just leaving." She slid out of her chair.

"You don't have to go on my account."

"I'm not."

Ms. Smith smiled at her. "Please, don't go. Are you a friend of Foster's?"

"I wouldn't say that exactly."

"Oh. There's really no need for you to leave. I won't bother you if you're reading."

It was clear Ms. Smith was making polite conversation and Tori realized she was being standoffish for no reason. If Foster had taken another lover, that should have been no concern of hers. But Tori couldn't figure out why he'd go to the trouble of bidding for her in that stupid auction when he had someone else. "Actually, I wasn't reading anything in particular. I was just scrolling through some images."

The woman stepped forward with an outstretched hand. "I'm Aya, by the way."

"Tori."

"It's nice to meet you. Have you known Foster long?"

"Too long."

Aya raised a brow. Whatever the other woman would have said in response was lost because Foster stepped into the room. His gaze briefly fell on Tori before looking at Aya with affection. "Hello, short stuff. What brings you here today?" He walked over and gave the other woman a quick peck on the cheek.

Again that unwarranted dislike of Aya spread through her. Tori had no reason to feel this way about someone who seemed very friendly, but she couldn't shake this irrational feeling.

Aya grinned at Foster and poked him in the chest. "What did I tell you about calling me that? I may be short, but I will kick your ass."

He chuckled. "You'd have to catch me first. To what do I owe the honor of your presence?"

Aya glanced over her shoulder at Tori. "Uh..."

Foster glanced Tori's way and waved his hand dismissively. "It's okay to say what you have to say in front of Victoria."

She could have been a piece of furniture for all Foster seemed to care. Without a word, she walked out the room, but once she was out of sight, she halted. Tori didn't understand what masochistic force made her want to eavesdrop.

"I hope she didn't leave because of me. I don't think she warmed up to me very well."

"Victoria is dealing with a few issues of her own. Don't take it personally."

"Is she your girlfriend?"

"It's complicated. But you and I both know I can't afford to get involved with anyone right now, not when I'm so close to finding the truth."

"What have you learned so far? Are you any closer to finding Macy?"

Tori froze. No. It couldn't be.

"I can't really say. I have some very interesting tips and an address to a drop off location. I plan on checking it. I also have a man tracking some accounts that may lead to whoever Macy was sold to. In the meantime, I've learned the name of the company behind the trafficking. I don't know with absolute certainty if they actually run the auction or just sell the women and children to the actual auctioneers."

"That sounds like promising information but is it getting you any closer to finding Macy? She's been gone for months now, and her family is running out of hope of ever seeing her again. They've already lost her older sister who may or may not be dead. I'm so worried about her. She once told me that if she ever went through another ordeal like she did with Rat Face, she said she'd either lose her mind or she'd do something to end her suffering."

"Aya, I made a promise and I intend to keep it."

Tori had heard enough. She had to know. She stepped back into the living room. "Macy who?"

Foster looked up first. "What?"

"Macy who?" Tori demanded. "I need to know." Macy wasn't an uncommon name but it was the mention of a sister who had gone missing that had caught Tori's attention.

"She was—is my friend. I met her when we participated in The Run together. She volunteered to support her family because her father is disabled and her sister had disappeared after she'd done The Run a second time," Aya answered.

Tori gasped. "No!"

Foster strode over to Tori and grasped her by the shoulders. "What's the matter?"

"Macy. That's my sister."

Chapter Thirteen

Foster stared at Victoria and it finally all made sense. He'd always felt an instant connection to Macy because she reminded him of someone else but he could never place his finger on who. Now he knew. It was Victoria. The only reason he hadn't made the connection was because of the two different skin tones. Where Victoria's skin tone was a rich bronzish-brown, Macy was pale like alabaster. Macy's eyes were violet where Victoria's were hazel. Despite these superficial differences, the resemblance was there. His keen observation skills were one of his strengths, so he could smack himself for not seeing this before.

"Sisters?" Aya was the first to speak after the revelation.

"We have the same mother but different fathers. She married my stepfather when I was very little so he's basically the only father I know. That's why we look so different."

"Not as different as you think," Foster murmured. "You never mentioned you're her sister."

"I told you I have two sisters and three brothers," Tori pointed out.

"But you never mentioned their names."

"I guess I never got around to it. But what is this about her being missing? And her involvement in the Run?" She glared at Foster. "Did you hunt my sister down in The Run?"

"No I didn't, but I did see her that day. She was taken by someone else. A really bad man who hurt her." Foster was careful not to say too much. It was clear Victoria was already in distress knowing her sister was missing, but if she knew the type of abuse Macy had suffered at the hands of West it just might break her.

During her first stay with him, Tori would mention her siblings and how much they meant to her. Though she'd never said their names, there was one sister in particular whom she'd allude to as being very naïve and innocent in a world that wasn't kind to people without enough money or influence to navigate it. He remembered the way Victoria's eyes would light up when she spoke of her sisters and brothers.

"You're not telling me something. How are you connected? Why are you looking for her?"

Aya placed her hand on Foster's arm. "I think you should tell her everything. It's her sister. She deserves to know."

He sighed. It wasn't his intention to drag Victoria into any of this. The less she knew the better off she'd be, but he realized she wouldn't rest until she had answers. "Maybe you should start, Aya."

Aya nodded. "Tori, I think it's best if you sit."

Tori shook her head defiantly. "No. Just tell me. What's going on with my sister?"

The way that Tori glared at Aya gave Foster the impression that she felt some sort of resentment toward Aya. If he didn't know better, he'd think she was jealous, but he didn't have a chance to dwell on those thoughts because Aya began to speak.

"Like I said before, I met Macy when she and I both volunteered for the Run. Obviously I didn't know what to expect. I'd only heard about it. I didn't think I'd ever participate in something like that. As you can imagine I was scared out of my mind, but Macy approached me. She was very kind, even though I could tell she was frightened herself. She was already familiar with the process because she said that her older sister, you Tori, had been through it before and had told her what to expect."

"I only told her about it because she wouldn't let the subject go until I gave in. It wasn't my intention to prep her for it. Did she say why she was there?" Tori demanded.

"She said she had to support her younger siblings and that your father was sick and unable to work."

Tori snorted. "More like sick of working." She shook her head. "I'm sorry for interrupting. Please continue."

Aya nodded. "You basically know how things went after that. I had the idea that if she and I could stick together, we'd have a good chance of fighting off anyone who tracked either of us down. The plan seemed to work well at first, we had each other to get through the grueling trek but then she fell and hurt herself. I wouldn't leave her but she wanted me to go. I couldn't. She'd been way too nice to me. I tried to take her with me as best I could but Macy being injured had slowed us down significantly. I was caught and so was she. But I remembered the man who had captured Macy had given me a really bad vibe earlier when the patrons came to inspect the volunteers. Dare, the one who took me, was able to negotiate with him to get her back and he hired her to be my companion. When Dare eventually let me go on my own recognizance, I returned to work at my uncle's bar and my uncle gave Macy a job. She was working at the bar and things were going great until she disappeared."

Though Aya was speaking, Foster watched Victoria's expression the entire time. Her eyes were bright and damp with unshed tears and her lips quivered. He wanted to pull her into his arms and offer her the comfort she needed but he didn't think she'd appreciate it.

Tori remained silent for what seemed to stretch on for minutes until she finally spoke. "Thank you, Aya, for being my sister's friend. But I get the feeling that a lot is being left out." She turned to him then. "How do you fit into all this, Foster? Why are you actively looking for Macy if you only briefly met her at The Run?"

"I was with Dare when he made his negotiation with West. There was a reason why this man gave off bad vibes. It's because he's not a good man. In fact...." he paused, wondering if he should tell her everything.

"He hurt her, didn't he?" Tori asked in a whisper. "Please, just tell me."

"Yes. He tortured her. When we got her back from West, she was cowering in a corner in her own excrement. There were scars all over her body and she had a few missing fingers. He'd also shaved her head."

"No." Tori shook her head as if she were in denial. The tears she held back earlier now flowed down her face. "Not her. She didn't deserve that."

Aya walked over to Tori and rubbed her back. "You're right, she didn't, but she got the best medical treatment money could buy, thanks to Foster. He saw to it that every single one of her wounds were healed. She even got her fingers back."

Tori flinched away from Aya's touch. "Physical scars are one thing, Aya, but what about the psychological ones? You don't understand. Something like that would destroy my sister."

"She was in a bad way when we found her," Foster continued. "Dare didn't have much success with getting her to come with us, so I talked to her. Macy seemed to take to me and she clung to my side and wouldn't let go. I think she saw me as her savior. I was there through all of her medical treatments and I became somewhat of a guardian to her. She's my friend and that's why I care about her. I made a promise to protect her so that nothing bad ever happens to her again, but I failed her and she was taken. I should have moved her and the rest of your family out of that area. And now she's missing but I'm going to get her back."

Foster didn't know what Tori would have said because Mrs. Gordon stepped into the living room with a brooding Dare following close behind. "Mr. O'Shaughnessy is here, sir," she stated the obvious.

"Thank you." Foster nodded his head in dismissal.

Instead of greeting Foster, Dare zoomed in on Aya. "You were supposed to go straight to my house."

Aya shrugged. "But I came here first. I needed to see Foster."

"Seems the two of you have been spending an awful lot of time together lately," Dare pointed out.

Aya sighed. "You know why. Can you not do this right now?"

Foster would have told Dare to cool it, but Victoria scrambled out of the room, visibly upset. He wanted to follow her but felt he needed to handle this situation first. He'd deal with Victoria later.

Dare walked over to Aya and grasped her by the wrist and tucked her underneath his arm. She did not look pleased.

"Dare, what the fuck is your problem, man?" Foster asked.

He and Dare had been friends since they were children, but no one knew better than Foster that Dare could be an asshole. Since his friend had been with Aya, he seemed to have softened a little, but every now and then the asshole would come out. He was extremely possessive over Aya. Foster understood the possessive part; it was the same way he felt toward Victoria even though he wasn't in a current position to show it. But Dare seemed to take it to another level. Foster hadn't known Aya as long, but he knew enough about the pint-sized woman to know she wouldn't take it for much longer.

"As I said, the two of you seem to be spending a lot of time together and I'm wondering what you could possibly be talking about that you're having secret meetings in Aya's apartment."

Aya glared at her lover. "That was one time, Dare, and we were talking about Macy. If you're going to be a jerk, I could just go back to my place tonight. Right now, I think I'll go check on Tori if Foster doesn't mind."

Foster shook his head. "No. Go ahead. She's in the west wing. Take the spiral staircase, third door on the right."

"Thanks." She squirmed out of her lover's hold and marched out of the room, leaving the two men alone.

Foster turned to his friend. "You have got to stop doing that. First of all, you know neither Aya nor I would do something that would jeopardize your trust in us. There's only so many times you can keep doing that to her before she has enough."

Dare narrowed his gaze and balled his fists at his sides. For a moment, Foster thought his friend would throw a punch but instead, Dare relaxed his stance and released a deep sigh. He raked his fingers through his dark hair. "You're right. I'm sorry. It's just...I'm so used to being in control of everything I don't know how to handle all the emotions she makes me feel. She says she loves me but she's so damn independent. She won't move in with me, won't even let me take care of her. She insists on working at her uncle's bar and living in that tiny apartment. I could give her anything she wants but she refuses it."

"Has it occurred to you that maybe all she wants is you? You have to stop treating her like a possession and maybe she'll be a little more receptive to living with you."

Dare raked his fingers through his hair. "I don't know what I'd do if I lost her."

"Aya loves you. You need to stop worrying so much and calm the fuck down."

"I'm kind of new at this love thing. I feel like I'm at its mercy and it makes me confused and angry."

"Love can do that sometimes."

"I guess I got a little jealous when she mentioned that you had visited her apartment, and then when she wasn't at my house when I left the office I was disappointed. I'm sorry."

Foster raised a brow. "Excuse me? Is the great Alasdair O'Shaughnessy actually apologizing?"

"Fuck you, Foster."

Foster chuckled. "So is there any other reason why you came here other than to claim your woman?"

"Yes, actually. Something strange has been happening lately. I was reading the news on the holopad this morning and I noticed an article about people going missing. It might have been an insignificant blip but I remember you mentioning in a previous conversation about your last encounter with West. People were using The Run to filter woman into this auction thing. Since I've shut down the game, I've been hearing about a lot of missing women. When I was in Aya's part of town, there were a handful of flyers posted on billboards. It's one of the reasons I've been paranoid about Aya's whereabouts. Macy was taken so I'm making sure it doesn't happen to Aya. She's not to go anywhere without having one of my drivers to take her around. She thinks I'm being overbearing and maybe I am, but as long as it keeps her safe, I don't care."

"Shit." Foster realized this thing was even bigger than he thought. "West is involved in this."

"I thought you'd already established that."

"Yes, but apparently he's more heavily involved than he had led on. The thing is, he has completely disappeared. No one has seen him in over a week."

"Can't he be tracked down?"

"I have someone working on it but I haven't heard anything back yet so it doesn't look good."

"What's your next move?"

"I'll have to go to the source."

"Look Foster, I know you don't like to talk about your past but have you fallen back into your old habits?"

"Don't ask questions you don't want the answers to, Dare. I'm doing what I have to do to get Macy back."

"Just remember if you slip back into that lifestyle, you might find it's not so easy to get out of a second time."

"I'll be fine."

"You don't have to do this alone. I'll help you."

"No. I can't get you involved in this."

"But I want to."

"Dare, if I need your help I'll ask for it."

Dare held up his hands. "Okay, fine. But if you need me, just ask."

Foster was already in deep and the deeper he went the more dangerous it was. He had to do this on his own because as Dare had pointed out, this time there may be no coming back.

<><><><><>

Tori threw herself on her bed and cried in frustration. This was the worst thing that could happen. The reason why she'd participated in The Run was so her sisters didn't have to. And she'd failed in that mission.

Tori had spent most of her life trying to protect her siblings, so learning about her sister's disappearance was devastating. What was worse, out of all her brothers and sisters, Macy was the most fragile. Her sweet, loving younger sister was the sensitive one. She didn't eat meat or even kill bugs because she valued all life. She was the one who took their mother's death the hardest. She was the one who nurtured their younger siblings while Tori took different jobs to earn money for their family.

Macy even had a soft spot for their good-for-nothing father. She overlooked his alcoholism and slovenly ways, making excuses for him because in her heart she didn't want to see him for the bum that he was. Macy saw the good in every situation and every person. The thought of Macy suffering the same fate Tori had gone through, tore at her insides. She blamed herself for not being there for Macy.

A knock on her door alerted her to someone waiting on the other side. She wasn't in the mood for company. It was probably Foster and she didn't want to see him. Besides, she was still confused about why seeing him with Aya had made her feel so uncomfortable.

"Tori, are you in there?" It was Aya.

She quickly sat up and wiped away her tears. What did the other woman want? "Yes?"

"May I come in?"

Tori slid off the bed. She didn't want to be rude, after all, Aya was someone who had and still cared about her sister. "Sure."

The door opened and Aya walked inside. "I'm sorry to intrude again but I just wanted to check in on you. I notice you looked upset and it's understandable. Macy is very special."

Tori nodded. "She is. I had no idea she and Foster were friends."

"Yes, he's looked out for her. He's sending money to your family so they don't have to worry about food or any other necessities."

Tori raised a brow, surprised by this news. "Really?"

"Yes. You look like you don't believe me."

"No, it's not that. You have no reason to lie to me, but I guess the Foster you're talking about isn't the one I know."

"I haven't known him for very long but he's become a good friend to me as well. The Foster I know may pretend like he doesn't have a care in the world, but I suspect it's just a façade. He's a good guy."

"If you say so."

Aya crinkled her nose. "I'm sorry, but can I ask you something?"

Tori shrugged. "I can't stop you from asking me anything."

Aya furrowed her brow. "There's that attitude again. Have I done something to offend you?"

Tori sat down on her bed with an exaggerated flop. She realized she was being unfair to Aya who had been nothing but polite toward her but she didn't want to admit the reason. "I'm sorry, Aya. I guess I'm just feeling a little stressed. Hearing about my sister's abduction doesn't really help matters."

"I bet. Just for the record, Foster and I are just friends. And that really overprotective Neanderthal who burst into the living room is my boyfriend. I became friends with Foster through Dare. They're best friends."

Tori shrugged with a nonchalance she didn't feel. "Oh, well that doesn't have anything to do with me."

Aya raised a brow. "Are you sure about that? I know this is none of my business but I noticed how the two of you were staring at each other."

"You're right, it's none of your business." The second Tori said it she regretted it. "I'm sorry. I'm being a total bitch right now, but bottom line is there can never be anything between me and Foster. The two of us do have a history together but not in the way you think. The first time we met was through The Run. He played games with my head and just when I'd fallen for him, he got rid of me. And this time around, I'm only here because he was the highest bidder in that stupid auction."

Aya didn't reply right away.

Tori bowed her head and folded her hands in her lap. She'd probably said too much. "Now I suppose you'll run to Foster and tell him what I said."

"No. What's said in this room stays here. And I mean that. Look you're painting a completely different picture of the Foster I know but I'm not going to defend him. What I will say is right now Foster is completely focused on getting Macy back and I don't think he'll rest until he does. In the meantime, whatever grievance you have with him I think the two of you need to talk it out."

"You make it seem like I'm talking about some lovers' quarrel. He bought me at an auction and now he won't let me go home. How exactly can I work anything out with someone who's holding me captive, let alone someone who's hurt me as badly as he did?"

"I understand how you feel."

"You couldn't possibly know."

"Well, I've been a volunteer in The Run. It wasn't exactly fun and the one who caught me was not only a patron, but was the owner of the entire game."

"You're here, so he let you go."

"Yes and no. He's actually downstairs with Foster now."

Tori frowned. "Wait a minute. He released you from your contract and you stayed with him."

Aya nodded. "I fell in love. Yes, he can be a bit brutish but when the two of us are together, it's different. How we started out wasn't ideal but we've managed to make it work so far. I'm telling you this to say that I've seen how Foster looks at you, and I can't imagine why he'd have you here unless he cared. I don't condone whatever he did to hurt you, but as far as bidding on you in the auction, I know he probably went there to see if there was a way to get Macy back. He probably could have bid on any number of women but he bid on you. I'm sure he has his reasons."

Though she didn't want to give Foster any credit, Aya had a point. Why did Foster bid on her? "Maybe so, but there's nothing to work out."

"Well, that's your decision but in the meantime, if you need someone to talk to, you're always free to call me. I'll give you the coordinates."

"Why?" Tori asked. "I mean, I haven't exactly been that friendly toward you."

Aya reached over and patted Tori on the hand. "Considering the circumstances, I understand."

"Thank you, Aya. And I'm sorry for being rude. You've been very kind."

"No problem. When I needed a friend, Macy was one to me so the least I can do is return the favor to her sister."

Tori was suddenly overcome with emotion and started sobbing. This time she couldn't stop. Aya wrapped her arms around Tori. "It's going to be okay. Things will work out. Foster will find Macy."

Tori sniffled, trying to compose herself enough to get the words out. "It's n-not just that. You're the first person who's been nice to me in a very long time."

Aya rocked her back and forth. "I'm not doing anything special, just being there for a friend and I do hope we can be friends, Tori. I know things look bleak right now, but everything will work out. You have to believe that."

For the first time in a long time, Tori felt an emotion she didn't think she'd ever feel again.

Hope.

Chapter Fourteen

Long after Aya and Dare had left, Tori couldn't stop worrying about Macy. She wanted to believe that her sister would be brought back safely, but Tori couldn't stop thinking about all the things that could go wrong. But if Foster did find Macy as he'd promised, what condition would she be in? Tori knew how the Elites worked. They toyed with people from disadvantaged classes like hers for their own amusement because they could. There was little to no consequences for their actions. All they had to do was throw their money around to make their problems go away.

Unable to stay cooped up in her room, Tori found herself wandering around the house, heading in no particular direction. She finally ended up in the living room only to see Foster staring at some documents on his holopad. He wore a ferocious frown and he seemed to be intensely focused.

She still had trouble reconciling Foster to the man who'd broken her heart with the caring protector he apparently was to Macy. It was as if the man had two personalities, one she despised the other that intrigued her.

Tori slowly backed away from the room so that he wouldn't notice her, but she was too late. Foster raised his head and once their eyes locked, Tori couldn't move. What was it about this man that gave him such a hold on her? She resented the hell out of the fact that she couldn't simply turn off her feelings at will.

"You don't have to run off. I'm surprised you're up this late. I thought you'd be asleep by now."

"Who can sleep after learning what I did?"

Foster swiped away the document holograms and put his holopad down. He stood up and walked toward her but abruptly halted. He stuffed his hands into his pocket. "Yes. But like I said, I'll find her."

Tori had tensed when Foster approached her, but then a keen feeling a disappointment swept through her when he stopped. She couldn't figure out what the hell was wrong with her and why she continued to experience these conflicting emotions around him. She shook her head to rid herself of all thoughts about the two of them. That was the past and all that mattered now was finding her sister. "So those documents you were staring at when I walked in, do they have anything to do with your search?"

"Actually they do. They're just some financial transactions I've been trying to cipher through for the past few hours."

"You really do care for my sister don't you?"

"Of course I do. She's very special to me."

"Was there...anything between the two of you besides friendship?" Tori hated herself for asking but she couldn't help herself.

Foster sighed. "I know you have a low opinion of me Victoria, but I wouldn't stoop so low as to take advantage of a woman who was clearly broken and in need of lots of medical attention.

"I'm sorry. It's just—"

He rubbed his temples. "I know. You're worried about her but believe me, nothing happened between me and Macy. Look, I'm running on about an hour of sleep so I'm going to turn in because I need to get up early to conduct a few business meetings."

Tori had hurt him and it bothered her that she even cared. When he would have walked past her, she grabbed him by the arm. "Wait. I'm sorry for asking."

He shrugged. "I understand why you would. You care about your sister and I don't have the best track record."

"It's not just that. Ever since our mom died, I've basically been in charge of my siblings. My father was never the best provider but he completely fell apart when she was killed because a rich man's son decided to plow down a bunch of Dregs in his new car. We were all broken up over not only that she died, but how it happened. We got no justice because her killer's family paid off the city official. It nearly tore our family apart. My father took up drinking and picked up all kinds of nasty habits. He and I were never really that close but he became verbally abusive and mean, especially toward me because I wouldn't let him direct his ire toward my younger siblings. I've been their protector and watched out for them. I love all my brothers and sisters but Macy has a special place in my heart. I'm not sure if it's her sweet nature or the fact that she looks the most like mom out of all of us. But knowing that someone else had to look out for her because I wasn't around makes me feel bad. I should have been there for them."

Foster's expression softened. He closed the distance between the two them. "Blaming yourself isn't going to bring her back. You've done all you could." He wiped away a tear she didn't realize had slid down her face.

"Thank you for watching out for her."

"It's my pleasure. I've always felt a special connection to her."

"Why?" Tori couldn't help asking.

"Because she reminded me of someone who was and still is very special to me. But I fucked things up with that person so thoroughly, I doubt I'll ever be able to fix it."

Tori's heart started pounding. He couldn't be talking about her. Could he? "Foster…"

"Forget I said that." He backed away from her. "Goodnight, Victoria."

This time when he walked past her, she let him.

As soon as he got the call, Foster hurried to the main branch of his bank. When he stepped into the building his personal assistant ran to greet him. Her usual calm demeanor was replaced with a frazzled expression. "Mr. Graham, I tried to hold them off as best as I could but they had a warrant and told me if I tried to stop them, I'd be arrested. I'm so sorry."

Foster nodded. "It's okay, Serena. It's not your fault. Let me handle this."

"I've contacted our legal representatives. They should be joining us shortly."

"Thank you. You've done all you can do. If anyone asks you for codes, do not give it to them."

"But Mr. Graham, they could have us arrested."

"No one is going anywhere. Now go back to your office and handle any business matters like nothing else is going on."

Serena looked uncertain but walked away as instructed.

As Foster walked farther into his building he noticed men in black suits swarming the building, demanding computer codes from harried employees.

A tall, painfully thin bald man appeared to be giving the orders. Foster walked over to him. "What's this all about?"

The head agent turned on his heels and gave him a long accessing stare through small raisin-like eyes. "Ah, Mr. Graham, perfect timing. I need the codes to access all of your business and personal correspondence."

"For what?"

"You're being investigated for running an illegal gaming operation that hasn't been cleared through the licensing bureau. Now, if you don't mind, I have an audit to conduct and you're holding me up. I need those codes please."

"I need to see the warrant."

The agent waved his hand dismissively. "One of my men has it."

There was definitely something wrong here. His bank was clean as were his other business holdings. The only reason the licensing bureau would have been called was because they had some kind of tip, and usually those tips were ignored even if the business did participate in shady dealings. The only way an establishment like his would ever be under scrutiny was if someone with a lot of pull had been the tipster. Foster could smell the bullshit.

"Now," Foster demanded.

The bald man raised his brow. "Excuse me sir, but you have no idea who you're dealing with, so I suggest you offer up those codes, or we'll take this to the next step which will be for me to contact the enforcers and haul you off to jail for obstruction. And then we'll freeze all of your business assets. It would be a shame if you're not able to maintain that fancy lifestyle of yours." A smug smile of satisfaction curled his lips once he delivered his threat.

Foster refused to be intimidated. "You can do that, Mr..."

"Williams. Earl Williams, Head Investigator for the Department of Licensing and Corporate Regulation."

"Mr Williams. You can do that but I promise you that if I go to jail, you'll be out of a job by morning."

Williams narrowed his eyes. "Are you threatening me?"

Foster moved close enough to get in the other man's face. What he had to say was only for Williams' ears. "No. I'm making you a guarantee. You see, I know your type. You probably weren't born into money so you had to scratch and fight your way into the high ranking position you have now. Maybe you even had to suck a few dicks to accomplish your goal, but you and I both know that this fancy title you hold so dear is meaningless because it only takes a transfer of a few credits and something like this goes away. But in the meantime, you take joy in causing a little discomfort because you resent people like me who live the life you've always wanted. You'll go home tonight to your mediocre life in your below average home and think about me and all the things I have that you can only wish for. You see, I know why you're here, and I'm going to find out who's at the bottom of it. And when I do, I'm going to come back for you. So you have to decide if you really want to do this. Is it worth it to you to lose that fancy title and your mediocre possessions all because you picked the wrong person to fuck with?"

Williams gulped. All color drained from his face. "You have to understand, Mr. Graham, that we were handed some very damning evidence. We have to look into every claim we get."

"Is that so?"

Before the other man could answer, Foster spotted his legal team walking toward them. "What's going on here?" Foster's head attorney, Howard Robb, demanded without preamble.

Williams sputtered. "We're in the middle of an audit and your client is being unreasonable. Perhaps if you convinced him into seeing reason, this will be over quicker."

"Do you have a warrant?"

"Of course, we wouldn't be here without one."

"You should be able to produce it."

"One of my men has it."

Howard gave Williams a stare that clearly said he didn't believe him. "You should be able to produce this warrant on a holo device. I notice you're wearing a holowatch. Let's see it."

"Well, I may not have downloaded it to the system yet."

"A warrant can be downloaded and in our correctional system within an hour of its issuance. According to Ms. Riggs, you and your men have been here for more than that time. So what you're telling me is that you have no warrant but you're here harassing my client?"

"I'm sure it was being downloaded before we arrived." Williams was lying, that much Foster was sure of. So the fact that this wasn't a real raid made him suspicious. He had no doubt someone had put Williams and his men up to this. Whoever it was had to know Foster would demand a warrant. With so many agents swarming around, it might have been a way for this mysterious tipster to get any information they could gather on Foster and his holdings. There was only one other explanation he could think of for why someone would do this to him. Because they could. To make him aware that he was being fucked with simply because they wanted him to suffer. For a weasel like Williams to risk his position, the fee must have been hefty.

Foster doubted Williams even know who his donor was. That person would be way too smart to directly connect himself to this man.

"Howard, I want Williams and all his men out of my building." Foster then turned to the bald man. "I suggest you tell whoever it was who put you up to this that it won't work. And if I see you in here again, you'll live to regret it."

Foster's holophone began to vibrate. He pulled it out of his breast pocket to see who the caller was. There were only a few people who had his personal holo coordinates so he frowned when it was a number he didn't recognize. He then remembered the mysterious call he'd received before.

"Excuse me. I need to take this." He walked off until he found an unoccupied space out of everyone else's earshot. He pressed the engage button to receive the call. Like the last time, no image popped up.

"I see you got my surprise this morning." It was the same disguised voice from before.

"I suppose it would be a waste of my time to ask who this is."

"You'd guess right. By tomorrow morning, everyone in your circle will have heard about the raid on your business. You know people in the Elite like to gossip. Imagine what it will feel like to be the center of it. What if they all think you have something to do with the recent wave of disappearances and you're just using your bank as a front? That could possibly ruin you. No one would want to associate with a known trafficker." The owner of the mysterious voice chuckled. That was one of the big ironies of their culture. Most of the people he knew had skeletons in their closets and had done some very bad shit behind closed doors, but it was never talked about in polite society.

But once those secrets were 'exposed' to the public, that's when it began to supposedly matter to the people who didn't want to associate with trash. They wanted to maintain the appearance of their own images and to do that, most of them had no problem throwing said trash under the bus. Foster wasn't concerned about what other people thought of him. If there was damage to his reputation after this, then so be it.

Foster didn't bother to reply to that taunt because he wanted to see what else would be revealed.

"You have nothing else to say? Not so smug anymore, are you? You may think you have the upper hand just because you've managed to get some information out of a man who is no longer any use to me, but remember I'll always be one step ahead of you. You might employee your grandfather's thug tactics, but you won't come out on top this time. Enjoy that pretty little exotic you have hidden away."

The reference to Victoria got a rise out of him. "You don't have to tell me who the fuck this is because I will find you and you I'll have your fucking tongue."

His threat was met with a chuckle before the connection ended.

"Shit!" he yelled in frustration.

Foster wasted no time leaving the building. He didn't wait to see if all the agents had cleared out of his building. That's what he was paying his legal team to handle. He needed to get back to the house. Clearly someone was having his place watched if they knew about Victoria. At all costs he would keep her out of harm's way. As he slid into his vehicle and pressed his thumb against the print analyzer to jumpstart the ignition, his holophone vibrated. He was going to ignore it but thought better of it. He pulled it out of his pocket and clicked engage. Serena's image popped up.

"Mr. Graham, there's some trouble at the west end branch, and the commodities building downtown."

"Is this something you'll be able to handle?"

"It's more serious than that. They've been bombed. There have been some reported deaths."

In that moment, Foster realized this wasn't just about his digging for information on the auction and the trafficking. This was a vendetta and whoever was behind it was coming for him.

Foster had done a lot of bad things in his life. Very bad things. But there was a line he'd dared not cross to keep his humanity intact. But now this was no longer about him. Innocent people had been involved, people he was in charge of. And for that he would become that monster that he'd kept hidden within himself for so long.

He would make them all pay.

Chapter Fifteen

It had been four days since she'd seen Foster. The last time she had laid eyes on him was the morning after the visit from Aya and Dare and their brief conversation. He had said he wanted to talk and though she wasn't ready to have another cryptic conversation with him, she met with him in his dining room for breakfast. It was then he received a business call that had him hurrying off with a promise to continue their conversation later. She hadn't seen him since.

She was almost certain he hadn't been home and it shouldn't have bothered her as much as it did. Tori didn't want to care, but she was worried. Something about that call had frazzled him and she wondered if it had anything to do with her sister. She found it hard to determine who the real Foster was. Was he the man who had treated her so callously or was he someone who actually looked out for and protected people like Macy. She believed him to be another predator who used people like her for his own sick amusement. The last time they spoke left her more confused than ever. If she didn't know better she would have thought he was confessing his feelings for her. But that was crazy. She had to admit however, that Foster was full of surprises.

It also astonished her to learn that he was financially supporting her family, people he had no obligation to simply because of his friendship with Macy. Even though he'd denied it Tori couldn't help but wonder if there had been more between Foster and her sister. The thought of Foster doing things to Macy that he done to her brought back that sick angry feeling. It was an emotion she could no longer deny. It was jealousy.

Tory had convinced herself that she hated him. When he'd tossed her out of his home in such a cruel way Tori had cursed his name. She blamed him for having to do The Run a second time. She hated him when she was taken by a man who used her as his own personal whipping post and outlet for all of his perversions. She hated him for being sold off to a bunch of sadistic monsters who forced her to their will, only to be put on an auction block and sold like an animal.

Even though he wasn't directly responsible for all the woes she'd endured over the past couple of years, she still blamed him. In her mind, they should have been together just like he said they would be. She hated that despite the blame she placed at his feet that she didn't really hate him at all. Those residual feelings from a time when he'd made her happy were still there and she couldn't shake them.

Now here she was driving herself crazy with worry for a man who ignored her presence half the time he was in residence. She still couldn't figure out why he'd bothered to buy her in the first place, if he was just going to keep her here as a glorified houseguest. Aya had seemed so sure that Foster's motives were altruistic but Tori doubted it. She'd learned that Foster was good at projecting an image he wanted people to see.

Tired of wandering aimlessly around her room, she headed downstairs. Tori found herself heading to a room she hadn't visited since her return, Foster's library. She pressed the panels to reveal the old hardback books. She ran her fingers along the spines and thought about the first time he'd brought her here. Despite this being the place where the lies began, she felt a certain sense of peace.

She took a book from off the shelf without reading the title. It didn't matter. She liked the feel of it, and how when she opened it, the black words neatly lined each white page. It seemed much more intimate to read from printed paper than a holographic image.

"I used to do that a lot when I was younger."

Tori jumped, startled by Foster who walked into the room without warning. The first thing she noticed were the large dark circles beneath his bloodshot eyes. His hair was in disarray and his clothes were rumpled. Stubble lined his chin and jaw indicating his need of a shave. Foster looked as if he hadn't slept in days. He was someone who took pride in his appearance and Tori had never seen him look anything less than impeccable.

She opened her mouth, but no words came. What could she say to him when they hadn't seen each other for days and with him looking like he was on the verge of passing out?

When she didn't speak in return he walked toward the bookshelf and scanned the books. "I liked to take each book off the shelf, and run my fingers over it and just look at all the words. It was fascinating to me." He pulled down a red book and tapped it. "This was my favorite. I still read it in times of necessity."

Tori leaned forward to catch a glimpse of the title. *The Art of War.*

There was something in the way he rubbed the cover back and forth, almost compulsively, that alarmed her. Though she told herself not to care her conscience wouldn't allow her to not ask. "Foster. Is everything okay?"

He stared at the book without looking up. "It will be."

"What's that supposed to mean. What's going on?"

He lifted his head then and gave her his signature smirk. "Careful Victoria, if you keep asking questions, I just might begin to think you care."

"I'm just trying to be polite. But…seriously. Are you okay? You don't look well. You haven't been home for days and the way you're holding on to that book, I'm scared for you. Does it have anything to do with Macy? She's not... Did you find out something about her?"

"No. I still haven't been able to track her down, but I haven't given up. Victoria, do know what this is?" He held up the book.

"It says *The Art of War*. Why did you pick that one?"

"For strategy. I've found myself fighting a losing battle, but I've been going about it all wrong."

Tori wasn't sure if it was his apparent lack of sleep talking or if he'd actually lost his mind, but something was going on with him and she didn't like it one bit. "I don't understand what you're talking about."

"I got sloppy. Didn't cover my tracks." He spoke so softly, Tori had to strain to hear him. There was a glazed look in his tired eyes and he had her worried.

"Foster. What's been going on with you? What happened?"

"I'm going to have to wake him."

"Who?"

"The monster."

She took a step back. "Foster, you're starting to scare me."

"I should scare you, Victoria. I'm not a good person. I should have never brought you here, not even the first time. But I thought..."

She clutched her hand over her heart wondering what he was going to confess before his words trailed off. "Foster?"

He stared into space for several moments, stroking the book in his hand before focusing on her. "I'm going to fix it. I'm going to do what I should have done a long time ago." Even though he was looking directly at her, she had the distinct impression that he wasn't actually seeing her. He had to be delirious.

Tori took another step away from him. It had to be the lack of sleep talking.

"I think you might be having a breakdown of some sort. Maybe I can get some help."

"You think I'm crazy don't you? To be perfectly honestly, I haven't seen this clearly in a very long time."

"Then tell me what's going on. If it involves my sister, I have the right to know."

"Victoria, I'm going to get her back but this thing has become bigger than finding her."

"What do you mean?"

"It doesn't matter. Just know that I'll take care of it. I'll do whatever I have to in order to get her back." He turned away from her and looked as if he was going to walk out the room book in hand, but Tori grasped him by the shoulder.

"Wait. Foster. You can't leave like this."

He stiffened. "Victoria, remove your hand." His voice was expressionless but she wanted answers. Something was going on that he wasn't telling her and she was tired of being left in the dark.

"No. Tell me what's going on with you. Why won't you tell me?"

"Because you don't really want to know the truth. You know that I'm dealing with dangerous people based on your own experience with them, and when you get in league with them sometimes you have to do bad things. You don't want to know the bad things I've done." He turned around suddenly, effectively dislodging her hand. "Or maybe you do. Maybe you want to know so you can give yourself a reason to keep hating me."

"I don't hate you," Tori blurted out before she had a chance to think about her words. She hadn't meant to tell him that, but now that it was out there was no taking it back. Besides, she didn't hate him, these last few days alone with nothing to do but think had made her realize that.

He gave her a humorless smirk. "I bet if I told you what I did, you would. You'd despise me and spit on the ground I walk on. Do you want to know what I used to do, Victoria?"

She backed away. "Don't."

He narrowed his gaze. "I didn't think so."

"I just want…"

The almost dead look in his eyes stopped her mid-sentence.

"You want to what?"

"Whatever it is you're going through right now, I want to help."

He raised a brow. "Help me? In what way do you think that you can help me right now? What do you plan on doing exactly?"

"I don't know, I mean, I can do something other than staying cooped up in this house all day. I've been bored out of my mind."

"Have you?"

"Yes, there's only so much holovision I can watch or books I can read. Frankly I don't even know why I'm here. It's not like we…" Again Tori stopped, realizing she'd said way too much.

"Then far be it for me to leave you without something to do." Without further warning, he tossed his book aside and grabbed her by the wrist and pulled her against him. Tori opened her mouth to protest but his mouth was hot and heavy on hers before she could get the words out.

Tori beat against his shoulders in an attempt to break his tight hold. His arms were like chains around her, almost making it hard for Tori to breathe. Foster pushed his tongue against the seam of his lips but she pressed them closer. Every other time Foster touched her, Tori's body went up in flames but this time around she was determined not to give in.

"Open your mouth," he muttered against her closed lips but Tori remained firm in her resolve.

When she failed to comply, he gripped her by the hair and yanked so hard she gasped in pain and surprise. Foster thrust his tongue in her mouth, sweeping and seeking, claiming her.

Again she tried to push him away, but he molded his erection against her pelvis, grinding aggressively. Foster had been forceful with her before. He was a dominant lover, but there was something different right now. He seemed to be driven by some intangible force. Whatever was going on with him, it had taken over and it scared Tori because she didn't have the strength to fight him off.

She'd survived being starved, beaten, raped and tortured, but if Foster continued on like this, Tori wasn't sure if she would recover.

Foster released the tight grip he held on her hair to tear at her blouse. He yanked it off without ceremony. "Please don't do this to me. This isn't you."

His response was to rip away her bra, exposing her breasts. He tweaked one nipple and then the other.

Tori felt a stirring within her core, sending a wave of warmth throughout her body. No. She couldn't give in to him. Not like this. It didn't feel right.

"You're better than this." Tori tried to appeal to any sense of decency he had. No one had ever hurt her as bad as Foster, but even when she was at her lowest, she didn't believe that he was all bad.

He raised his head then. "You only think I am. But I'm a really bad man, Tori."

There was so much pain in his voice that she could almost feel it herself. He was hurting and she didn't know why. Whatever issues the two of them had could be dealt with later but now, she had to help him somehow. She relaxed her body within his hold. "I doubt there's anything I can say to the contrary."

"You're absolutely right about that. After all, every time we encounter each other even if it's briefly, you let me know by your words or the angry glares that you hate me and that I'm the lowest form of life."

"I don't think that, Foster, but how am I supposed to act after what you did?" She shook her head. "Look, that doesn't matter now. Just let me help you. Whatever you want me to do, I'll do it."

"Oh, yeah?"

"Yes."

"Take off the rest of your clothes." Tori hesitated for a moment. He watched her with an unreadable expression. It was like he was testing her. He stared into his eyes and it was almost as if he wasn't even there but if this is what it took to reach him then she would do it. She undid the fastening of her pants.

"Slowly."

Tori eased her pants down her hips before kicking them off. She then removed her panties at the same slow pace, never breaking eye contact with Foster. When she stood before him completely naked, she barely managed not to cover her nudity. He'd seen her naked before but the way he stared at her now, unnerved Tori a bit. She moistened her suddenly dry lips with the tip of her tongue.

"Now get on your knees."

Once she did as he ordered, Tori waited for his next command.

Foster looked down at her and stroked her hair almost as if she was a favored pet, but the look in his eyes remained dead. "You're so beautiful. When I first saw you Victoria, I had to have you. Do you know why?"

She shook his head. "Because there was something in your eyes that told me that despite your circumstances, you weren't going to let it get to you. You were unbending and brave among a bunch of women who looked like there was no hope left. I saw a light. I wanted that light for myself." His words though touching was delivered with zero emotion.

Seeing him like this made her question everything she believed about him. Who was the real Foster Graham? She placed her hand on his thigh and stroked it in comfort. She grazed the outline of his cock with her thumb. Foster inhaled sharply as if her touch had shocked him.

"Undo my pants and take out my dick."

Tori unfastened his pants and slid them down. His shaft bobbed slightly when she set it free. He was long but not as much as he was thick. His cock was red and veiny. She gently cupped it with one hand and gently stroked it with another. She rubbed her thumb against the helmeted tip before leaning forward and circling it with her tongue.

He moaned, encouraging her to continue with her exploration. Tori licked him from root to tip and then repeated.

"Stop fucking teasing me and put it in your mouth."

Tori wrapped her lips around his rod and slowly took him into her mouth an inch at a time. He placed his hands on either side of her head and thrust forward. She relaxed her throat muscles as he pushed his cock to the hilt, enabling her to take him whole.

She didn't need to move much because he took over, fucking her mouth hard and fast. He grunted and groaned as he moved in and out of her mouth. It was almost as if she wasn't there. Foster seemed to be exorcising some demon and she was his vessel.

He surprised her by suddenly pulling out. "On your hands and knees," he grunted.

Foster didn't wait for her to comply. He grabbed her by the waist and positioned her the way he wanted. He was behind her in an instant. She felt his cock at her entrance before he slid into her. Foster gripped Tori by the shoulders and plowed into her. She could feel his thrusts deep inside of her, each one harder and faster. And despite the fact that he didn't seem to care about her pleasure or even his, her body loved it. She'd be sore when this was over but the fire inside raged on, sending her to the edge. Her climax was quick and fast, but he kept going. His grip remained firm on her shoulders, digging into her flesh. She was sure there would be bruises in the morning.

Foster kept going on and on, in an extraordinary show of stamina. He continued even though her arms were too weak to hold her body braced. When Tori collapsed to her elbows, he caught a handful of her hair and kept fucking her. The only sounds he made were animalistic grunts and growls. The ache between her legs came next. She bit her lip to stop herself from crying out. She wasn't sure how much time had passed but she knew this was longer than anything she'd ever experienced. Any pleasure she'd felt before was gone. Tears stung her eyes as he kept going. Foster was no longer a man but a machine with no emotion, no feeling and no ability to grow tired.

Each time her body sagged, the tighter he gripped her hair. He pulled so tight she thought she he might yank it out. "Foster," she cried out his name. "Please. I can't." Either he didn't hear her or he ignored her. Every part of her body ached. Her back, neck and knees screamed for relief. Bright dots danced before her eyes and the room started to go dark. Just when Tori thought she'd faint, Foster pulled out.

A damp gel-like substance suddenly coated spots on her back and she realized he'd released his seed on her body instead of inside of her. She crumpled to the floor and pulled herself into a ball. The tears streamed down her face.

It barely registered when she was lifted off the floor and carried out of the room down the hallway and up the stairs. Her mind was completely numb when he took her to the bathroom and cleaned her off. Her mind, body and soul were completely exhausted when he placed Tori in her bed and tucked her inside the covers.

Foster leaned over her and lowered his mouth until his lips nearly touched her ear. "I told you I wasn't a good guy."

And then he left.

Chapter Sixteen

Foster swallowed the contents of his glass in one gulp before reaching for his bottle of scotch to refill it. The bottle was nearly empty and he decided he wasn't nearly as drunk as he wanted to be. He wanted to be so drunk that he could no longer feel or remember anything. He wanted to fall into a sweet oblivion, at least temporarily.

He'd hurt her again. No matter what his intentions, he always ended up doing the thing he said he wouldn't. Why the fuck couldn't he get it right? Foster wasn't lying to her when he said that he wasn't a good person but even still, he didn't know what had driven him to do that. One minute he was trying to put his distance between them so he wouldn't say or do anything stupid and the next he'd turned into the monster he feared. His intentions had been honorable, but when she touched him so gently, looking so sweet and more perfect than anything he ever deserved, something inside of him snapped.

Foster had wanted to consume that goodness, to feel something other than the rage, pain and fatigue of the last several days. Once she placed her mouth around his dick he'd lost all control. By the time he'd come back to his senses, he realized what he'd done. Foster wasn't sure how he could face her. He couldn't even look at himself in the mirror.

The specter of his father's memory seemed to taunt him. When he squinted, he could almost see his father looking at him with disapproval. "You warned me, didn't you? But I didn't listen. I wanted to prove that I was a man. And now look at me." He snorted before taking a healthy gulp from his glass.

The agents at his banks were only the beginning of his problems. Several of his businesses had been bombed, injuring several of his employees and killing ten. If that wasn't enough two of his personal accounts were completely wiped out. It had taken Gareth days to track it down and place the money into encrypted accounts that made it difficult to hack. All while this was happening, his search for Macy had taken a detour. Every single one of his contacts had wound up dead. Peter West, who had gone missing, was found in a hotel room beheaded. Ruben Meyer had been gutted from nipple to navel. The three men West had named were also found dead, one murder more gruesome than the next. It was clear someone was trying to send him a message.

That someone wanted him to know that they could get to him from anywhere at any time. They could hurt him in his business and personal life. With each incident the mystery caller had gotten through to him to let him know that he was still watching. The final straw was when enforcers accompanied by the city commissioner had hauled him away from his office to take him downtown for questioning surrounding the death of West. Thankfully his assistant had contacted his legal team and had gotten him out of that situation. The hefty bribe he had to pay to the commissioner to make sure those questions were never asked again hadn't hurt either.

Foster had had the week from hell. All the sins of his past had finally caught up to him, and there seemed to be no way of digging himself out of this hole. Any hope that he had with working things out with Victoria was gone. There were moments when he believed that she still had feelings for him. He figured he could explain why he did what he'd done and prove to her that he was sincere. But he doubted she could forgive him for what he'd done to her in the library. He didn't blame her because he couldn't forgive himself.

Foster was in the middle of pouring himself another drink when the door to his study opened and Dare stormed inside. His brows were knitted together and the scowl that lined his face was deep.

"What the fuck is going on with you?"

Foster poured liquor into his glass until the bottle was empty. "And hello to you too." He held up his glass in a salute.

"Don't play games with me. Is there any reason why you haven't been answering your phone and why Mrs. Gordon claims you're not home when I stop by? If I didn't charge past her today, you would have kept avoiding me."

"It's not Mrs. Gordon's fault. This is actually the first time I've been home in days."

"Really?" Dare asked skeptically.

"I have no reason to lie."

"You look like shit, man."

Foster took a sip of his drink. His vision was starting to blur. "You sure know how to flatter a guy."

Dare stalked over to his desk and grabbed the glass out of Foster's hand. "This is no time for jokes. It's all over the news how your businesses were bombed and you were being questioned for murder."

Foster slouched in his chair. "Oh, that made the news as well?" Not that he cared. His world was so fucked up right now that one more thing didn't matter.

"No. I actually did some snooping around myself. Foster, what's going on with you? You have me worried. Aya's been asking about you as well. I've never seen you like this. Look, I may not be the most open person and I apologize if you felt you couldn't come to me with any problems you're going through, but I want you to know that I have your back."

"I doubt there's anything you can do."

Dare took the seat facing Foster's desk. "Tell me about it."

Foster wasn't sure if it was the alcohol or the heavy burden he carried, but he felt the need to confess. He rubbed his temples to relax the tension of an oncoming headache. "These people behind the auction have made it clear that they don't want me snooping in their business. They've spent the better part of the week trying to destroy me. Before that, I've been getting these mysterious calls from an anonymous source that's taking credit for all the chaos happening. But it's just not about me trying to get Macy back. This is personal, otherwise I think they would have tried to kill me by now."

"Why would someone go after you, Foster? You're probably one of the most laid back people I know. I've never heard of you having an issue with anyone."

"Of course not, because I was very good at what I did. Anyone who knows the real me is either too scared to speak up or has disappeared."

Dare narrowed his eyes. "What are you talking about?"

Foster sighed. "'You know a little bit about my family's background. My grandfather wasn't born into wealth. He fought for every single credit he earned, and because of that he became respected and admired for bettering himself. He was held up as the gold standard citizen, someone from the slums who didn't constantly have a hand out. He'd made something of himself and amassed a fortune that a lot of people envied."

Dare nodded impatiently. "Yes, I already know this."

"My grandfather wasn't the man everyone thought he was. People wanted to believe that someone from poverty could actually make something of themselves with just hard work just so they can point to the other poor people and call them lazy. They were willing to look the other way in regards to how my grandfather made his fortune. He was a big, intimidating guy so he got a lot of work as a bodyguard. He was also extremely street smart. He realized he could use his natural assets to get what he wanted. He started making small loans off the grid and charging an exorbitant interest rate. Years ago, they called it loan sharking."

"Really? I guess that would make sense. How else would he have been able to amass a large enough amount to start a bank? That would take a lot of capital. "

"And influence. I wish I could say that illegal loans was the only thing he was involved in, but he dabbled in intimidating small businesses for protection money, blackmail, drug dealing and gambling. You name it, he was probably involved in it in some way. By his mid-twenties he was one of the biggest crime bosses in the country, but he was cunning about the way he went about things. See, it was always his plan to make a name for himself within the Elite. He wanted to rub elbows with the very people he hated. My grandfather said it was his goal that no one would ever look down on him again."

"I can imagine he didn't have it easy growing up."

Foster shrugged. "No one who grew up where he did had it easy. He just chose the path he saw fit. The thing about my grandfather is, even though he left the slums, the slums never left him."

"How do you mean?"

"Even after he started the bank and built it to what it is today, he still continued his underground activities. Not all of them just the more lucrative ones, like the gambling, illegal loans and blackmail. When people didn't pay him back, he had an interesting way of collecting."

"What did he do?"

"He'd torture them."

Dare raised a brow. "And no one ever found out."

"The ones who did were paid off and the ones who couldn't be bribed were either blackmailed or they disappeared. My grandfather wanted to build an empire and he was willing to do it by any means necessary. Along the way he took over other businesses and got rid of the competition. That's one of the reasons there are so many Grahams banks in this region. I think most of the people he associated with either feared or revered him and sometimes a little of both."

Dare nodded in his understanding. "I remember your grandfather always being larger than life whenever I was in his presence. Even my father deferred to him and we both know that my father did that with no one. Do you think my father knew what he was up to? I wouldn't put it past him."

"I honestly don't know. I've only seen your father and my grandfather together in social settings. Whether they had any dealings in my grandfather's illegal activities will remain an unanswered question since they're both gone now."

"And your father?"

Foster shook his head. "Wanted nothing to do with my grandfather's underground business. He wanted the businesses to be completely legitimate. He felt that Grandfather could leave that world behind because frankly, a lot of people my grandfather dealt with were dangerous. Of course my grandfather refused to listen. It didn't matter that he'd built his empire like he dreamed, he still held on to his street mentality. As long as the money was good why walk away? Besides, I don't think he could have even if he wanted to."

Dare frowned. "What do you mean?"

"That life was in him. He liked it too much, that control, the need to have someone's life in his hands. He was addicted to the power."

"Did he tell you this?"

"No."

"Then how do you know?"

Foster took a deep breath. He didn't know if what he was about to confess would change how Dare felt about him but he was tired of living this lie. If the past few days had taught him anything it was that no matter what you did to cover your tracks, your past would always come back to haunt you. "Because he brought me into that life and I loved it."

"Get the fuck out of here. Not you. I mean I know you used to look up to your grandfather and he was a mentor to you, but you were involved in the illegal stuff?"

"Just the collection and intimidation part."

Dare narrowed his eyes. "In what way?"

Foster raked his fingers through his hair and released a heavy sigh. "Well, remember, I already told you that my grandfather had secret businesses that weren't completely legitimate that I was involved in."

Dare snorted. "Yeah, I thought you mean illegal trading or some shit like that, not that you were leaning on people. I want to know everything."

Foster sighed again. When someone didn't pay back one of Grandfather's under-the-table loans, that's when we needed to give the mark a reminder. I was thirteen years old when I watched him beat a man to near death and threaten his family if he didn't get his money. I was fucking terrified. Here was a man I looked up to and wanted to be like and he had turned into some kind of beast. I didn't understand what was going on but I didn't want to speak out either because like I said, he was my hero. I didn't want him to think I was a wimp so I kept quiet. I didn't even tell my father what I'd seen."

"Grandfather said he wanted to toughen me up and that he didn't want me to end up soft like my father. So I witnessed things that most people only ever see in movies. My grandfather once had a guy chained to the wall and made him watch while he raped the man's screaming wife. And so it went, whenever he came by to collect me for some quality time, it was always on one of his runs. After a while I became desensitized to the violence. In my mind I justified it by saying these people shouldn't have borrowed money they couldn't pay back, or they shouldn't have crossed my grandfather. I convinced myself that these people deserved it so I wouldn't end up seeing my grandfather for the monster he was. And then it happened."

"What?"

"He took me to our regular location and then told me to pick one of the weapons off the wall and use it. You see, the very first time he took me to one of his sessions, he made me participate, but he ended up doing most of the work. This time around, he wanted me to do the entire job on my own. Watching was one thing but taking part was another. I wanted to run away but more than my fear of hurting that man who'd never done anything to me was the fear I felt of my grandfather's reaction. I didn't want him to look at me the way he looked at my father. I didn't want him to direct his disappointment toward me. So I took a small knife off the wall and my hands were shaking. Every step I took toward that terrified man, I'd shake ever more. I could barely hold the knife steady. I was about to tell my grandfather that I didn't want to do it and then his voice cut through all my resistance."

Foster began to shake as the memory took hold of him. *"Don't let me down like your father. Make me proud."* More than anything he wanted to please his grandfather, so he swallowed the bile that threaten to spill from his mouth. He ignored the tears flowing down the bound man's face. He shut his ears to the pleading and took the knife and slipped it down the side of the man's face. He'd watched his grandfather do this a countless amount of times so he knew just how deep to cut.

"And then what?" Dare broke into Foster's thoughts.

Foster didn't realize he'd drifted away. "And then I began to make precise slices all over his body. He screamed and begged but I didn't stop. I kept looking back at my grandfather and all I could think about was how happy he seemed. But that wasn't the worst part. The worst part was that there was a piece of me that liked it. It gave me an adrenaline rush. It became my addiction too. There were men after him. I became good at what I did. I even studied up on torture techniques and what tools or maneuvers I needed to use in order to produce the most pain. I was so efficient, my grandfather started to defer to me. I handled all the enforcing. I became immersed in this world, dealing with a bunch of criminals. I became feared in my own right and I loved it. I became an even bigger monster than my grandfather. But it was at the cost of my humanity and my relationship with my father. When he found out about my involvement into the seedier side of Grandfather's business, he never looked at me the same again." Foster grabbed his glass and downed the remainder of its contents before tossing it across the room. The glass hit the wall and smashed into several pieces.

He dropped his head into his palms. "And the really fucked up part about all of this is I'm not sure if I had a chance to do it all again that I wouldn't."

A long silence surrounded the room and Foster sunk deeper into his misery. He wouldn't be surprised if Dare walked out the door without a backward glance. To his surprise, he felt a heavy hand fall on his shoulder. Foster raised his head to see Dare standing over him. "Don't beat yourself up over this. You were a kid."

"I was a kid who became a man who enjoyed doing sadistic shit. And because of the stuff that I was involved in my father was killed. We did a good job of covering it up and calling it natural causes, but there was no doubt in mind or my grandfather's that he was murdered. By that time, I'd seen enough to recognize when something was natural or not."

"Really? Do you know who did it?"

"I never did. But my grandfather did and oddly enough, he never told me who. He just made some cryptic statement."

"What did he say?"

"A son for a son." Foster had begged his grandfather to tell him what that meant but he'd refused. It was odd that the Foster's father's death was the thing that had finally broken his grandfather. The old man was never the same again. It was clear the man had a lot of regret, especially involving the relationship between him and his son.

"What does that even mean?"

"I don't know. I never really got a chance to find out because with my father gone, I had to take over his business duties. I realized that I couldn't go back to that life. It was the least I could do to honor his memory, and besides, I realized the longer I continued, the more of my soul I lost. I busted my ass to separate all of our legitimate business interests from the illegal ones. Night and day this was my goal. I paid a lot of people off, rearranged a few things. I even had to do a few more jobs as favors. It took me a few years to be completely free of any underground activity. You know what happened next, my grandfather died. This time it was natural causes. I checked. Grandfather was getting up there in years but he was an otherwise healthy man. I think he died of a broken heart. I'd like to believe he regretted the rift between him and my father.

"To distance myself from my criminal past, I cultivated this charming playboy persona. I attended the right parties, always had a beautiful woman on my arm. I even participated in The Run because it was something that people in our circle did. Most of those women I tagged, I didn't even touch. I'd let them spend the night at one of my other houses and then let them go. I made it appear that I spent the majority of my time living a life of leisure when in fact I worked just as hard as anyone else with this much responsibility. I even had you fooled. I was determined that no one could associate me with the man I used to be."

Dare raised his brow. "So was any of this real?"

"You mean our friendship?"

Dare nodded his head in the affirmative.

"That was one of the only real things in my life. You and Victoria. You and I have been friends since we were children. Nothing will change that unless you decided you don't want to deal with someone like me."

Dare began to pace the office. "So everything that's happened to you in the last few days was because of your past?"

"I have no doubt. I thought it was because I began to dig into the auction and all the missing women and children. I'm not proud of it but to get some information I had to resort to my old tactics. But all my findings have come to a dead end because every single one of my contacts is now dead. I almost got sent to prison because of one of those deaths. I've done a lot of fucked up shit in my life, but I've always stopped short of murder."

"Shit, man. Why didn't you contact me?"

"Because I didn't want to get you involved in my bullshit. My father and grandfather are gone. I'm not going to have your death on my conscience as well."

"Your grandfather made his own choices. As far as your father, that wasn't your fault. You didn't kill him, someone else did."

"But I might as well have. Maybe if I hadn't involved myself in that life he'd still be alive today."

"Or maybe if your grandfather hadn't involved you. Look Foster, you're in over your head right now and you need help. I'm quite capable of handling myself. Besides, I'm not without my own resources. I'm sure that if we put our heads together we can come up with a plan together."

"I'm already in too deep, Dare. I can't drag you down with me. Besides, if you get involved you could inadvertently be involving Aya. I know these types of people, they'll try to get to you through the people you care about. I know this because that's why my father is dead. He wasn't even involved in that life. It was what my grandfather used to do. It was what I did. Someone has a personal vendetta against me and it's stressful enough trying to keep Victoria safe. I wonder if she would have been better off if I'd left her on the block than bringing her home with me."

"Why did you bring her here? Who is she to you?"

"Someone I don't deserve. But at this point it doesn't matter. She's here so I can keep her safe."

"How about you let me worry about Aya. I'm perfectly capable of protecting her myself. She's stubborn as hell but maybe I can convince her to spend some time away at one of my houses. I can hire a team to guard the perimeter. Perhaps you should consider letting your Victoria stay with Aya and that way we'll know they're in a safe place while we sort out this mess."

Foster's first instinct was to protest but Dare actually made sense. There was no telling who was watching the house. If he could get Victoria out of here safely and away from harm that would be one less worry he'd have.

Foster sighed with defeat. "Okay. We'll go with your plan."

"Good. I'll make the arrangements to get everything set in motion by nightfall. That will be the best time to get her out of the house. In the meantime, get yourself together. I'll be in touch." Dare turned to leave.

"Dare."

His friend turned to see what he wanted.

"Thank you."

"Anytime. Foster, I know I have a reputation for being an asshole and I may not express my feelings well, but you're the closest thing I have to a brother. And if someone fucks with you, they're fucking with me. If you ever need anything just don't wait so long to come to me for help. Now go shower. You fucking stink."

Once Dare was gone. Foster hopped out of his seat. His conversation with Dare had given him the spark that he needed to get his shit together. He'd been on the defensive for far too long.

It was time to launch an offensive. This was war.

Chapter Seventeen

"You haven't touched your food and you didn't eat anything for lunch either. You're worrying me." Aya looked at her with concern.

Tori picked up her fork and stuffed her mouth with mixed vegetables. She was sure it was delicious but right now it could have been dirt for all that she could tell. She had no appetite but she didn't want to upset Aya, who had been nothing but kind to her in their forced confinement. But she couldn't help but think she'd traded one prison for another. Shortly after that incident in Foster's library, Mrs. Gordon had come to her room to help her pack. Her initial thought was that it was happening all over again. Foster was kicking her out after using her. Tori thought Foster would let her go home but that wasn't the case. She had been informed that she was being moved to another house, and transportation would be around to collect her.

Tori had found it strange that she was carted off in the dead of night with three burly bodyguards surrounding her. When she'd arrived here it had surprised her to see Dare and Aya in residence. They informed her that this was one of Dare's vacation homes and she would be staying with Aya until further notice. That had been two nights ago.

This house wasn't as large as Foster's mansion but it was just as beautiful and expensively decorated. It was outside of town right on the beach, which gave the air a crisp, slightly salty scent. The view was beautiful and the sunset was awe-inspiring, but she couldn't feel any joy in seeing it. In most circumstances she would have fallen in love with a place like this, but all she felt was numb.

Aya tried to keep her amused but Tori just couldn't bring herself out of the deep depression that had taken hold of her. Nor could she stop thinking about her last encounter with Foster. The way he had so callously taken her without any regard to her feelings or well-being should have been another reason for her to hate him, but Tori couldn't bring herself to do it. If anything it had confused her even more about how she felt toward him. He had seemed to be in so much pain but there was no way of reaching him.

Who was the real Foster, she asked herself for the hundredth time. Was he the charming loving man who'd made her body and heart explode into flames? Or was he the cold, calculating beast who took pleasure in hurting her? But there was another side he'd revealed: a man who was in so much pain that the only way he could express himself was hurting other people. He'd told her that he wasn't the man she believed him to be. Maybe she should have listened.

Tori inhaled and exhaled deeply, trying to catch her breath from the exertion of Foster's forceful lovemaking. She didn't know when it had happened but she'd become addicted to the way he moved in and out of her, the way his hands grazed her skin, the way his tongue made her forget her own name. He collapsed next to Tori and pulled her into his arms.

She rested her head against his chest, reveling in the way she felt so protected and safe. Foster had turned out to be full of surprises. When he'd tagged her on The Run, she wasn't sure what to expect, but it certainly wasn't this.

He casually drew circles on her arm with the pad of his thumb. Tori let out a soft sigh of pure content.

"Tell me what you're thinking," Foster said suddenly, breaking the quiet of the moment.

Tori hesitated at first. She was still guarded with him, not sure whether he would use her words against her. "Nothing really. I guess I never imagined this."

"Imagined what?"

"Us like this. At The Run, you came on pretty strong."

"That was kind of the point."

"Why me? There were other women there way prettier than I am. You could have had any of them."

"Don't sell yourself short, Victoria. Big beautiful hazel eyes, gorgeous skin, great body, why wouldn't I pick you?"

"Do you have thing for exotics like me?" She asked, using the word she hated so much in a sarcastic tone.

"I'm not a fan of that term. It makes you sound more like an animal than an actual woman. And no, I don't have a preference. A beautiful woman is a beautiful woman. I saw you and I wanted you." There was a way he spoke that made Tori think there was something more to his statement but he didn't seem willing to expound on it.

"But for how long?"

"Let's not worry about time and enjoy the now, Victoria."

Tori wasn't sure how she felt about that. Already she was beginning to develop feelings for him. It had started that day in his library. And then there were the moments he'd make her laugh, just by telling her a joke out the blue. He'd take her places, showing her a side of life that she never thought would be available to her. But her favorite moments were the times when they would talk for hours about everything and nothing at all. She forced down the pang of disappointment she felt at his nonchalant response.

It wasn't like she wanted to be here with him forever. She had a family to worry about. If anything, she should count herself fortunate that she didn't suffer the fate of some of the other women she'd encountered. There had been men at the game who had given off really bad vibes, making her think that some of those women would be severely abused. The only hand Foster had ever raised to her was to give her a spanking in the midst of their steamy sexual encounters.

She shivered at the thought of his skilled lovemaking. It excited and confused her that she could want someone so badly who basically she was indentured to.

"*Cold?*" *he asked while rubbing her arm vigorously.*

"*No. I was just thinking about my family.*"

"*Oh? What about them?*"

"*I'm just wondering how they're holding up. I don't know if it was a good idea sending those credits to my father. There's no guarantee that he won't blow it all on alcohol and other unnecessary stuff. If I could have, I would have sent the money to my younger sister. But maybe she can get him to do the right thing. She seems to be the only one my father has a soft spot for out of all of us.*"

"*Do you resent that?*"

"*No. Not at all. My sister is actually quite lovable. She's the kind of person to see the good in everyone, even my father who is selfish and lazy. She makes excuses for him and he takes advantage of her good nature. Around her, he sort of pretends he's something better but he never really follows through. My sister is the one who still has hope when the rest of us lost it a long time ago.*"

"*She sounds like an amazing person.*"

"*She is. So kind and fragile. She wasn't made for our world.*"

"*Too naïve?*"

"*Yes and no. She's wise about what's going on around her but she would prefer to look on the bright side of things.*"

"*Is that really a bad thing?*"

"*I guess not. I just fear that she's in for a huge letdown. Enough about me. Tell me something about you that you haven't told me already.*"

Tori was very curious about him. She realized that he knew a lot about her background but she still had a lot to learn about his. Foster didn't answer at first and she didn't think he would. She raised her head took to look at him and he seemed to be in deep thought. "Foster?"

"*It's just so hard to pretend sometimes.*"

His cryptic message confused her. She furrowed her brow. "I don't know what you mean. Why do you have to pretend?"

"*Because if people saw me, they wouldn't look at me the same.*"

She lay her head on his chest. "*Foster, I don't know the man you think you are but I do know the one I've seen and I like him. A lot.*"

"*Perhaps I'm just showing you who I want you to see and not who I really am. I'm not a good man, Victoria.*"

"*I don't believe that.*" She lifted her head again to look him in the eyes. "*Foster, when you brought me here, you could have done anything you wanted to me. I've heard horror stories about women never being seen again after The Run and some who come back who are so badly beaten and bruised that they're unrecognizable. I can't imagine you ever hurting me.*"

His lips curved. "*I like that you have so much faith in me, Victoria. I hope I never let you down.*"

Tori wasn't sure why that conversation played over and over in her mind. He'd warned her that he wasn't a good person but she didn't believe him. But then she remembered the pain behind those words; it was the same hurt she'd seen when he'd had his breakdown in the library. Why couldn't she simply close her heart to him?

"Tori, sweetie, what's the matter?" Aya's voice broke into her thoughts.

"Nothing," Tori denied and attempted to put more food in her mouth, but her throat wouldn't cooperate. She grabbed a napkin and spit it out. "Sorry, guess I don't have much of an appetite.

"You're crying."

Tori hadn't realized that tears flowed unheeded down her cheeks. "Sorry."

Aya got out of her seat and walked over to Tori. She placed her arms around her and gave her a hug. "It's okay. Let it out."

Tori rarely allowed herself the luxury of tears but they came tumbling out with forceful sobs as Aya rocked her back and forth.

"It's okay," Aya whispered.

It took several moments before Tori was able to compose her words. "I don't know what came over me. I'm not usually a crier."

"We all cry sometimes. Do you feel better?"

"A little. So much has happened in these past couple years and I guess it all came crashing in on me."

"Tell me about it."

"I've already told you a little bit about my time with Foster. I fell in love with him and right before I was about to tell him, he told me he didn't want me anymore. And not in a way where he tried to let me down gently, but in the most humiliating way possible. He made me feel like a fool for believing in something that wasn't real. My trust isn't easily placed and I had intended to entrust him with my heart. After he kicked me out, I fell into a deep state of depression. I couldn't eat or sleep and when I wasn't sitting somewhere in the corner staring off into space, I was crying. I was home with my family where I thought I wanted to be, but I couldn't stop thinking about Foster."

"It's understandable. You loved him," Aya reasoned.

"But I had never experienced anything like that before. I couldn't seem to get out of the emotional hole I'd fallen into. And what was worse, I started neglecting my family. Instead of looking for work and ways to earn money to help put food on the table, I just sat around the house. I was just as bad as my father. Then my little brother got sick. It was a bad viral infection that required a special medication that we couldn't afford. We'd already gone through the money I'd earned from The Run, so my only option was to volunteer for the game again. Macy tried to talk me out of it but I needed to do it as a way to atone for neglecting my responsibilities."

"I felt guilty that while I was living a life of luxury with Foster, they were suffering. So I thought returning to The Run was how I could make it up to them. The guy who tagged me the second time, very abusive and demanded complete obedience. He would beat and starve me, and make me suffer if I stepped a little bit out of line. And even through all the abuse I felt this was no better than what I deserved for neglecting my family and falling for a man who only wanted to use me."

"It sounds like you're still blaming yourself for something you couldn't help."

"But I could have helped it. I shouldn't have given into Foster so easily. I should have known that someone like him could never be serious about someone like me. He even told me he wasn't a good guy and I refused to believe him."

"Tori, it's not your fault. Whatever Foster did to you was not on you, it was on him. But even still, maybe he had a reason. I can't imagine someone who didn't care would put us up in a safe house for our protection."

The rational part of Tori's brain could see the sense in Aya's logic but the other half was controlled by a hurt that tore at her soul. "Or maybe he's keeping me safe because he thinks I can give him some useful information about the auction."

"Has he even asked you about your experience at the auction?"

"No. We haven't talked about much actually. We basically stay out of each other's way and he's only touched me…"

"What?"

"A couple times but the last encounter was…I'm not really sure how to explain it. It was different. He seemed to be void of all emotion, kind of like he wasn't even there. Even as he was inside of me, I feel like I could have been anyone."

"I doubt that's true. I'm sure he knew it was you. But, he's had a rough time lately. Look, Dare thought it would be best if I didn't tell you this because he didn't see the merit of you being in the know, but Foster has had a lot of bad things happen to him lately."

Tori froze. "Like what?"

"Dare wouldn't tell me everything but for the last several days Foster has been under attack. Dare speculates because he started digging into the auction and all the trafficking. It seems to have pissed some very powerful people off. They've hit his businesses and hacked his systems. Millions of his personal credits vanished into thin air and he nearly went to jail for someone's mysterious death. And even going through all this, he still hasn't given up searching for Macy. And he doesn't intend to stop until he finds her. The reason why you're even here is because he wants you out of harm's way."

Tori frowned as she tried to figure out the significance of what Aya had just told her. "He's gone through all this for Macy?"

"Yes. The two of them became very close. But not in the way you're thinking right now so wipe that frown off your face. There's no denying that Macy has a bit of a crush on Foster but I always got the impression it was more of a hero worship thing. And he sees her as a kid sister. He was always looking out for her. He took her disappearance the hardest, harder than me even."

It was the enigma of Foster it seemed. Was he the cold calculating brute or the loving man she once believed him to be? Tori simply couldn't figure it out. "I still don't see what I have to do with this."

"Don't you?" Aya asked gently.

Tori shook her head. "No I don't. I mean, wouldn't it have been easier for him to let me go? I could go home to my family."

"Except there's no home for you to go to."

She froze. "What are you talking about? What's happened to them?"

Aya smiled. "Nothing. I shouldn't have worded it like that. What I meant was that Foster had them moved to another safe house when he moved the two of us here. You're here because he wants to keep his enemies from getting to you. That's why this place is surrounded by so many armed guards. Do you think a man who didn't give a damn about you would go to so much trouble to protect you? Tori, whether you believe it or not, and even if he hasn't said it, that man has feelings for you."

Part of Tori wanted to believe that but her cynical side simply wouldn't allow that belief to come to fruition. She'd seen too much, suffered more than most. She shook her head. "Aya, I see the sense in your words but my interactions with him say otherwise."

Aya sighed. "Then I guess there's nothing else I can say. But you have to ask yourself, are you going to willingly walk away when this is all over?"

Chapter Eighteen

Foster had spent the better part of the week trying to learn everything he could about Hemmel Corporation, how it was run, who went in and out of the building and their financial dealings. So far he had nothing. All paths he'd taken had led to dead ends. The actual headquarters for that particular building was an abandoned warehouse, and the supposed CEO Edison Wallace simply didn't exist, at least not on the grid. From the looks of it, this person was made up for the purpose of giving this ghost business some legitimacy. He should have guessed this was a straw company because he'd never met anyone who actually did business with that place.

Another clue was the fact that Myers had been so quick to give that information up. Perhaps the man had known less than Foster had supposed, but there was nothing he could do about it because Myers, just like the rest of his leads, were dead. What was worse, he'd had the building where the trafficking exchanges took place surveyed by a team of hired mercenaries he'd assembled, only to learn that it was no longer in use. Someone had obviously gotten wind of the fact that he knew of the location. Perhaps Myers had tipped them off before he died. It was as if they were one step ahead of him.

He wracked his brain to think of all the people who had been in attendance at the auction. The only person he could remember was Winthrop, who was very insignificant. Since their families had dissolved their business ties, the Winthrops no longer had the pull they'd once had in their circles. Barely anyone saw Eli II in public anymore. The other people he recalled seemed to be foreigners and a few others he didn't recognize.

He thought about the woman Zee who seemed to be running the entire operation, but Foster doubted she was the one in charge. It wouldn't have been good business to be the face of that type of outfit and own it as well. There was too much of a risk of being recognized.

Foster placed his hand in his palms. The more time that elapsed the harder it would be to get Macy back. And then there was Victoria. He couldn't image what she must think of him. He thought that maybe after all this was over and Macy was safely back home he might be able to convince Victoria to stay with him but after what he'd done to her he doubted they could reconcile. He just kept hurting her over and over again and for that he didn't deserve her. The first time he'd done it was for altruistic reasons but the last time... Foster shuddered as he remembered the image of her scrunched in a ball on his library floor like a wounded animal. He would never forget the way she'd looked at him. He saw the hurt, disbelief and the confusion on her face as if she were simply trying to make sense of what had just happened to her.

Foster couldn't figure out why he'd done it either. He'd felt so empty and then she touched him. He wanted to consume every bit of her to feel whole again, but all that incident had done was make him feel like an even bigger piece of shit.

The very last thing he wanted her to do was to relive any painful memories but he needed to know this information or else. With a heavy sigh, he dialed the coordinates to the holophone he'd left for her to use in case he needed to contact her. She didn't answer and it didn't surprise him. His number was the only one programmed in that phone so she had to know it was him. Foster didn't blame her for ignoring him, he'd put her through a lot of shit.

Foster then tried Aya. She answered quickly. Her holographic image popped up. "Foster. I wasn't expecting you to call. I just finished talking to Dare, he said the two of you haven't had much luck yet." She seemed a bit wary instead of her usual upbeat self. It was almost as if she wasn't happy to talk to him.

"No, we keep hitting brick walls." He paused for a moment to study her stiff demeanor. "Is everything all right, Aya?"

"As fine as they can be expected. Why are you calling?"

He raised a brow. "You kind of sound as if I'm the last person you want to speak with. Have I done something to upset you?" Having Aya mad at him was another problem he didn't want to deal with. He had to resolve whatever issue she had with him right away.

She sighed. "It's nothing you've done to me per se, but I think you and Tori are going to have to talk when this is all over."

"Victoria? That's actually who I was trying to contact but she's didn't answer the call I just sent her."

"Because she's taking a nap. She's exhausted from crying most of the morning."

"Crying? What the hell is going on?"

"Maybe she's crying because she's been through a lot these last couple of years, and on top of that you don't have the balls to tell her what the hell is going on. Don't you think she has the right to know why she's being held in a safe house? Not only that, she deserves to know how you feel."

"So you're upset with me on Victoria's behalf?" Aya had always been a little spitfire who was fiercely loyal and protective of those she cared about. Foster never imagined he'd be on the end of her ire. As sweet and generous as Aya Smith was, she was never one to hold her tongue.

"What did Victoria say about me?"

"What she told me was in confidence. You'll have to ask her. And no, I'm not upset with you but I am disappointed. I just don't understand you. I can think of no other reason why you bought her at the auction or put her up in this place other than the fact that you care about her. But Tori doesn't seem to know that. She thinks you're playing some cruel game with her feelings. Are you?"

"Of course not. You know why the two of you are there. I need to keep her safe in case someone tries to hurt her to get to me. And since Dare has become involved, he insisted you be there with her."

Aya crossed her arms over her chest. "But the only way someone could possibly hurt you by hurting her is if you had feelings for her. Why doesn't Tori know this?"

For such a petite woman, Aya had a way of looking at a person that made them feel an inch tall. At the moment Foster felt half an inch. He released another heavy sigh. "Because I don't want her to know."

"Why?"

"Because when this is all over she'll go back to her life. It's for the best."

"Really? The best for whom? Because the way I see it, the two of you have feelings for each other and neither one of you are willing to act on it. I get why Tori won't. She's in a lot of pain, pain that you've caused, and it's going to take a lot for you to earn her trust back. So all the power rests in your hands. Why if you care about her would you let her go?"

"Aya, some things are better left alone."

"Why?"

"Aya..."

"Why?"

"Because I don't deserve her!" He yelled, his chest burning with the pain and anger of having to admit out loud what he'd known all along. "That's why. So there's the truth. Are you happy?"

Aya placed her hand on her chest. Her eyebrows rose in her apparent surprise at his outburst. Then gradually her features softened to an expression of compassion. She reached out her hand as if to touch him even though she couldn't. "Oh, Foster, I'm so sorry."

"What for? You're only looking out for your friend. That's what you do."

"I guess... I just didn't realize that maybe you're hurting too. I should have recognized that."

"It's nothing," he dismissed it, in no mood to explore his feelings.

"You know if you ever want to talk about it, I'm always willing to listen. I know Dare isn't huge on discussing feelings, just know you have a friend who is."

"While I appreciate the offer, Aya, there's really nothing to talk about. I've made up my mind as far as Victoria is concerned. I'm doing what's best for her."

"Is it really for the best or just what you *think* is the best? Like you pointed out before, you're going through a lot right now. Don't make any rash decisions until everything is settled because when you do that, you end up making mistakes."

Foster chose not to reply to that statement because deep down, he knew she was right. "Is it possible you can get Victoria? I know I'm the last person she wants to speak with right now but it's extremely important that I talk to her. I need some information I think possibly only she has access to."

"I finally convinced her to take a nap so that could be why she didn't answer. That was over two hours ago. I can check on her and see if she's awake. She might be up. How about I check on her and call you back either way."

"Sounds like a plan." Foster signed off without waiting for Aya to respond. That woman was far too astute for her own good.

Tori had only pretended to sleep to get Aya to leave her side. Even if she wanted to rest, all the thoughts buzzing in her mind wouldn't allow her any rest. Was Aya really right about Foster actually caring for her?

There was a knock on her door, breaking into Tori's thoughts. "Tori are you awake?" Aya called out.

Though Tori was tempted to feign sleep, she was tired of lying down. She was getting restless and needed to stretch her legs. She let out a loud, exaggerated yawn. "Yes. I'm up. Come in."

Aya entered the room with a smile. "Are you feeling better?"

"Tons. I'm almost completely refreshed." Tori felt bad about lying but she didn't want the other woman to continue worrying.

"That's great." Aya took a seat on the edge of the bed, a slight frown drooped the corners of her lips. "Look, I just received a call from Foster. He said he tried to call you earlier but you didn't answer."

Tori's heartbeat sped up. "Oh I, left my phone downstairs. Did he say why he called?"

"Foster said he needed to ask you some important questions about the auction. He and Dare are having trouble tracking down any solid leads and he thinks that whatever information you can give him might provide them with some clues."

Tori moistened her lips that had suddenly gone dry. "I don't know what I can tell him. I didn't see any of the other girls and I don't know how that place was run. I basically lived in isolation for the few weeks that I was there."

"I don't see the harm in talking to him, especially if it helps to get Macy back. Who knows, you might actually have seen or heard something that could be helpful to them."

"You have a point. I need to go downstairs and get my holophone. I didn't have it on me because I didn't think I'd have to use it."

"Don't worry about it. You can use mine." Aya handed her the four inch rectangular disk. "Foster's coordinates are already programmed in. Just say last call and it will automatically contact him."

"Thanks."

Aya nodded. "I'll give you some privacy." When she turned to leave, Tori scrambled to the side of the bed and grabbed her hand.

"No. Please stay with me. For moral support."

"Are you sure?"

"Yes please." Tori felt that with Aya at her side, she might not completely crumble into a big ball of quivering emotions from talking to Foster. He was so unpredictable she didn't know what the conversation would lead to.

Aya took a seat next to her and gave Tori an encouraging pat on the knee. Tori took a deep breath and followed Aya's instructions to contact Foster.

When his holographic image popped up, Tori had to bite her bottom lip to keep herself from gasping. Though he was shaved and cleaned up from the last time she'd seen him, there was no doubt that the stress had taken a toll on him. There were large bags, under his eyes and he looked as if he hadn't slept in months. He seemed thinner and she wondered if he was eating.

"Victoria," he said simply.

"Uh, yeah, Aya said you wanted to speak to me? She's next to me by the way."

"Yes, I know. I see her sitting there."

"Oh." Holophones were a luxury that she had yet to get used to. Growing up, her family had never been able to afford one. She like the rest of the people in her neighborhood had to rely on old technology from the twenty-first century to contact each other and that was only in cases of absolute necessity. "So what did you want to talk to me about?"

He raked his fingers through his hair. "I didn't want it to come down to this but I need to know what happened while you were at the auction."

She gulped. Tori had tried to forget about that horrible place. She didn't want to relive those memories and how scared she felt not knowing what her fate would be. But she realized she'd have to tell him what she knew, especially if it helped to get Macy back. "What do you want to know specifically?"

"Anything you think would be of importance. Give me names that you heard." Foster pulled up a holographic keyboard.

Tori took a deep breath. "Well the main person was a woman named Zee. She seemed to be in charge of everything. Everyone who worked there took orders from her. She also punished me whenever she felt I was out of line."

Foster's jaw tightened but he typed away at his keyboard. "What else? I'm just taking down what you say so I don't forget anything."

Tori nodded in understanding. "There was Shia. She was the girl who was basically the go between. She would groom me and relay any order Zee didn't give me directly. She brought my meals and told me what to expect. She was just a child really, only fifteen years old. Apparently, some of the women these people took were pregnant. When the women come to term, they deliver the babies and sell the mothers off. Shia was one of those children. The organization raises the girls to be servants and sometimes they sell them off too. The boys they sell as children, around the age of eight."

"Disgusting," Aya whispered, shaking her head as she listened in.

"Zee always had two guards with her," Tori continued. "One she referred to as Bronte and the other Xander. There was also another man name Dino who would be with her occasionally but I didn't see him often."

"I've met Dino. He was there on the night of the sale. Anything else?"

She bit her lower lip and shut her eyes as she remembered being in those cold white rooms. "Everything around me was always bright. After I was given my meals in the morning I would sit in a sensory deprivation room until I thought I'd go crazy. Then I was escorted to a room where I was made to sit in front of a screen and given what Zee calls instruction time. It was basically a video of everything that was expected of me when I was given to my new master. I had to watch the same footage three times a day, every day until I could recite it word for word. It was torture in and of itself. Once when I fell asleep during instruction time, Zee had me strapped to a wall. Her guards doused me a bucket of water and she proceeded to electrocute me with this wand. It was horrible." Tori began to shake as she remembered screaming for mercy while that evil bitch watched her without blinking an eye.

Aya placed her arm around Tori's shoulders for comfort.

Foster stopped typing and eyed her solemnly. "I'm sorry that happened to you."

Tori shrugged with a nonchalance she didn't feel. "Well, there's nothing we can do about it now."

"I beg to differ about that, but are there any other people you remember interacting with. Anyone else mentioned?"

"Those were the only four people I ever saw. I couldn't even tell you where we were located. There were no windows and I was only ever in three rooms. I didn't even see the other women there but I know they were around according to Shia. I believe they each had their own attendant. Oh, and they never referred to me by name. They called me Rose. According to Shia all the women who went on the block were given flower names. I don't know how significant that is or not but I once asked Zee why. Maybe she was feeling generous that day because she was never forthcoming with information, but she said it was what the boss preferred."

Foster seemed to be mulling over Tori's statements before he spoke again. "So there was a mention of someone else in charge. Hmmm. And he was never mentioned by name?"

"No. He was just the boss."

"I know this part may be painful for you but how did you come to be at the auction? You mentioned being in The Run again and I can only assume it was one of the times when I didn't participate, but is the man who tagged you the one who sold you off?"

She nodded as tears burned her eyes, and she remembered that evil asshole who seemed to get off from torturing her and the other girls there. Tori wondered if the other women in his house had met the same fate as her. "I was with that sadistic bastard for months and I never thought he would let me go, at least not alive. And then one night he said to me that it will be our last night together. I experienced the most pain I'd ever endured in my life that night. I passed out afterwards. The next thing I remember is waking up in this big white room."

"Who was he?" Foster's tone had taken on an aggressive edge. His chest heaved up and down and he looked as if he wanted to commit murder.

"I only ever knew him as Mr. X. Even his friends called him X. And before you ask, his friends were always referred to by letter names. They always used some kind of code with names. I wish I could tell you more about him. His features were pretty nondescript except for this nasty mole on his right cheek. It was the size of a thumb and it was hairy. He called it his beauty mark but I always noticed it because that's usually the type of blemish a person with his money would have had lasered off. He seemed quite proud of it."

Tori noticed Foster's sudden change in demeanor. All color had drained from his face.

"Foster, are you okay?" Aya asked.

"Uh, yeah. Thank you, Victoria. Your information has been helpful. I'll be in touch." He signed off before she could say another word.

Tori looked at Aya. "What was that about?"

"I don't know but here's hoping he found your information useful."

A cold sweat broke out along his skin. It couldn't possibly be. Once he ended the call between him and Victoria, he contacted Dare.

"Any news?" Dare asked without preamble when his image popped up.

"I know that it's been shut down, but do you still keep records from The Run?"

"Yes, why?"

"Because I believe I've finally found the son of a bitch behind the trafficking."

Chapter Nineteen

Foster looked over the transactions from The Run from the last two years which had been provided to him from Dare's assistant Ronald.

"Have you found what you were looking for yet?" Dare asked, looking over his shoulder.

"Not yet, but I think I'm going to narrow it down to the days I know I didn't participate as a patron in The Run."

"You were in quite a few of them. It's kind of odd you wouldn't be at the one this guy was in. Most of the patrons were returning clients according to Ronald."

"Exactly. Not to sound paranoid, but it almost seems like he was avoiding me on purpose."

"If that were the case, the question remains, how would he know which ones you'd participate in and which ones you didn't? Do you think he might have paid someone on the inside to get that info?"

"I thought about it." He moved his finger around the holographic screen. "Remove all dates with Foster Graham," Foster said to the computer.

The words and numbers on the screen began to scramble and several lines disappeared and everything was rearranged until only six lines remained. He tapped the first line under the patron's tab and a list of names unfolded, revealing thirty-five patrons. As Foster scrolled down the list, he came across the name he was looking for. He then went to line two. Again that name popped up. It appeared again on the next line and the subsequent ones. "Got him. That son of bitch. Why didn't I see this before? I should have seen the clues but I've been so single-minded."

"What, Foster?"

"It was Winthrop all along."

"Winthrop?" Dare frowned. "As in Eli II?"

"Yes, him."

Dare widened his eyes in apparent surprise. "No one has seen him in years. It's like he dropped off the face of the planet even though I know the Winthrop property never went up for sale after Eli Winthrop the First died. There was a rumor that that the Winthrops experienced some financial problems after they sold their interest in the bank. I haven't thought about him in years. I remembered we used to associate with Eli III. He disappeared one day. I heard he was shipped off to a school overseas. Are you sure it's Winthrop? He's always struck me as a mousy guy."

"It all fits now. He was at the auction on the night I was there. It struck me as odd that he would be there as well. Like you said, word was out that the Winthrops were broke, but in order to be in a place like the auction one would have to have significant wealth and some connections to the underground. I was quick to write him off because I didn't see him as a threat. But then I spoke with Victoria. She told me about a Mr. X. He was the man who had tagged her the second time she volunteered for The Run. It wasn't until she described a mole on the side of his face with significant amount of hair on it did I make the connection."

"The Winthrop curse," Dare whispered.

Exactly. The birthmark on the side of Eli II's face was apparently hereditary because his father had it as well as his son. Foster and Dare used to tease Eli III for it, but their childhood friend didn't seem to mind. Eli III seemed to think of it as something of a family crest. Foster and Dare had called it The Curse.

Foster nodded. "As much as I've participated in The Run, don't you think it's odd that every single time Winthrop participated I wasn't there? Not only did it seem like he was avoiding me he might have had me watched."

"But I never saw him at the games either."

"You let Ronald run it for you. You were hardly ever there. There was less risk of running into you than me. But I think this specifically has to do with me. I'm beginning to think there may be some hard feelings about the dissolution of my grandfather's partnership with his father. Maybe he feels cheated out of his cut. His words had been very cryptic to me when I spoke to him at the Auction. Shit!" Foster exclaimed now that he saw everything so clearly.

Dare frowned. "What?"

"That mysterious message he gave me about being in his territory. Fuck, that bastard was hiding in plain sight all along. All this time I was chasing all these leads that were getting me nowhere and it was fucking him. Shit, I bet he was the one who's been leaving me those calls. He attacked my banks; he's the one who nearly had me thrown in prison. And he threatened me all those months ago."

Foster hopped out of his seat, raging mad. Winthrop had cost him more than he could ever know. Money, time and inconvenience aside, Winthrop had cost him Victoria. Had he not gotten that threat a while back, he and Victoria would still be together. But he'd done what he thought best for the sake of her safety.

He pounded his fist into his palm and roared with frustration. This had never been about the auction but some vendetta in the mind of a madman. He wouldn't put it past that asshole that he had set his sights on Victoria out of spite to somehow hurt him. When he got his hands on that man, Foster would hurt him in ways that he'd never done with anyone else.

"You mean you were getting threats before all this started?"

"Yes. It was only one threat but it worried me enough to take precautionary measures.

"Why didn't you tell me?"

"I didn't want to get you involved, and frankly I wondered if it's my penance for what I did in the past. All those people I tortured and beat up were bound to come back to haunt me. I'm just surprised that you're still willing to associate with me after I told you what I did."

"Like I said before, I've done some pretty fucked up things myself. It's not like I have that much room to talk."

"Yeah, but you've never carved your name into someone's chest with a laser."

"Shit, man, that's hardcore. Look, I'm not judging you. I know what it's like to be under the influence of someone with a strong personality. Even though I hated my father's guts, a part of me always wanted his approval. So I get that you did those things because you looked up to your grandfather."

Foster snorted. "Yeah, but I started to like it too much. I've avoided going back to those ways, up until now. I thought Myers would be my last victim but apparently I have one more."

"Winthrop?"

"Yeah. It's time for a little payback."

<><><><><>

Tori wasn't sure what to make of how her call had ended with Foster. He'd ended it so abruptly she wondered what she'd said to make him sign off so suddenly. "That call was strange, wasn't it?" Tori mused out loud.

"You're still thinking about that?" Aya asked looking up from her holopad. They had settled in the living room by the fireplace after dinner. Aya had refused to let Tori leave the table until she'd eaten a decent portion.

"Yeah. I didn't think anything I told him would be that helpful but maybe he's found a clue."

"Maybe. You'll just have to trust that he's working as hard as he can to get Macy back."

"Yeah," Tori replied more to herself than to Aya.

"Dare!" Aya jumped up from her seat. "What are you two doing here?"

Tori had been so deep in thought she didn't hear anyone enter the room. She turned around to see Dare with Foster trailing behind.

Dare nodded in Tori's direction but stalked toward Aya with purpose. He grabbed the petite woman by the arm and proceeded to drag her out of the room. To Tori's surprise she went with him without protest or a backward glance. With Dare and Aya gone, she was left alone with Foster.

Foster's lips were tilted in a half-grin. "My friend is not one to waste time when there's something he wants."

The way Dare had dragged Aya out of the room left no doubt in Tori's mind exactly what he'd taken her out of the room for. "Well, we have been here for a few days," she said a bit uneasily. She wasn't sure how to behave around him. There was a time when they could tease and joke with one another but not anymore.

"So did you two come by with news?"

"Yes and no."

"Which is it?"

"As you've already seen, Dare was eager to see his woman. And I wanted to tell you about what I learned."

"What?" Her heart began to pound. "Are you any closer to finding my sister?"

"I don't know, I do know who's behind the auction so at least now we can find out how to gain access to finding Macy."

"Who is it?"

"Your Mr. X turns out to be an old acquaintance of my family."

She gasped. "You know him?"

"Not well, but his father and my grandfather were once business partners. After the partnership dissolved we didn't hear from them again. In fact seeing him at the auction was the first time I've seen him since I was a kid. I wrote him off as insignificant because of how little pull he had in our circles. I was so single-minded that I didn't stop to ask myself why someone like him would be in a place like that, particularly someone who wasn't supposed to have the wealth it took to get into the auction in the first place. When you mentioned that birthmark on his face, something clicked."

"You figured that all out because of a birthmark?"

"Yes. It's very distinctive, isn't it?"

Tori shuddered as she thought of all the times that thing had been close enough for her to touch. "It was a disgusting hairy mess."

Foster nodded. "He had a son with the exact same mole. Dare and I used to tease him about it but apparently it was hereditary. That's why it came together. Look, Victoria, would you mind having a seat?"

"Why?"

Foster hesitated for a moment, seeming unsure of himself. Victoria wasn't sure if she'd like what he had to say next. "Because I think after everything you've been through, you deserve the truth and it's time you finally heard it."

He seemed sincere enough but she couldn't tell if this was some kind of trick. With Foster she never knew. "Why can't you tell me while I stand?"

"Because it's a long story. Look, I know I haven't given you much reason to trust me but please, could you take a seat?" He gestured toward the couch.

Tori let out a labored sigh as she complied. "Okay, I'm sitting. What is it you have to tell me?"

"Around the time I started digging into the trafficking organization that funneled women into the auction is about the same time I began to receive threats. I started getting anonymous calls and all of a sudden my businesses, finances, and reputation, were under attack. I believed at first it was because of my snooping, but it was more than that. I realized it was personal. They were trying to destroy me in a way in which I could never recover. I believe the person behind all my mysterious calls was the same person who'd threatened me a couple years ago. That person was the reason I made you leave."

Tori shook her head vigorously. He didn't get to twist the truth to suit his needs. He was playing with her heart again, to bend her to his will. But she refused to play this time. "You made me leave because you got tired of me. You said so yourself. What do you think you're trying to accomplish with this revisionist history?"

"I told you what I wanted you to believe. I was purposely cruel. I did it so you would move on with your life and forget about me. Sure it would hurt at first but then as you healed, you could find someone worthy of you."

"I don't believe you."

"You don't have to believe me but it is the truth. Someone had set one of my banks on fire. The security in my building was impeccable so I realized it had to be someone on the inside. Once I found out the culprit, that person decided to take their own life than to tell me who paid them off. It was then I realized how dangerous the mastermind behind it had to be. I wasn't worried so much for myself as I was for you. If they were attacking my businesses it wouldn't be long before they tried to get me through my heart. That person hinted that that he was watching us."

"What are you trying to say, Foster? Don't tell me you actually had feelings for me, because the way you pushed me aside was not how someone shows they care."

"That's exactly what I'm telling you, Victoria. I fell for you hard, almost from the moment I saw you. There you were in a room full of women who all seemed to have every ounce of spirit zapped out of them while you stood there with your head held high. You looked at each and every patron in the eye daring them to steal your dignity. You were a queen among peasants, a beacon shining in the darkness. And I wanted that light. Needed it. I had to have you at all costs. I rationalized to myself that if I didn't claim you someone else would. So I took you and for a while I believed that we could have something special. I thought maybe you were starting to feel a little for me too. And I intended to tell you and make it real, but then the bank burning happened. And I felt my past coming back to haunt me. I didn't want you in the crossfire so I let you go. If you believe nothing else I say believe that because I loved you. I still do and after all I've been through, and all I put you through, I owed this explanation to you."

His sapphire eyes glistened with the suspicious gleam of tears, and even though Tori wanted to call him a liar she couldn't deny his sincerity.

A sudden burst of anger swept through her. She hopped off the couch and stalked toward him. Before she realized what she was doing she smacked him across the face with an open palm. She did it again. And then again. Foster for his part stood there and took it. His passiveness pissed her off even more. He didn't get to play the victim after all she'd been through.

Tori balled up her fists and punched him in the chest over and over again. Tears streamed down her face and all the pain she'd suffered because of him came pouring out. "You stand there and tell me that you got rid of me for my protection? You rip my heart out and crush it and say you did it all for me? You didn't even fucking talk to me. You took the coward's way out. Have you any idea what I've dealt with after your so-called protection? I had to do the damn Run again! Day in and day out I lived under the thumb of a sadist who took pleasure in causing me pain. He'd beat me if I didn't entertain his guests, he'd beat me because I didn't do something quickly enough for him. He tortured me because he couldn't get it up without the assistance from a mechanical implant. He nearly killed me when I didn't want to service one of his smelly friends and then he sold me off like I was some inanimate object. I was separated from my family, wondering how they were getting along without me. And despite it all, the worst part was that I couldn't get past what you'd did to me. I'd cry myself to sleep at night wondering what it was about me that was so unlovable. I wondered how I could give my heart to someone who didn't give a shit about me. And now you stand there and tell me that you got rid of me for my protection? Fuck your protection, Foster! And Fuck you!" She collapsed to her knees.

All this time she'd hated him for the wrong reasons. "Coward," she whispered. "If you cared about me you would have told me. Maybe we could get through it together but out of some misguided sense of chivalry, you threw me away like garbage without giving me a say in my own fate. Please just leave me alone. I don't want to look at you." She couldn't raise her head. To look at him would be to fall for him again, and she couldn't afford that. He'd cost her too much.

"I understand. I just wanted you to know how I felt. If I don't see you again at least you'll know the truth." Foster walked off, leaving Tori to her misery.

Chapter Twenty

"Are you sure you want to do this?" Dare asked.

When his men had sent him word that they'd caught Winthrop and had taken him to his old location he knew what had to be done. "It's the only way. How else are we going to find Macy? Besides, I have to take Winthrop out of commission before he can do any more damage."

Dare nodded. "And end his trafficking operation. Just remember once you cross this line, there's no turning back."

"I know. I've thought of nothing else since that bastard had been caught. I need to know why he came after me. I get that he wanted to warn me off from finding out the truth. But it began way before this. He's out for blood so now it's either him or me."

"I could go in there with you."

"No. I need to do this on my own. I can't involve you in this."

"Fine, but I'll be outside waiting and if you're not back within an hour, I'm coming in and you won't be able to stop me," Dare warned.

"Okay." Foster slid out of the vehicle tools in hand. He looked over his shoulders to make sure he wasn't being followed as he walked across the street to where it all started. This was the old main branch that he hadn't stepped inside of for years. One of the first steps he'd taken to completely legitimize all of his business assets was to close this building down. There were too many memories attached here. It housed his grandfather's torture chamber. Foster had his own spot but he felt it was more fitting to bring his prey here.

Walking down the empty corridor he thought he felt the specter of his grandfather's ghost. "You old bastard. How could you do that to me? I was just a kid," Foster spoke out loud. "I can't lay all the blame at your feet. I was willing to do anything to please you. I could have said no. But it ends here tonight. After this I'm done with you, Grandfather. Do you hear me?" Foster yelled. "I'm done with you, Grandfather!"

The echo of his voice resonated in the dark hall. Once he'd let all other emotions drain he calmly headed to his destination.

Foster wasn't sure why he'd left the building in working order. Perhaps, like his toolkit, he'd kept it because deep down he knew he'd use it again. A certain calm came over him as he took the elevator to the bowels of the building. When he stood in front of the door that led to what his grandfather once referred to as the work room, Foster took a deep breath.

This was it.

Foster walked inside and headed to the little table in the center of the room. He didn't bother to look at the man chained to the wall. He was sure his men had followed through. That's what he paid them for. Foster opened his bag and lined his tools on the table. He then shrugged out of his jacket and walked over to the far corner of the room to hang it up.

He made sure to take his time with each task he performed. Foster had learned that it drove his victims crazy. Once he'd donned his gloves and goggles he turned to Winthrop, who eyed him with a malevolence that nearly made Foster take a step backward. Stealing his emotions, Foster finally approached his victim.

Foster eyed the handiwork of the mercenary he had hired. He had left specific instructions on how he wanted the other man bound. Winthrop had been stripped naked and he was secured against the wall. His wrists and ankles were held by chains that were securely bolted. These weren't ordinary chains, however. With the press of a remote, they could heat to temperatures as high as

400 degrees. It was hot enough to cause third degree burns as well as cut through muscle and bone.

Winthrop's mouth was covered with a special adhesive tape that would take off at least three layers of skin once it was yanked off. Foster made a mental note to give his mercenary a bonus for a job well done. He was sure it hadn't been an easy task taking down the guards who probably surrounded this maniac.

Once he was satisfied with his inspection Foster took the chair that was tucked into the table and pulled it in front of his waiting prey. Foster stared at the man who had caused him so much grief, and his first instinct was to take one of his sharp razors and gut Winthrop from throat to bellybutton but he decided against it. He needed the information and he was determined to have it. He wouldn't let everything that happened be for nothing.

"So here we are," he began. "You're on my territory now. I don't know why I didn't guess it was you. But then again, you were so insignificant you had me fooled. And it was awful clever of you setting up that dummy corporation under the name of Edison Wallace. That was very tongue-in-cheek of you to make a fake name with your same initials. Bravo for a hand well played." Foster gave Winthrop a slow ironic clap.

This seemed to incense the chained man. He fought against his restraints and attempted to yell but all that came out were muffled grunts.

Foster chuckled. "What did you say?"

Winthrop glared.

"Oh, I'm sorry. Let me fix that for you." Foster got out of his chair and halted directly in front of his victim. He caught the edge of the tape and yanked it off with a forceful tug.

Winthrop howled. "You mother fucker!"

Foster examined the sticky side of the tape and sure enough there was a thick layer of skin on it. He looked to see that the chained man now bled where the tape had been. His lips looked swollen and abused.

"Oh, that's not nice, Winthrop. And here I thought we would be great friends."

"Fuck you, Graham. You're just like your dreg grandfather. I should have killed you when I had the chance."

"Well, I guess that was your mistake now, wasn't it?"

"Do what you will to me because whatever you want to know I won't fucking tell you. You don't scare me because I know what you're capable of. Yeah, that's right. I know exactly what kind of man you are and have always been."

"Is that so? Well, we're only just beginning. So I guess we'll find out." Foster returned to his chair and proceeded to stare at Winthrop who continued to curse him several times. No matter what he said, Foster couldn't lose his cool. With just one slip of the hand he could end up dealing a fatal blow before he obtained the information he needed to know.

It was only when Winthrop seemed to run out of insults to hurl at him did Foster leave his chair to go to his tool table. "You know, I could have easily forgiven you for a number of your crimes, like for being an uninspiring dipshit. I might have even forgiven you for messing with my businesses or even me. But you fucked with two people I care about, one of whom you will tell me the whereabouts of. Make no mistake, you will not leave this room alive, but just how painful your death will be is up to you."

"You sick son of a bitch. Go ahead and kill me now. I already told you I wouldn't talk."

"They all say that, you know." Foster spoke without bothering to look up. He eyed the tools, wondering which weapon he'd use first.

"I'm curious, though. You seem to be on a one man vendetta against me. You could have easily killed me as you said. Any particular reason why?"

Winthrop snorted. "You have me chained like an animal and you dare ask me that question? You know what your family did. You fucking know it. Your dreg grandfather made sure to destroy us in a way that he knew we'd never recover from. I'm sure he bragged about what he did to get my father to practically hand over the controlling interest of the bank. He cheated my father out of his fair share of the bank they started together."

"All this because you're bitter over something that happened over twenty years ago?"

"Don't you dare pretend that you don't know what he did! He had my son's severed head delivered to my father in a gift-wrapped box! My son was innocent and your grandfather killed him. And then that evil son of a bitch threatened to do the same to me if my father didn't sell his shares. My son is dead because of your grandfather's greed!"

Foster froze. When Eli III had disappeared, it had happened so abruptly that he briefly wondered if some foul play had been involved. But he'd quickly rid himself of those thoughts once the rumors of Eli III getting shipped off to boarding school overseas had begun to swirl. Never in a million years had he suspected his grandfather would stoop so low as to decapitate a child to get what he wanted. No matter what Eli II had become, the Winthrops had at one point been decent people. Foster wanted to call Winthrop a liar but then he remembered what his grandfather had said to him when Foster's father had died. *A son for a son.*

Foster narrowed his eyes. "You had my father killed, didn't you?"

"Without any regret and I'd do it again if I could."

Foster reached for the serrated blade. "My father had nothing to do with grandfather's business."

"And you think my innocent son should have been beheaded? Fuck your father!"

It truly was a fucked up thing his grandfather had done, but apparently Winthrop intended Foster to pay forever. He stalked over to his victim with the knife raised. Foster had every intention of stabbing that bastard in the heart for what he'd done but halted. He had to remember his mission.

Foster took several calming breaths before he returned to his tool table. He lay the knife down and picked up the heated blade.

After this, he was done with his grandfather's ghost for good and he'd be able to mourn his father properly.

"Winthrop. I had no idea about your son. I was a boy myself when it happened. I didn't realize what my grandfather did in order to force the dissolution of his partnership with your father and I offer my sincere apology. What I'm not sorry for, however, is this." He pressed the button on the heated blade. Foster jabbed the knife into his captive's thigh, digging to the point where he sliced through muscles but not enough to reach the bones.

Winthrop screamed but Foster wasn't finished with him. He slowly pulled the blade out and stabbed the other thigh. "This used to be an old favorite of mine. It keeps the victim alive for the most part because as it cuts, it also cauterizes the wound."

"You bastard, what do you think you're going to gain by doing this to me? You might be enjoying this, but I bet not as much as I enjoyed fucking your bitch. Oh yeah, that's right. I knew about her. I was watching you, waiting to strike. I was watching her too. I knew it wouldn't be long before someone like her would enter that game again. Isn't it funny how you were called away on urgent business that weekend so you couldn't participate?" Winthrop taunted.

Foster stabbed Winthrop in the thighs several times, drawing a scream each time. What he'd done to Tori was just another reason this asshole would die tonight. When it seemed like Winthrop would pass out from the pain Foster backed off and took a seat in his chair, giving the man a chance to recover. He intended to drag this out for as long as possible. "Oh yeah, you must be so proud of yourself. We had a good laugh about how you use a device to get hard. That's pretty pathetic, even for someone like you."

"Fuck you," Winthrop whispered.

Foster chuckled. "Defiant until the end I see. You look a little cold, let me heat you up."

Foster replaced the knife with the remote control to the chains. "Here's what's going to happen next; I'm going to press the button on this remote control and then those chains are going to get hot. Every time I press a button, they heat up another twenty-five degrees. They'll eventually get so hot that they'll start melting your skin. After that happens, it will burn through your muscle tissue and then your bones. The chains will no longer be able to hold you because your hands and feet will fall off. But thankfully you won't bleed out because they'll be cauterized. I can guarantee you with absolute certainty that it will be the worst pain you've ever experienced in your life. Trust me, it's better for you to talk to me now rather than later. So what will it be? The easy way or the hard way?"

"I'm not weak like my father." Winthrop spat in his direction. Foster barely managed to sidestep the huge glob of phlegm that sped his way.

"The hard way it is." Foster turned on the button.

"How do I access the transactions to find a particular girl who was sold on the auction?"

Winthrop remained stubbornly silent.

Foster turned up the temperature. "Ready to talk?"

"Never to you."

Foster adjusted the heat again.

After two more rounds, Winthrop began to squirm uncomfortably.

"Ready to talk?"

"Turn the heat down!" Winthrop demanded.

Foster turned it up. "Excuse me, what did you say? Were you telling me how I can access the names of the buyers and who I'm looking for specifically?"

By now, Winthrop's flesh began to sizzle, and Foster could tell it would take a massive amount of pain tolerance to not be bothered by that.

"No!"

Foster sighed. "You're only making this hard on yourself." This time he pressed the button until it had gone up fifty degrees more.

Winthrop yelled out, "I have a safe in my home office that contains all the digital files of our buyers that can be cross-referenced with who they brought. Now turn it off!" The skin around his hands was blistered and peeling.

Foster turned off the chains.

"That wasn't so hard now, was it?"

"Even if you find this woman it doesn't mean whoever bought her will simply hand her back. These people guard their property under lock and key."

"Hmm," Foster murmured in response. He put the remote down and picked up the serrated knife again.

When he stood in front of Winthrop Foster grabbed the other man by the chin and dug the knife down the side of his cheek. He proceeded to carve off the birthmark that Winthrop took so much pride in all while ignoring the ear-splitting wails.

"Noooooo! Not that. It's my family crest!"

"Fuck your crest. This is for Victoria. For all the times you beat her because you're an inadequate little fuck."

Foster made sure to really dig the point of the knife into Winthrop's flesh. By the time Foster was done, there was a large hole in the crying man's cheek. "That thing was disgusting anyway. Now tell me how to gain access to the safe or it's your balls next. I will chop them off and feed them to the first dog I find."

Winthrop shook his head.

Foster shook his head. "Why do you have to make this so hard on yourself?" As he promised he grabbed Winthrop by the sack and sliced them off with one clean swipe. "Next I'm going to saw off a finger and then another and I'm going to do it with a dull knife."

Winthrop quickly rambled off the code to his safe and how to access his files.

"What I'm going to do is contact my man who is currently watching your house. He'll check this information and verify whether or not you're telling the truth. If you're not say goodbye to those fingers. All of them. Maybe your toes too."

Foster produced his holophone from his pocket. "That was a neat trick you pulled by the way, hacking into my coordinates to call me. You must have hired a hell of a hacker to do that."

Winthrop whimpered and moaned as Foster placed his call. It took several moments before he was able to verify the information but finally he was satisfied. "That info is now being downloaded to a link that will go directly to my system. One more thing. Tell me about the money trail. Where does it go and how do I access it?" Foster didn't want Winthrop's money. He had plenty of his own. But he wanted to cut off the funds to this trafficking business once and for all.

"There will be others. You can kill me but I won't be the last one. If Zee doesn't hear from me, she'll take the operation overseas." Winthrop's voice was weak and he began to shake.

"Right now, all I'm concerned about is your funds. But since you mention it, I want now know where I can locate Zee. Sounds like she needs to be taken out of commission as well. I also want to know where the women are kept."

"This won't end," Winthrop repeated.

"I'll give you one more chance. Start talking."

Winthrop whimpered in response.

Foster balled up his fist and delivered a hard blow to the ribs. "Please just kill me."

"Tell me what I want to know."

"Kill me," Winthrop begged, his voice getting weaker still.

Foster stormed over to the table and picked up a demobilizer. It would send a jolt of electric currents through Winthrop's body. Without hesitation he pressed it against the man's neck. "Talk."

This time Winthrop told him what he wanted to know but Foster turned the demobilizer on anyway and kept it against his Winthrop's skin until smoke came out of the device. Winthrop screamed as drool and blood poured out of his mouth. Blood also flowed from his nostrils, the corners of his eyes and his ears.

He screamed until no more sounds left his mouth. Foster finally pulled the weapon away.

As Winthrop's head drooped, he whispered, "I'm sorry, son."

Those were his final words.

Chapter Twenty-One

Once Foster had gotten all the pertinent information he'd needed from Winthrop he'd stood back and watched the life drain from his body. He'd never allowed one of his victims to die before but he made an exception for this man. In a way, Foster felt a little sorry for Winthrop, who had basically started his vendetta to avenge his son. Winthrop had lost a son and Foster a father, and all because of the greed and malice of one man: Andrew Graham. It had been a while since Foster viewed his grandfather as a hero, but now knowing the truth he could never view him as more than the monster he was. Innocent lives had been wasted for nothing more than the façade of respectability. It sickened Foster that he'd tried to be like him.

Despite all that, Winthrop had to go. Regardless of what happened in the past, it had been his choice to become a trafficker, and his decision to capture, rape and brutalize women. Winthrop was the one who'd decided to hurt people Foster cared about and for that Foster felt no remorse.

Foster didn't doubt the other man's words that there were more out there like him. Unfortunately, trafficking was a huge business and there were syndicates all over the world, some more ruthless than the next. There was no way possible he could take them all down. But he could hemorrhage the organization that Winthrop had started.

Once he'd checked Winthrop's pulse to confirm he was indeed dead, Foster had calmly peeled off his gloves and goggles and tossed them onto the floor. He walked out of the room without a backward glance, leaving his toolkit behind. Foster never wanted to see them or that room again. Once he got back into the vehicle with Dare, he'd called his cleanup crew who had rigged the building to implode. Foster watched with satisfaction as the building crumbled to dust, destroying his grandfather's final legacy. It was like a funeral of sorts, because he was determined that it would be the last time he ever mourned that old bastard.

It took nearly a month to sort through the mess that Winthrop and his crew had created. Foster spent time working with his teams to wipe this syndicate out. The first crew he worked with were hackers who had taken the money the organization made and transferred it to untraceable accounts. His second crew was the rescue and recovery group that found the location for the auction. They'd found the women housed in an old converted office building, each in their own separate prisons. Every woman, child and servant were put in safe houses that were purchased with the money the hackers had put in the anonymous accounts, and was then further distributed to each of the victims so that could either return to their homes or start new lives for themselves. Sadly some of the women and children had never stepped out of that building of horrors, having been raised to serve. Many of them opted to stay in the safe houses because they had nowhere else to go.

Foster saw to it that money would be distributed for their education and job training so that one day they might have a chance at a normal life. He realized many of them would never leave as they'd been brainwashed from the time of birth, but at least they would have funds for their upkeep.

The final team was the locaters who hunted down Zee and all the guards who'd worked the auction. Foster's only instructions to his men was to persuade every single one of them to leave the country. He didn't care how they did it. He didn't want details, he just wanted the job done and confirmation when it was complete. A week later, he received photographic proof of Zee being helped onto a plane. She was noticeably battered and bruised. It looked as if one of her arms was missing but he couldn't be sure because of the angle of the picture. He'd received proof of departure of her men as well. He'd been told that they were more easily persuaded, probably because they'd seen what had happened to their boss.

It had been an absolute nightmare to go through that ordeal but it was about to meet its fruition. He had one more task to accomplish. His driver pulled up to the opulent home with gushing fountains in the front. Gold gilded stone lions rested on either side of the grand iron door.

He took a deep breath and slid out of the vehicle and walked up the cobblestone path to the front door. Before he could knock however, the door opened. A tall dour man dressed in gray answered the door. "Mr. Graham, Master Richie is waiting for you in his office."

He didn't expect to be received so eagerly. It had taken a few days to get through all of Winthrop's files of his victims before he'd found Macy's record. Because they weren't listed by their actual names and their vital chips had been removed, he had to find them through facial recognition. Macy's code name had been Daisy. She hadn't been an easy find because apparently there had been several Daisys who'd been sold through the organization. Once he'd located Macy, finding her buyer had been another challenge. They were only traceable by bank numbers which had been scrambled. If Foster could say nothing else about Winthrop, he could say the man kept her files in a way that was damn near impossible to decode. Though it had been a daunting task, he'd finally located the buyer.

It turned out to be a man by the name of Beauford Richie, a low level criminal who ran an illegal gambling ring. He was also one of his grandfather's old associates. It was apparent from the house he lived in he'd come up in the world.

Gray Suit, whom Foster assumed was the butler, led Foster through one of the most ostentatious houses he'd ever been inside. It was filled with expensive paintings covering the walls and ornaments lined on the shelves and tables. And despite the obvious wealth of its owner, there was nothing tasteful about it. It was the house of someone who had recently come into money and wanted to show off. That was how his grandfather's house used to be.

Finally the butler stopped in front of a room with an door open. "You may go in, sir."

Foster nodded his head in acknowledgement before stepping inside. A corpulent man stood in the far corner of the room. Each of his meaty fingers sported a ring. He smiled at Foster. "Welcome friend. I must say it's an honor to have you in my home, although when you contacted me, I was surprised that the likes of you would want to associate with me. I was dear friends with your grandfather by the way. He was such a good man."

Foster was in no mood for social niceties with this creep. "We both know my grandfather was a lowlife piece of shit, so there's no need to try to make him out to be something he wasn't."

Foster's rebuttal seemed to take his host by surprise. "Oh, well uh, to what do I owe the pleasure of this visit?"

"I won't waste your time or mine. You have something I want. I'm willing to compensate you for what you're out."

Richie raised his brows. "That's surprising. I'm not sure what I could possibly have that someone like you would want. I mean after all you're one of the wealthiest men around. Surely you can—"

"You purchased a girl a few months back at an auction. I'd like for you to hand her over to me. As I've stated, I'm willing to pay you for whatever you're out."

Richie straightened his tie with a look of distinct discomfort. He shifted on his feet from side to side. "Uh, I think you have the wrong man. I don't deal with girls in my business. I'm just trying to make an honest living like you."

Foster stalked across the room and didn't stop until he was nose to nose with the other man. "I'm not sure if you heard me properly. You have a girl who I want. You have five minutes to get her or I will fuck you up in ways you can never imagine. Every minute you hesitate, I'll deduct from the sum I'm willing to pay. If those five minutes expire, you won't get shit and I will tear this place apart. And don't think about pressing that button on your gaudy as fuck ring to call in your men because I've already paid them off. So if you start screaming they'll pretend like they don't hear shit."

Richie turned bright red. "Look, you don't understand. These people...I mean they're dangerous people to make enemies of. You have no idea what it took for me to even get an invite. If they find out I ratted them out they could kill me."

"That sounds like a you problem." Foster didn't bother to let the man know that he had nothing to worry about.

"Okay, but I paid two millions credits for her." Richie whined.

Foster had no respect for the man who didn't bother to put up even a minimal fight. "It will be transferred to you before I leave. But first get the girl and make it quick."

Richie scrambled out of the room as if his ass was on fire. Foster waited impatiently for his return, taping his feet. He couldn't wait until this was all over so that he could get home.

For a moment his mind drifted to Victoria, who hated his guts. He hadn't seen her since he'd told her how he felt. He couldn't blame her for her reaction, after all, she'd been through so much, and all because he'd been too much of a coward to tell her the truth from the beginning. Though he told himself that he had gotten rid of Victoria for her protection, deep down he knew it was because he was afraid for her to see the demon inside of him and her rejecting him because of it. In the end she'd rejected him anyway.

After all she'd suffered through the least he could do for her and her family was to make sure they were financially secure. One of the things he'd done was to purchase a home for her family in a safer neighborhood and set up an account for them to maintain the place and for all their necessities. He even hired a small team of servants for them. He made sure all funds would go to Victoria and not their father because as Victoria had pointed out, he'd only spend it on alcohol and gambling. He felt it was the least he could do to compensate for some of his sins.

Victoria had reunited with her family and he hoped at least she would be happy. According to Aya she seemed to be at peace but was a little sad. He assumed it was because he hadn't recovered Macy yet but that would be rectified shortly.

Footsteps alerted him that someone was approaching. He looked up to see Richie standing in the doorway. "As promised, here she is. We're square, right?" he asked nervously.

Foster nodded briefly before focusing on the slender woman behind Richie.

Macy walked into the room, her steps unsure. She looked thinner than he remembered and the see-through red dress she sported left nothing to the imagination. Other than that she didn't look too worse for wear. She looked at Richie with uncertainty before zooming in on Foster.

She took a step toward him, her violet eyes wide. "Foster?"

"Yes. I've come to take you home." He opened his arms to her and she raced across to room and jumped into his embrace.

She began to sob noisily. "I knew you would come for me."

He held her tight and buried his face against her hair as he stroked the back of her head. "I made a promise that I would always look out for you," he whispered.

And despite all the hardship he'd endured in this ordeal, having Macy safe made it all worth it. Gently, he lowered Macy to her feet and wiped her tears away. "Come on, it's time to go home."

"Foster why won't you tell me what my surprise is?" Macy questioned.

After Foster transferred the two million in credits to Richie, he was glad to get Macy out of that eyesore of a house. Their first stop had been to a boutique in the shopping district where she was given something proper to wear. He'd purchased several outfits and opened a credit account for Macy for whenever she wanted to return and purchase more items.

Afterwards, they dined at one of Macy's favorite restaurants, where she not only ate what was on her plate but half of his as well. It was apparent that pig didn't feed her enough. Foster should have punched that bastard in his face but getting Macy home safe had been his priority.

Macy didn't volunteer whether Richie had abused her nor did he ask. There would come a time when she would want to talk about her experience and Foster intended to be that friend she needed whenever she was ready. Right now, Foster couldn't wait to show her what he had in store for her.

"If I told you it wouldn't be a surprise now, would it?"

She pouted, crossing her arms over her chest. "You're being a big meanie."

"That's funny. You weren't saying that when you were stuffing your face," he teased.

"Oh, don't remind me. That was the first decent meal I'd had in weeks. Beau said that women should have a pleasing figure for her man, so I was only allowed to eat tiny portions while he would pile food on his plate."

Foster hadn't intended to ask but he needed to know for his peace of mind. "Did he hurt you?"

Macy sighed. She placed her hand on his thigh. "After what I've been through with West, Beau was nowhere near as bad; in fact, he seemed kind of sad. He acted as if I was his girlfriend who actually wanted to be there. Enough about him, I'm eager to get home and see my brothers and sister again. But we're going the wrong way. You said you were taking me home."

"I am and here we are."

His driver pulled up in front of a large beige home.

She looked at him with silent question in her eyes.

Once the vehicle stopped, the chauffeur opened the door for them. Foster held out his hand to Macy. "Let's go."

She took his hand as she slid out of the car. "Why are we here?"

"This is your new home. Come with me. I think there are some people who are eager to see you."

Her jaw fell opened. "You bought me a house?"

"Not just you. You have housemates. Now stop gawking and let's go." Foster dragged her along.

When they entered, the first person to greet them was a little girl who looked like a miniature version of Macy. "Macy!" She screamed with glee.

"Cary!" Macy embraced her little sister, laughing and crying at the same time. Thus began a wave of people who came forward to welcome her home. Each one of Macy's siblings hugged and held on to her as if they didn't want to let go.

Aya was next. The two women hugged each other fiercely. "I'm so glad you're home safe."

Arthur and Mac from the bar then greeted her. Even Dare gave her a perfunctory hug although it was clear he'd done it at the behest of Aya.

Her father Carl was last. Foster had given the man a stern talking to, letting him know that he had to get his shit together or Foster would have him removed from the house. Apparently Carl had taken his words to heart.

"Glad to see you home, baby girl." There were tears in the older man's eyes and even if he wasn't exactly the best father it was obvious that he cared about Macy.

Finally when everyone had hugged and welcomed her home, Macy went to Foster and wrapped his arms around her waist. "This was an amazing surprise. I can't begin to thank you for all you've done for me. There's nothing that could make this moment more perfect."

Foster grinned. "Oh, I beg to differ. Aya, could you go get Macy's other surprise?"

Aya nodded with a big smile on her face before rushing out of the room. She returned with Victoria in tow.

Foster barely registered the shock on Macy's face before she fell to her knees with the enormity of the moment. All Foster could see was how beautiful Victoria was. Her honey brown curls framed her lovely face and her outfit skimmed her curves perfectly. It was almost as if he was seeing her for the first time again. He loved this woman with everything in his being but she wasn't meant for him. She deserved someone who wasn't so thoroughly broken and fucked up inside.

Her hazel gaze briefly cut toward him. Foster couldn't read whether she was pleased to see him or not but it didn't matter because soon she only had eyes for her sobbing sister. She raced forward and slid on the floor with Macy.

They two sisters held on to each other as if their lives depended on it. It was a beautiful scene that brought tears to the eyes of many occupants in the room.

His mission was finally accomplished and he was no longer needed. He slipped away unnoticed and headed out the door. With each step he took his heart broke a little bit at a time.

Chapter Twenty-Two

Tori didn't think she'd ever get used to living in such a nice place. If she'd only had herself to consider, she would have refused to move into the house that Foster had bought for her family. It seemed like some kind of payoff. Her father always said she had way too much pride for her own good. Maybe she did, but pride was all she had. It didn't help matters that everyone sang Foster's praises. All of her siblings seemed to think he was great, especially Macy, who believed that the sun rose and set on Foster. It was always Foster this and Foster that. Even her father, who she hadn't seen take a drink since they'd moved into to the house, thought Foster was a great guy.

She'd resorted to taking long walks just to avoid being inside and thinking about him. But no matter what she did or how hard she tried he was never far from her thoughts, especially at night when she closed her eyes. Her dreams were haunted by him and how it had felt to be in arms. She'd wake up expecting to see him there only to realize it had all been a figment of her imagination.

But then she had those days when she wondered if what he'd told her was true. Did he really love her? It was hard to believe him after he'd hurt her so badly. She was so conflicted where he was concerned that she didn't know what to do.

Tori stepped inside the house and stretched. She'd walked for at least five miles to clear her mind and though Foster remained centered in her mind, she at least felt better physically. The house was eerily quiet. Usually there was lots of activity with her siblings either lounging or running around the house. But now all the younger ones were enrolled in one of the fancy schools where the Elite sent their children. Her father had actually met a widow in the neighborhood who he seemed to be smitten with. He was spending so much time with her that there were nights when he stayed at her place. Macy still worked at Arthur's Bar because she said she'd be bored otherwise. Tori knew the feeling. She planned on looking for work soon. Aya had offered her a job at the bar as well, but the place wasn't very large. She felt she'd be getting in the way and taking a check she didn't deserve.

It looked like she had a place to herself for a while. But as Tori walked further into the house she was surprised to see Macy on the couch reading a paper book. "Hey Macy, what are you doing home? I thought you had to work at the bar today."

"I did but Foster came by to take me out for lunch. Arthur said I could take the rest of the day off. Before Foster dropped me off here, he said he had to pick something up at his house so I was waiting in his living room and saw a paper book laying on the table. He showed me this amazing library. Did you know he owns over a thousand paper books? It was pretty incredible. He said I could borrow this one as long as I'm very careful with it. This book is pretty good."

Tori remembered him telling her that he'd only ever shown it to her and Dare. At the time it had made her feel special. She didn't know why it bothered her so much that he showed Macy. But bothered wasn't the right word. She was jealous and before Tori could think about her words she said, "He showed me his library? Did he take you upstairs to his bedroom afterwards, too?" The second she said it, she regretted it.

Macy's eyes widened and her mouth fell open as a bright red blush swept her entire face.

"I'm sorry. I shouldn't have said that. I...I don't know what's wrong with me. That was out of line."

Macy put her book down and walked over to Tori. She grabbed Tori by the hands. "What's going on with you, Tori?"

Tori shook her head. "Forget I said that, okay?"

"No. I mean, I'm not angry at you. But I'm concerned. Where did that come from? You know that Foster and I are just friends. I admit that I did have a huge crush on him at one point but I realized that it mainly stemmed from my gratitude to him for saving me from that monster who had tagged me in The Run. Now he's like the big brother we never had. He's come to mean a lot to me. But believe me, there has never been anything romantic between the two of us. How could there be when he only has eyes for you?"

Tori pulled her hands away from her sister's. "I don't know what you're talking about." She had never mentioned her time with Foster to anyone in her family. All they knew was that she'd been with some mysterious man that she refused to talk about. The irony of Macy and Foster becoming close wasn't lost on Tori, but she never wanted to come between their friendship because it was clear that it made her little sister happy.

Macy gave her a knowing smirk. "Oh, but I think you do."

"Has he said anything about me?" Tori couldn't help but ask even though she didn't want to care.

"All the time. Nothing specifically but he asks how you're doing a lot. He always manages to work your name into a conversation. Look Tori, it isn't hard to figure out that he was the one you'd met when you did you first run."

"How?"

Macy sighed. "I'm not stupid, Tori. I know you try to protect me from things you think could hurt me, but I'm a big girl now. This past year has taught me that I'm stronger than I thought I was. You've done so much for me. You let me cry on your shoulder when I had that nightmare the other night. You've taken care of me all my life. Let me be here for you for once."

Tori shook her head. "You wouldn't understand."

"Stop patronizing me, Tori. You might as well talk about it with me because the way you've been moping around the house has everyone concerned. Even Dad has questioned your state of well-being."

Tori snorted. "Never thought he'd notice anything beyond his own self-interests."

"Would you stop being such a bitch? You and I both know that Dad isn't perfect but he's trying. You, on the other hand, disappear for hours at a time, and when you are here you sit in a corner and stare out the window. I hear you cry yourself to sleep at night. You barely eat, you don't interact with the rest of us and then you stand here and patronize me. Cut the bullshit, Tori. If you're not willing to talk about it, fine, but you need to get yourself together, not only for the kids but for yourself."

Tori's mouth fell open. Macy had never talked that way to her before or anyone for that matter. And there was nothing Tori could say to dispute it because everything her sister said was absolutely right. One of the reasons she's kept her distance from her family was because she didn't want them to see how miserable she actually was. She lowered her head as a tear slipped from her eyes. "I'm sorry. I didn't realize how my mood had been affecting everyone."

Macy pulled Tori into her arms and gave her a tight squeeze. "Oh hon, it's okay. I'm just worried about you. I love you so much and it hurts me to see you in so much pain. Please, won't you tell me about it?"

Tori nodded her head and allowed her sister to guide her to the couch. Once she sat down, the words came tumbling out. Every now and then she'd pause so that she wouldn't break down. All the while, Macy held her hand and listened without interruption. Tori left nothing out, from how she and Foster had met during The Run, how she felt about him and how he'd hurt her. She shared her experience with the auction and through it all she never forgot about Foster. Finally she confessed the last conversation she'd had with Foster and how she reacted. By the time Tori was finished with her tale, she was exhausted and all out of tears. "So that's basically all there is to say about it. I fell in love with him, and even though he's given me so many clues not to trust him I stubbornly didn't listen. After all I've been through he tells me that he loves me as if he didn't rip my heart out. His only excuse is that he was trying to protect me. He doesn't get to change things around like that."

Macy remained silent as if she seemed to be in deep thought.

"Well?" Tori prompted. "Aren't you going to jump to Foster's defense?"

"Is that what you want me to do?"

Tori was a bit taken aback by her sister's response. She was sure Macy would tell her to believe in Foster. She wondered why Macy remained silent now. "Of course not."

"Then I won't. I was under the impression that you needed me to listen and that's what I'm doing. Sometimes talking things out makes you feel better. How are you feeling?" Macy rubbed Tori's arms in an up and down motion.

"A little better. But I'm still confused. I don't understand how he can be a certain way one minute and then the next this cold, unfeeling jerk."

"We both know that people aren't the same all the time. You certainly haven't been your usual upbeat, happy self since you've been home which is understandable. You've experienced things that would have broken most women."

Tori stood up. "Tell me what you think."

Macy tilted her head to the side. "I think you already know what the next step is but you're too scared to take it."

There was no use in pretending that she didn't know what Macy was talking about. Deep down she knew what she knew what she had to do in order to get some type of closure or else she'd drive herself crazy with wondering what if. "I can't. It hurts too much."

Macy sighed. "You're my sister and I'll always be on your side no matter what. But I don't see the point in your torturing yourself like this when the person you should be telling these things too is just a call away. You're hurting and from the looks of Foster, he is too. So let's say he was telling you the truth when he explained why he did what he did to you. You're justified in your anger because he didn't have the right to take that decision about your future into his hands. But on the other hand how long can you stay mad at him if his intentions were noble?"

"You're right. I guess I've known all along but I'm scared. Scared of how intense my feelings were for him and of getting hurt again. I don't ever want to feel what I did when he discarded me."

"I don't know much about being in love, but I do know that love is about taking chances and if you really love someone they're worth the risk. I'm not telling you what you should do, but like you said, if you talk to him at least afterwards you can finally heal. That's parts of the problem. Your emotions were left into such a tailspin, you've never had the chance to fully recover. You owe yourself the opportunity to heal, no matter how things turn out between you and Foster."

"You're right, but do you believe him?"

"It's really not my place to believe him. But I can tell you this, the Foster I know is someone who will go to any lengths to keep a promise. He told me that he would always look out for me after he saved me from that bastard who used to torture me until I wished I was dead. And he's come through for me ever since. When I was kidnapped on my way to work I was scared out of my mind. Through it all, the grooming process, the conditioning, even going on the block, I never lost faith that he'd come for me. And he did. That's the kind of man I think he is. Now it's your turn to decide for yourself."

Tori narrowed her gaze. "When did you get so wise?"

"I learned from the best. I'll tell you what; I'll dial his coordinates on my holophone and tell him you'd like to have a meeting. On neutral territory of course."

Tori hesitated for a moment. Was this really what she wanted? Regardless it was what she needed. "Okay, yes go ahead."

Macy pulled out the holophone and asked it to contact Foster. The device chimed a few times before Foster's image popped up.

"Macy," he greeted. "What can I do for you today?" He then turned his head and looked at Tori. His eyebrows shot up in apparent surprise before he schooled his features to something unreadable. "Victoria," he acknowledged.

"Hi," Tori responded for lack of anything else to say.

"Is there something you wanted?" He directed his question toward Macy.

"Actually, I'm calling on Tori's behalf. She wants to meet up with you."

Foster turned his head to look at Tori. "Is that true, Victoria?"

She licked her lips that had suddenly gone dry. "Yes. I'd like to see you, Foster."

Chapter Twenty-Three

Foster couldn't stop fidgeting in his seat. He adjusted his tie and played with the buttons on his jacket to give his hands something to do. When it seemed like more time had elapsed, he glanced at his holowatch. It hadn't even been a full minute since he'd last checked it. He'd never been so eager for a meeting in his life because nothing ever mattered as much to him. When he'd received a call from Macy, he was surprised to see that Victoria had joined her. He was doubly shocked when she requested an audience with him but she'd insisted that it be in a public place.

He'd been certain that after their last meeting she was done with him. Even if she just wanted to see him to curse him out some more, he didn't care. He loved her so much that he was willing to take any crumbs she threw his way.

When the designated time of their meeting passed he began to wonder if she changed her mind. Just as he was about to give up hope, Victoria was escorted to his table by the maître d'. The moment he saw her approach no one else in the room existed. There was something different about her from when he'd seen her last. She seemed a little leaner and a bit tired. The bags under her eyes indicated her lack of sleep. They still didn't detract from her beauty.

He stood up as she approached the table and pulled her chair out for her before the maître d' had a chance to do it. "Thank you," she said softly.

He took his seat and barely managed not to pinch himself. He feared this was a dream he'd wake up from. Seeing her again made his heart race. Even if he only got to spend this little bit of time with her, he was happy. "You look well, Victoria."

"Thank you."

"Would you like to order anything? This food here is excellent."

"I'm not really hungry actually. I just wanted to talk."

"Okay." He folded his hands on the table. "What did you want to talk about?"

"I need to know if you meant it."

Foster immediately knew what she was talking about. After his confession had practically broken her all over again, he vowed he'd be completely honest with her and tell her anything she wanted to know, the good bad and the ugly. At least if she walked away from him because she couldn't handle the man he was, then he would have a clear conscience. "Yes. Every word of it. And I haven't stopped. I love you, Victoria. I think I have almost from the beginning."

"Why did you wait to tell me when you did instead of earlier?"

"Because love was so new to me. I barely understood it myself at first. How we met wasn't the ideal circumstances to start some grand love affair, but there I was, holding you in my arms at night after you'd fallen asleep, watching you and thinking that I'd found something precious in you. I didn't recognize that love at first because all of my life, most things came easy to me. Even women. Girls were throwing themselves at me even before I was a teenager and it was always just one meaningless sexual romp after another."

"Is that why you participated in the Run, because the women presented a challenge to you?"

"I've participated in that game over twenty times to my recollection. Part of it was the sport, but there was another reason that didn't really have anything to do with the women. But as far as the women I tagged went, besides you I'd only slept with maybe three of them and in each case they were the ones who initiated the encounters with me. Otherwise I would have sent them home. I took no pleasure in taking women who were frightened out of their minds and who were only in it for survival purposes."

"But I was scared and I made it quite clear that I didn't want to be there. Why me?"

"I wasn't lying to you before when I said I saw a light in you that I wanted to consume for myself. I don't know if it was what you called love at first sight but I knew I couldn't let you get away. I needed you near me at any cost. My possessive streak came out in full force. I didn't want any of the other men to have you because the thought of them touching you and holding you drove me mad with rage. You were mine and I was determined to have you. If that makes me sound like an asshole I apologize, but it's the truth and I don't regret it, because having you in my life was probably the best thing that had ever happened to me."

Victoria lowered her head and he couldn't tell what she was thinking. "I resented the hell out of you at first," she began, "but even as I told myself I hated you I became addicted to your touch. I began to hate myself for giving in to you so easily. But then you showed me a side of yourself that humanized you. I liked the Foster you showed me. I guess that's why it hurt so much when you got rid of me because then I had to reconcile with the fact that the Foster I'd fell for wasn't real." She didn't look at him as he spoke but the hurt was clear in her voice.

"That was the real Foster. I was always genuine with you until the end."

She raised her head and glared at him. The hurt was there and it seemed as if she didn't quite believe him. "I need to know what exactly you thought you had to protect me from. What was so bad that you believed my life was in danger?"

He took a deep breath. This was the part he feared telling her but now was the time to let it all out. "Do you remember when I told you that I wasn't a good guy?"

"Yes. I remember. I was so confused when you told me that and I couldn't figure out why you would."

"Guilt. I was debating on whether I should tell you how I felt but each time it was on the tip of my tongue my past taunted me, reminding me that I didn't deserve a happy ending. When my bank was set on fire I got a mysterious call that night that told me someone was watching. But what scared me the most was that this person indirectly threatened you. I don't think I would have ever forgiven myself if something were to happen to you based on my past. But I let you go and in the end that person harmed you anyway."

Victoria frowned. "What are you talking about? Who are you talking about?"

"My grandfather was a self-made man, which is a rare feat since it's almost impossible for a person living in poverty to move up in society unless they participate in illegal activities. My grandfather was determined to get out of the slums. He didn't want to be labeled a dreg for the rest of his life so he made his money by robbing, intimidation, gambling, trafficking, anything to earn him some credits. After a while that no longer satisfied him. He wanted status so he found a partner who happened to be going through some financial difficulties at the time. You see, he needed this guy because he had an impeccable family name and came from old money. My grandfather used him to start a bank. But eventually Grandfather forced him out of the partnership by having one of his partner's relatives executed."

Tori gasped. "Are you serious?"

"I wish I was joking. My grandfather wasn't exactly what you'd call a nice man. He was used to getting what he wanted and if someone stood in his way he took care of them. The ironic part of the whole thing in that once my grandfather made a large fortune and was wealthy enough to bend politicians to his will people viewed him as some kind of upstanding citizen. But what they didn't know was that he never stopped the illegal activities. Not only that, when I was thirteen, he dragged me into it. He told me I was getting soft like my father. He said I had no killer instinct, and you've got to understand, at the time, I believed my grandfather could do no wrong. He's the one who taught me that if I wanted something I was just supposed to take it. Only the strong survived. As an impressionable kid I ate up every word he said. I wanted to please him so much that I did some bad things, Victoria."

"Like what?"

"For the most part, Grandfather had given up the petty crimes, but his illegal loans and bribery operation still brought in a great deal of money for him. He didn't want to give that up. Anyway, if someone got behind on a loan or if he needed to intimidate a person, he would have them tortured or badly beaten. He taught me all his techniques and I became so good at it, I was better than him. He let me take over that portion of the underground business and before you ask, yes, I did hurt a lot of people. And in a lot of cases I liked it. At first it was just something I did to gain my grandfather's approval but then it became some sick addiction. I got off on making someone scream in pain. When I was doing those things it was like I had no soul. Part of me knew what I did was evil, but I couldn't stop. But I justified what I did in my head by telling myself that those people deserved it." He paused to gauge her reaction.

Tori stared at him with a look of utter disbelief. "Oh, Foster," she whispered in what sounded like a mixture of horror and sadness.

"I know. There's nothing I can say that can excuse what I did even though at the time I certainly tried to. Anyway, my big wake-up call happened when my father was murdered. I never knew who did it but my grandfather seemed to know. My father wasn't involved in any of the illegal stuff and he never wanted me to follow in my grandfather's footsteps. But I let him down over and over again. It caused a rift in our relationship. I essentially chose my grandfather over him because I wanted to prove that I was tough, and I'll live with that regret for the rest of my life. My father tried to lead me down the right path and I laughed in his face. I told him that he wasn't man enough to stop me from doing what I wanted to do."

Foster lowered his head in shame as he remembered the hurt in his father's eyes. That was the day Foster had broken his dad. He'd seen the hurt in the older man's eyes. In that moment Foster wanted to tell his father that he'd change but he couldn't because he was in too deep. That was one of the final conversations he'd had with his father. And then he was murdered."

"Foster...I'm sorry. It sounds like he meant a lot you," Victoria sympathized.

"I didn't know how much until he was gone. I finally found the strength to walk away from that life because even though he was gone, I wanted to be the kind of man he would have been proud of. My grandfather took Dad's death pretty hard. He lost all interest in running his various businesses after that and he gladly handed the reins over to me. With all that responsibility suddenly thrust on me, I worked morning, noon and night to go completely legitimate."

"I broke away from all my underworld contacts and made sure that every business venture under my control didn't have a hint of illegal activities. But even though I had distanced myself for my criminal past, I felt like there was this monster lurking within me and if someone looked close enough they'd eventually see it. So I wore a mask. I became the person people wanted to see, the nonchalant playboy who didn't seem to care about much beyond his own pleasure. I did what people in my circle did, spent a lot of money, attended the right parties and was seen with the right people. I even saw participating in The Run as a way to blend in because it was a source of amusement for people in my income bracket. All along, I knew I was shit. I was waiting for someone to expose me. And then I met you." He broke off.

Foster wasn't aware of what was going through Victoria's mind. She looked at him with an expression of mild disbelief, confusion and fear. "You were the best thing that ever happened to me. No matter how bad my day went, a smile from you made everything better. You were everything I wanted in a partner: beautiful, smart, and you weren't afraid to speak your mind. And every day you were with me, in the back of my mind I knew I didn't deserve you. So when my bank was under attack, I thought this was it. Here was my punishment for all my crimes. I didn't want what happened to my father to happen to you. I think I would have died myself if that were the case. But it doesn't end there."

A tear slid down Victoria's cheek and Foster was tempted to reach across the table to wipe it away but he didn't dare. She must have realized she was crying because she hastily rubbed it off. "I...I don't know what to say."

"You don't have to say anything else. Just listen. Because the next part is a bit more complicated. So once I let you go, I was beside myself. I drank too much, ended up with random women, and through it all I couldn't get over you. But eventually I knew I had to get myself together and I did my very best. There were no more attacks on any of my businesses so I thought that was the end of it. But then Macy went missing. Even though I vowed I wouldn't, I had to get in touch with my old underground contacts. I was able to get an invitation to the auction where I saw you. I thought maybe, just maybe, you were there because fate was giving us a second chance. So I bid on you so someone else wouldn't. It was my goal to keep you with me until I found Macy. In my head I figured once everything was over, I could tell you the truth and we could work it out. And then the attacks started happening again, but worse. Once again I feared that you were a target. At first I didn't associate the attacks with the one I had two years ago because I thought the more recent ones had to do with me making inquiries about the trafficking."

"But they were connected."

"Yes. There's so much that happened that I could be here all day telling it to you but the gist of it is, I had to do some things, really bad things to get the information I wanted out of people."

"Did you...torture them?" Victoria seemed hesitant with her question.

Foster nodded in the affirmative. "Yes. I told myself that it was because I was determined to get Macy back and mainly that's the truth, but part of me enjoyed it. A little too much. That's when I realized that monster I'd tried to keep at bay all those years was still lurking. I had no future with you. I didn't deserve you. It hurt like hell to admit it but there you have it.

"When I found out who was behind the trafficking and was able to rescue your sister, I let you go. But know that it was one of the hardest things I've ever had to do."

Victoria remained silent to the point where Foster didn't think she would respond but finally she asked, "For my peace of mind. Who was behind it all? The auction, I mean."

"Turns out it was the son of my grandfather's former business partner. He was the father of the son my grandfather had killed. He had his eyes set on revenge for years. His name was Eli Winthrop III. But you might know him as Mr. X."

Victoria gasped as her eyes widened. "He was behind it all? The trafficking and attacks on you?"

"Yes. He tagged you on The Run because of our association. So you see, everything bad that's happened to you is my fault. And now that you know this, I understand if you completely hate me. But if it's any consolation, you can't hate me as much as I already hate myself." Just staring at her, knowing that all his dreams would never come true where Victoria was concerned, was too painful to endure.

Abruptly he pushed his seat back and stood up. "I'm going to give my apologies because I have to leave. But if you need to order anything put it on my account." Foster didn't wait for her to say anything else because he was too focused on getting out of the restaurant.

He didn't want to see the look in her eyes now that she knew him for the monster he was.

Chapter Twenty-Four

Tori remained frozen to the spot long after Foster had left the restaurant. She wasn't sure what she'd been expecting to hear but it certainly hadn't been that. Everything she had suffered through was horrible but she could also see that he had dealt with many issues himself. How could she condemn him for something that he was pushed into at an age where he didn't fully understand the ramifications of his actions?

She had only been able to focus on her own pain bypassing his suffering. Tori would never forget the look in Foster's eyes as he relayed that story to her. She knew then what she had to do. Tori contacted her driver. It still took some getting used to that her family had servants. All thanks to Foster. There was no reason for him to go above and beyond the way he had, but he did. Foster had always been generous but it was something she'd taken for granted.

"Where to, Miss Preston?" Keith, the driver, asked when she slipped into the back seat of the luxury vehicle.

"Could you please take me to Foster's house? I mean Mr. Graham's."

"Certainly."

Tori's heart beat faster the closer she got to her destination. By the time Keith had pulled up to Foster's gate and got authorization to enter, Tori was a nervous wreck.

Tori was surprised to see Mrs. Gordon waiting for her at the door. "Ms. Preston, please come in. Mr. Graham hasn't returned home yet but you're welcome to wait inside."

Tori frowned. "He's not back? But he left the restaurant before me."

The housekeeper shrugged. "He didn't inform me when he'd be back but I'm sure he'll be home soon enough. Please come in." She stood back enough to allow Tori entrance.

She walked inside and followed Mrs. Gordon to the living room.

"Can I get you anything to drink or eat?"

Tori shook her head as she took a seat on the couch. "No, thank you. I'll wait here."

"Okay. Please don't hesitate to contact me if you need anything."

"Thank you."

Once she was alone, she waited anxiously for Foster, but after an hour he still hadn't returned. She turned on the holovision and found a program to watch while she waited. Before she realized it another couple hours passed. She turned it off and contemplated her next move.

The next thing she realized, someone was shaking her. Tori stretched her arms over her head. Shit! She must have fallen asleep. She sat up to see Foster standing over her. His eyes were bloodshot and his hair was messy as if he'd raked his fingers through it several times.

She stood up and smoothed her clothes down. "Foster. I uh, was waiting for you."

"I can see. Mrs. Gordon contacted me to say you were here, otherwise I would have been on a jet out of the country."

She moistened her lips with a quick flick of her tongue. "You were going to leave?"

"Not forever. I was going to visit my mother overseas."

Tori raised a brow. "Your mother?"

"Yes. I do have one."

"You've never mentioned her before. I just assumed she was dead, like mine."

"No. She's very much alive and living quite happily with her latest lover. She and I had never been particularly close. She left my father and me when I was eight because she decided that being a wife and mother wasn't all that she thought it would be. She left the country to go on adventures, according to her at least. The truth is, she found an older trillionaire who pampered her and didn't make any demands on her. He eventually died and she got all his money and has been living quite nicely since. We've been in touch over the years but sporadically. Out of the blue she issued me an invitation to see her. This seemed as good a time as any to make that visit."

"Where overseas does she live?"

"Dulcinia, it's a small country that used to be a part of Italy before the war. She says it's beautiful there. She has a home right on the sea."

"Sounds nice."

He sighed before putting some distance between them. "So why are you here, Victoria? Do you want to yell at me? Or tell me how much I disgust you?"

It hurt a little that he thought she would be angry with him, but it was no less than what she deserved. He'd come to her before with his feelings and she didn't believe him. She understood why he'd be wary of her presence now. "Actually, I came by to talk to you. Not yell. Just talk."

"Then talk." He turned away from her, back stiff.

"Could you at look at me?"

"I can't."

"Why not?"

"Because it hurts dammit!"

Determined, Tori walked around Foster until they were facing. "Foster please, you're not making this easy for me and granted you have every right to think I wouldn't take what you had to say very well, but I just want you to know that I don't hate you."

"You don't have to lie. How could you not after I confessed what I did?"

"I admit that it's frightening to imagine you hurting people the way you described, but you were a boy under the influence of someone you looked up to."

"A boy who grew up into a man who sliced people up and took pleasure in doing it. You don't understand the enormity of my actions."

Tori reached out and placed her hand on his arm. Foster flinched but didn't pull away from her touch. "You're right, I don't understand any of it, but I do realize that you were driven by your hero worship of your grandfather and he used that to his advantage. And you may have even liked it a little but—"

"There is no may about it. I did like it."

"Sometimes we can get caught up in things that go against our true nature, but I don't believe that's who you were. If that was really who you are, you wouldn't be harboring so much guilt and being so hard on yourself. You did the right thing by wiping out your grandfather's legacy and that in itself tells me that you wanted to change. People aren't infallible. We make mistakes and yours may have been huge, but you tried to right those wrongs. Besides, an evil person wouldn't financially support a family he barely knows just because he knew they needed it. An evil person wouldn't make promises then follow through on them. The way you were relentless in your search for Macy, even while you were under attack, is something I will forever be grateful for. And even if in your misguided way you sent me away you were doing it for my protection. I didn't see it at the time, or didn't want to, but I do now. Those aren't the actions of an evil person."

He raised a brow. "Oh yeah? Do you want to know what I did with your Mr. X? I had that bastard strung up and worked him over until he drew his last breath."

"You killed him?" she whispered in surprise.

"Damn right I did and I'd do it again."

She thought over all he'd done to her and the other women in his residence. That man was sadistic for no reason at all. Learning about his son made no difference. She and his other victims had nothing to do with that, but he chose to mete out excruciating punishments time and time again. She remembered all the times he'd beat her or deprived her of food. He'd shown absolutely no remorse. She'd looked in the face of evil before and it wasn't Foster's. "Good," Tori finally answered. "He deserved it. Besides, if you didn't kill him he'd be torturing other women and having his people kidnap them off the street."

"You don't know what you're saying, Victoria."

"Oh, but I do. You have no idea how many nights I'd fantasize about murdering him. I'm just sorry you got to him before I did. Look, Foster, you can't continue to beat yourself over this. That's in the past. The only thing now is to look toward the future...and if your feelings for me haven't changed, I'd like to be a part of it."

He backed away from her, shaking his head. "Don't do this to me, Victoria. Don't fucking play games with me."

"I'm not. I was so wrapped up in the pain you caused me that I didn't realize you were hurting too. So when you told me how you felt, I didn't want to believe you because I was scared that you'd hurt me again. I've never felt for anyone what I feel for you. And when you sent me away that first time I was devastated. I couldn't eat or sleep, and despite it all I loved you through the pain. I've blamed you for all the misfortune in my life so long that all my emotions just came out in one big ball of anger."

"You love me?" he whispered in disbelief.

"I never stopped."

"You'd better fucking mean that because once you commit yourself to me I'll be damned if I ever let you go again."

Tori closed the distance between them and cupped his face. "I mean it. Every word. I love you, Foster Graham. Past and all."

"Good, because you'll always be my Victoria." With what seemed like a hungry growl, he gripped her hair and fastened his mouth on to hers. He kissed her with the force of a man who had been deprived for too long.

Foster wrapped his other arm around her waist so tightly, she could barely breathe, but she didn't mind it. One of the things she loved about him was the forcefulness of his lovemaking.

Tori dug her fingers in his hair, loving every second of being in his arms again. She'd dreamed about this moment since they parted, but her fantasies didn't come close to the reality. Her body went up in flames and her core ached with need.

The kiss went on and on but soon it wasn't enough. Tori was eager to feel his skin beneath her fingertips. She tore her mouth away, gasping for breath. "I need you."

She shivered as she spied the unbridled lust within the depths of his eyes. Foster's only response was to scoop her into his arms and carry her out of the room. Tori wrapped her arms around his neck and snuggled closer to him. Foster took the stairs two at a time and when he reached the top, marched across the hall, not stopping until they made it to his bedroom. He threw her on the bed unceremoniously and quickly undressed.

When Tori attempted to take her clothes off he halted her with a shake of his head. "If anyone is going to undress you, it's going to be me."

"But I want you right now. I can't wait." She cupped her breasts and slowly licked her lips to tease him.

"If you keep that up I'm going to spank that big beautiful ass."

Tori undid three of her buttons, deliberately disobeying him.

"Keep that shit up and your ass will be sore for weeks."

Tori grinned, undoing the rest of her shirt before shrugging out of it.

Foster narrowed his eyes until they were sapphire slits. He fisted his hard cock and stroked it back and forth as Tori continued her striptease.

Once she tossed her shirt out of the way, she rolled her pants down her hips and kicked them off.

Foster groaned when she unclipped her bra and let it fall off. Her panties followed leaving her completely naked to his gaze. She moved back on the bed and spread her legs for his viewing pleasure.

"You're a nasty girl, aren't you?"

Tori moaned as she massaged her clit. "You have no idea."

Before she realized he'd moved, Foster grabbed her by the arm and yanked her off the bed. "What did I tell you about teasing me?" He demanded.

Foster didn't wait for her reply. He placed Tori on her feet then positioned her facing the bed. "Bend over."

Leaning forward, she planted her hands on the bed. Before she could properly brace herself he smacked her ass with his open palm. Foster didn't give her a chance to recover before he brought his hand down on her other cheek. Foster proceeded to hit her ass in a relentless assault.

Her bottom stung like crazy but each time he smacked her, the tips of her fingers grazed her pussy. The mixture of pleasure and pain was nearly enough to make her come.

"This is what happens to bad girls who tease." And just as quickly as he began he stopped. Foster caressed her tender flesh, carefully rubbing and stroking Tori until she purred with pleasure. She looked over her shoulder just in time to see him kneel behind her. "Turn your head," he ordered.

Tori quickly straightened her head. The next thing she knew, Foster buried his face between her legs. He pressed his tongue into her wet channel and his thumb inside her sphincter. The sensation was incredible. Only Foster played her body this masterfully, sending waves of pleasure flowing through her body.

He was relentless with his mouth, tongue and fingers, bringing her to a hard and quick climax. "So delicious," he murmured. "You have the best tasting pussy. I miss this so much." Foster returned to his task of devouring her center until her pussy wept.

Tori collapsed when her arms could no longer support her. She was weak from the intense sensations. Foster was relentless like a man on a mission. Just when Tori didn't think he'd stopped he removed his hands and stood up.

"Get on the bed."

She crawled onto the bed and fell breathlessly onto her back.

Foster licked his lips. "Best meal I've had in months." He then crawled on the bed with Tori and moved between her legs. Once he'd placed his cock against her slit, he locked his gaze with hers. "After this, there's no turning back. You're mine."

Her heart swelled within her chest. She loved this man heart, body and soul. "I've always been yours,

Foster." She stroked his face with the back of her knuckles.

Foster maintained eye contact with her as he moved in and out of her with measured strokes. Tori wrapped her legs around his waist, wanting to pull him deeper into her still. They took each other by the hand, locking fingers. She never took her eyes off his face and he kept his focus on her.

They'd had sex, fucked, and even made love before, but nothing had ever come close to right now. It was as if their souls were touching. She'd never felt this close to anyone in her life, not even her family. Now that she had finally let go of her fear and allowed herself to love him she was free.

By the time they both reached completion, tears streamed from her eyes.

Foster gently wiped them away and kissed her on the forehead. "Why are you crying?"

Tori sniffed. "These are happy tears."

He smiled before placing a light kiss on her lips. "I love you, Victoria. I intend to spend the rest of my days loving and cherishing you. But don't think I won't spank that ass every now and then." His eyes twinkled with amusement.

Tori laughed. "I wouldn't expect it any other way."

Epilogue

Tori felt like a princess. She'd never worn anything so beautiful in her life. She'd stood in front of the mirror for nearly twenty minutes just staring at herself and twirling around. The peach colored gown was made of silk covered in tiny crystals that made it shimmer. Even the spaghetti straps were made of sparkly jewels. Though it was formfitting, it was easy to move in because of the slit that went all the way to the top of her thigh. It clung to her body so comfortably, she never wanted to remove it although she was certain Foster couldn't wait to do exactly that from the way he'd looked at her when she'd come down the stairs.

She couldn't believe the difference a few months had made. Tori couldn't believe that not so long ago her life was bleak, she was under contract to a man who took pleasure in psychologically and physically abusing her. She'd bore the scars on the inside and outside. Her soul had seemed hollow and she was to the point where she'd nearly been completely broken, but then Foster reentered her life. Tori had fought so hard against loving him again that she'd only ended up hurting herself. Now she was glad she'd given love a second chance.

Things couldn't be more perfect for her. She'd officially moved back in with Foster and they were talking about marriage although they'd decided there would be no rush. They had a lifetime together. They didn't need any legal formality to make their love any more real. Foster was the man who made her heart soar with just a tilt of his lips or the gentle stroke of his hand. She loved that he was the first person she woke up to in the morning and the last one she saw at night.

The lovemaking was incredible. Being fully committed to each other seemed to make it better. Often after one of their lengthy sessions, she'd weep from happiness as Foster gently kissed her tears away. While her love life was amazing, it made Tori happy that everything else in general seemed to be falling into place. Though Foster was extremely wealthy, Tori wasn't content to stay around the house all day or shop. She wanted to do something important with her life.

Since she'd worked most of her life and her family couldn't afford to send her to school beyond a certain level, Tori decided to complete her education. She wanted to learn how to manage her own business. She wasn't sure what she wanted to do from there herself because there were so few opportunities for women, but she was eager to find out.

Macy had decided to go to school as well even though she chose to stay at Arthur's part-time. Tori suspected her younger sister decided to continue working at the bar because she was getting closer to the errand guy, Mac. The two were adorable together although Macy claimed she and Mac were just friends. The rest of Tori's siblings seemed to be thriving in their new home and were excited about getting their education. Even her father had gotten his act together. He and his lady friend had amicably parted ways but he'd actually started working. Foster had offered him a job as a custodian to one of his buildings and to Tori's surprise, Carl had taken it. She'd even gotten reports that he was doing well at it.

She'd become closer to Aya over the past few months. Aya had turned out to be a true friend, although Tori worried about the petite beauty. Lately her friend always seemed deep in thought or looked sad. Every time Tori would ask her what the matter was, Aya would smile and deny anything was wrong. She wondered if it had anything to do with Dare who always seemed a bit short-tempered and scary to Tori. Foster had said his friend wasn't as bad as people thought. Tori could only take Aya at her word.

"We're here." Foster placed his hand on Tori's thigh.

Tori had been so deep in thought she didn't notice the vehicle had come to a halt. "Oh." She looked out the window of the people heading inside the grand building. Everyone was so elegantly dressed.

"Where were you just now? You seemed to be in really deep thought."

Tori looked at Foster with a smile. "I was just thinking about how happy I am. I can't believe we're at the Sapphire Ball! People talk about it but I never imagined I'd ever get to go."

Foster leaned over and kissed her neck. "Well you're here. And you're be the belle of the ball."

She giggled. "If you keep doing that, we'll never leave the car."

He wiggled his eyebrows playfully. "Oh yeah? Shall I put that to the test?"

"No way. This is my first ball. I want to see what's inside."

"Should I be upset that you chose this ball over me?"

"Of course not. No matter what I'll always choose you. It's just...you know, it's the Sapphire Ball."

Foster chuckled. "I guess I'll forgive you for your excitement this one time since it is your first ball. Shall we?" He gestured for the driver to open the door.

Once they were inside, Tori was in awe of everything she saw, from the glitzy decorations to the beautiful people scattered around the room. She'd even recognized several celebrities. Everyone seemed to be having a good time, dancing, drinking and some people were practically having sex on the tables. The women were all dressed in expensive dresses each one more scantily clad than the next.

Tori's gaze then landed on Aya. She was absolutely stunning in a silver and black sequined dress that seemed to be held up by sheer will. She wore a silver headband to match her amazing outfit. She was talking to a tall dark haired man. When she smiled at something he said her entire face lit up. The two of them seemed to be having a pleasant conversation. Tori wondered where Dare was, but just as the thought occurred to her, he popped out of nowhere and was instantly at Aya's side. He yanked the little woman roughly to his side, glared at the other man and practically dragged Aya away.

Foster must have noticed as well because he shook his head. "When is he going to learn?"

Tori gasped when Aya twisted out of her lover's hold and stalked away from him. "I should go after her. Maybe you should talk to Dare and calm things down."

Foster nodded.

Tori hurried to catch up to Aya who stopped only when she made it to the powder room. Tori entered just in time to see Aya go into one of the private stalls. As Tori got closer, she heard sniffling. She knocked on the stall. "Aya? Are you okay? It's me. Tori."

There was silence before the stall door opened. "Come in."

Tori walked inside and closed the door behind her. "What's going on?"

Aya's eyes were red and Tori spied the faint trail of tears on her friend's cheeks. "I'm sorry you had to see me this way. I take it since you followed me in here you saw my boyfriend acting like the complete jackass he is."

Tori nodded not bothering to lie. "What's going on with you two?"

"I'm not sure. At first thing were great but lately, Dare has just been...I don't know how to explain it really. He's always been a bit jealous and possessive. But lately, he's out of control. Maybe he's always been like this but I refused to see it because I love him. But my love can only go so far. He has me followed, he gets angry when I make plans for myself. He wants me to spend all my spare time with him and I can't even look at another man without him blowing up. He punched one of our customers in the face because Dare claimed the man was staring at my ass. He's unbearable. And I just can't take it anymore. I love him but I'm tired of being Dare O'Shaughnessy's possession." Aya dropped her head into her palms and Tori gave her a comforting hug.

"It's obvious the man is crazy about you. Isn't there a way the two of you could work it out?" Tori asked gently.

"Crazy is the operative word here. Maybe I'm overreacting and need to think about this some more, but that guy I was just talking to was simply apologizing to me because we accidentally bumped in to each other and Dare comes along and pulls me away like I'm some mindless doll."

Tori empathized with her friend and wanted her to be happy. She wasn't sure what advice she could give. Love was so complicated. "I'm sorry you're going through this. I can't tell you what to do, but like you said, just think about this some more and maybe talk it out. Tell him how he makes you feel."

"I wish it were that simple. If I tell him he's smothering me, he backs off for a few days and then he comes on even stronger." Aya sighed. "But you know what, we're at the Sapphire Ball. Let's go back out there and enjoy ourselves. I'm not going to let that jerk ruin my evening. I just need to repair my makeup. I must look like a mess. I'm not used to having all this stuff on my face."

"You look beautiful."

Aya smiled. "Thank you. You do too. That dress is fantastic. And I love how your hair is piled on top of your head like that. It looks very elegant."

Tori preened at the compliment. "Thank you."

Once Aya had fixed her face. The two women walked out of the restroom arm in arm. Their men were waiting for them on the outside. Dare seemed to look a bit remorseful as he held out his hand to Aya. Aya hesitated a moment before placing her hand in his and allowed herself to be led off.

Foster held out his bent arm to Tori. "May I have this dance, beautiful lady?"

Tori gladly took it. "Yes you may, handsome."

As soon as they made it to the dancefloor, Foster twirled her around. Tori laughed as he continued to whirl her around until she was dizzy. There were a few fast dances and then a slow one where Foster pulled Tori into his arms and held her tight. Tori wrapped her arms around his neck and as their eyes locked, he lowered his head and brushed his lips against her. Then he went back for more until they were kissing long and deep.

She finally pulled away to catch her breath. Tori happened to glance over Foster's shoulder and she saw Dare standing alone. She frowned.

"What is it?"

"Do you think Aya and Dare will be okay?"

"I'm sure they'll work things out eventually. That friend of mine can be quite stubborn. But enough about them. Did I tell you how sexy you look tonight?"

"About a hundred times."

"Well let me tell you a hundred and one. You looked sexy." He paused for a moment and cupped her face. "I love you, Victoria. I can't wait for the rest of my life with you."

Tears sprang to her eyes. She loved this man with every ounce of her heart, body and soul. "I love you, too Foster Graham. Always."

About the Author

New York Times and USA Today Bestselling Author Eve has always enjoyed creating characters and stories from an early age. As a child she was always getting into mischief, so when she lost her television privileges (which was often), writing was her outlet. Her stories have gotten quite a bit spicier since then! When she's not writing or spending time with her family, Eve is reading, baking, traveling or kicking butt in 80's trivia. She loves hearing from her readers. She can be contacted through her website at: www.evevaughn.com.

More Books From Eve Vaughn:

Whatever He Wants

Finding Divine

Run

Jilted

The Kyriakis Curse:
Book One of the Kyriakis Series

The Kyriakis Legacy:
Book Two of the Kyriakis Series

GianMarco:
Book One of the Blood Brothers Series

Niccolo:
Book Two of the Blood Brothers Series

Romeo:
Book Three of the Blood Brothers Series

Jagger:
Book Four of the Blood Brothers Series

Dante:
Book Five of the Blood Brothers Series

Giovanni:
Book Six of the Blood Brothers Series

Made in United States
North Haven, CT
19 May 2024

52715019R00137